MICHAEL RAPPAPORT

A WHITER SHADE of PALE

For Nicole, who makes everything possible.

PROLOGUE

I had been thinking about Danny Jacobs for half an hour or so when the phone on my desk rang.

It wasn't the special line to Waynesburg that had been put in for the occasion, but the regular line on which my calls came in every day. The phone didn't usually ring through directly—the governor of Pennsylvania has two or three people trying to minimize his contact with the public—but it was nearly 10 p.m. and my secretaries had gone home for the night.

I stared at the phone. I knew if I ignored it long enough, it would stop ringing. But I also knew who was probably on the other end of the line and I knew he wouldn't quit until he reached me. The next call would come to the cell phone in my shirt pocket. I picked up the phone and answered. "Governor's office, Rob Miller here."

"Governor Miller." The man on the other end of the line spoke with the nasal accent so typical of those who grew up around Phila-delphia. I don't have that accent, but I spent my formative years in the western part of Pennsylvania, in Johnstown. "Carl Kennedy. We met last week in Washington."

I remembered. Kennedy was a Democratic Party official who had buttonholed me at a White House reception for a returning war hero from my state. Everyone was praising the kid for the dozens of Iraqi insurgents he had killed, but the thing I couldn't get out of my mind was the fact that his right leg had been amputated just above the knee.

I had been to the White House only twice during my two years as governor. The president was from the other party, and my only other visit had been with 49 other governors after our annual conference. I had been shoved through the receiving line quickly along with the other Democrats. I didn't even get my picture taken with the First Lady.

Kennedy had grabbed me as I was getting my coat. He said he didn't want to talk then, but asked if he could call me in Harrisburg. I had told him I would take the call, and now it had come.

"What can I do for you, Mr. Kennedy?" I thought I knew why he was calling, but I wanted to hear him say it.

"I want to talk to you about what you're doing tonight," he said quickly. "You're not going to grant clemency to Tommy Wood, are you?"

This wasn't what I had expected, but I figured it all tied in together. "I'm not sure it's any of your business, Mr. Kennedy, but I haven't really decided yet."

"Did you know that 68 percent of Americans favor the death penalty in all cases," he said. "Eighty-three percent, including roughly the same number in your state, say they favor it in this particular case. Can you give me one good reason Tommy Wood shouldn't die tonight?"

I knew the numbers. I also knew that the crime for which Wood had received the death penalty was particularly grisly, a carjacking gone wrong in which he had killed a pregnant woman and two small children. There was no doubt he had committed the crime. He hadn't been abused as a child and he wasn't retarded.

No, when it came down to it, Tommy Wood was a truly bad person who didn't deserve ever to walk free again. He was either going to die at midnight by lethal injection or have his sentence commuted to life without parole. The decision was up to me, and there was no pressure to keep him alive. Only the most hard-core death penalty opponents were speaking out against this particular execution.

Only an idiot would commute Wood's sentence. The voters of Pennsylvania knew I was opposed to the death penalty and that I was planning to send a repeal bill to the state legislature in my second term. I thought I could educate people about it, but I knew this wasn't the case that was going to make my point.

My initial reaction was to tell Kennedy I was going to allow the execution to go ahead. I didn't want a long conversation with him, and that course of action was the logical one. Still, I wasn't sure. "I'm just making sure I've considered everything," I said.

"It could hurt you in two years," he said.

"Maybe, but I don't think so. We've balanced the budget, we've cut taxes and we've even spent some money on the infrastructure. Folks are pretty satisfied. I don't think giving one guy life without parole will cost me re-election."

"I'm not talking about Pennsylvania," he said.

"You're kidding," I said. "What else could you possibly be talking about?"

"Come on, governor. Don't tell me a popular governor of a major industrial state has never thought about running for president. If it's true, you'd be the first one ever."

Before I could say anything, Kennedy started on his prepared sales pitch. I didn't get another word in for five minutes. What it boiled down to was that after eight years of Bill Clinton and five of George W. Bush, the Democratic Party was desperately searching for candidates who were strong on the so-called "moral issues." I was a family man with a moderate pro-life position on abortion, and I had actually served in the National Guard as a young man. Kennedy and his cohorts thought I had the best chance of being competitive in the so-called "red states" without seriously offending the liberal wing of the party.

"You run and the money will be there, governor," he said. "You run and at least a few of the other potential candidates will get out of the way. But you can't stir up the death penalty crowd. You've got to let Wood die."

I sighed. It wasn't as if I didn't know the ramifications of acting in this case. I hadn't been a politician all my life, but I had served three terms in Congress before running for governor and I was aware of how volatile voters were.

I told Kennedy I understood, but that I wasn't going to be able to give him any more time. He seemed accustomed to being dismissed, and he hung up and left me to my thoughts.

More than anything, I wanted to be able to talk it over with my wife. But she and the children were in New York for a long-planned weekend, and they were probably sitting through the last act of a popular Broadway show. I wasn't going to be able to reach my wife before Saturday morning. I was on my own.

I picked up the phone again—the regular line—and punched in a familiar number. Even though it was well past dinnertime, I hadn't eaten. A takeout place three blocks from the Capitol building that my secretaries used frequently promised to deliver an order of kung pao chicken, some fried rice and a couple of egg rolls within half an hour. I thanked them, hung up and then called the guard at the front desk to tell him they would be coming.

I had some time to wait, so I reviewed the clemency request. Wood's lawyer pointed out that executions were extremely rare in Pennsylvania, that while we had put 1,040 people to death before 1976, only three had died since then. Indeed, five people on Death Row had been found to be innocent and released. The brief argued that what we had in the Keystone State was very close to a de facto repeal of the death penalty.

As much as I tried, though, I couldn't keep my mind on Tommy Wood. He kept getting mixed up with Danny Jacobs and what happened in Charlottesville, Virginia, nearly 40 years ago.

I never used to think that much about my time at Virginia even though I spent all four undergraduate years there. I didn't stay for law school. I came home to Pennsylvania and got my law degree from Penn State. I've tried to forget what happened in Charlottesville in the spring of my first year of college, but there's a part of me that will always remember.

In fact, I have a feeling I could live to be 100 years old and I would remember my first roommate. Danny Jacobs has been dead for a long time, and I knew him for less than nine months, but I still find myself wondering if there was anything I could have done to save him.

What happened to Danny was a big part of what shaped me into the man I am. I've got a beautiful wife and four terrific kids. I never planned to go into politics, but I spent a few years working with consumer groups to keep big business from gouging average people too deeply. I got some good publicity, and 10 years later, there are apparently people who think I might make a good president of the United States.

It's fairly strange. I have a reputation as an honest man. My late father was a Superior Court judge, and as someone mentioned at a testimonial dinner last winter, I must know something about "honor" since my undergraduate degree is from the University of Virginia. I'm glad I didn't laugh out loud. Folks know about Virginia's Honor System, and they respect it. I don't anymore, but that doesn't make them wrong.

I went years—maybe even decades—without thinking much about Virginia, but lately I find myself reminiscing about school—and about Danny—more and more frequently. Late at night, after my children are asleep and my wife has gone to bed, I sit up and ponder what happened during my first year of college.

When I do, I bring out my old record albums. No one I know owns phonograph records anymore. The only places you ever see them are at yard sales and swap meets. We switched to cassettes in the '80s and compact discs in the '90s. Now all the music my children collect is on their iPods, and the first time Alicia, my younger daughter, saw one of my albums, she asked me what it was.

I played "Abbey Road" for her, and when she heard the hisses and the pops, her reaction was that it sounded terrible and why didn't I listen to my CDs. I didn't say anything; she wouldn't have understood that the music sounded exactly the way I remembered it.

I don't listen to the Beatles all that often. They weren't our soundtrack in Charlottesville. We listened to the party songs—the Motown stuff that raised the consciousness of every white kid in America. I listen to Motown, and I listen to Otis Redding and Wilson Pickett, to the Soul Survivors, to Sam and Dave. I listen to the music everyone seems to think of when they think of the late Sixties. Jefferson Airplane, the Doors, stuff like that.

At some point, I always play one particular song. "A Whiter Shade of Pale," by Procol Harum. That's the song that evokes the strongest memories of my first year of college. We spent hour after hour arguing its meaning in dormitory bull sessions. I'm not sure we ever figured it out. The song has a mournful quality to it, and most of the time when I think about that year, I feel mournful.

The first year I spent away from home was one of the most eventful of my life. I made friendships I've maintained ever since. I joined a fraternity. I even lost my virginity with a truly special girl. And of course, there was Danny.

I suppose I would be a much different person—maybe even a happier one—if I never had met Daniel Aaron Jacobs. He and I were complete opposites. We were roommates, though. The housing computer had matched us. We never did figure out why the university bureaucracy thought we would be good for each other. Danny was a slightly built Jewish kid from the Washington, D.C., suburbs, and it was obvious the first time I met him that he had led a sheltered life.

I was born and raised in Johnstown, a shot-and-a-beer town in western Pennsylvania most famous for the 1889 flood. A town where half the guys in my graduating class chose between the steel mills and the Army after high school. Thirty-four guys in Johnstown High's Class of 1967 served in Vietnam. Twelve came back in coffins. Henry Donovan still is listed MIA in Cambodia more than 35 years after he disappeared on a reconnaissance mission and his parents have spent hundreds of hours and thousands of dollars lobbying the government for information. A lot of families got hurt in that war and most of them weren't real happy when Clinton went to Vietnam in the last year of his presidency.

I was lucky. I lived on the right side of the proverbial tracks because my dad, Robert Alan Miller Sr., was a judge. He went to Virginia, Class of '40, and I grew up wanting to follow him there. I never thought there would be any problem. My grades were good and I had SAT scores that were solid if unspectacular.

It didn't make things any easier when my dad died halfway through my junior year of high school, but Judge Miller had planned well. His life insurance paid off our mortgage and left enough money for my education. My mom went back to work, and I spent summers on a construction crew earning my spending money. I think having to work for what I wanted helped give me good values. Danny's parents took another approach. They kept him under a pretty tight rein, but they gave him all the money he needed. As I said, we were different.

I never did become friends with Danny, and many are the times I've wished I could forget him. I can't, though. I think of him a lot, especially when I sit in my den late at night and listen to Procol Harum singing plaintively.

" ... She said there is no reason, and the truth is plain to see. But I wandered through my playing cards, could not let it be. One of 16 vestal virgins that were leaving for the coast, and although my eyes were open, they might just as well been closed..."

On those occasions, I sit in my chair, close my eyes and listen to the song, and for a few minutes, I'm 18 going on 19, riding in a car with my friend Dave and heading straight into the most tumultuous year of my life.

1

"Hey, Bobby. Wake up." I felt someone shaking me roughly as I fought my way out of sleep. For a moment I was disoriented. I had trouble remembering where I was or what I was doing there. I'm a sound sleeper. Always have been. My mom used to say they could set off a hydrogen bomb in the next room and I'd sleep through it if I hadn't had my eight hours. "Come on, Bobby."

The hand was shaking me a little harder, and the fog started to lift. I realized I was stretched out in the back seat of a car, and we were stopped at a gas station. Then I remembered. I was on my way to college, and the person shaking me was my best friend, Dave Lyons. "Are you going to wake up or not?"

"Yeah, yeah," I said groggily. "I'm awake. Where are we?"

"Ruckersville, 16 miles north of town. I stopped for gas."

It was coming back to me. We had decided to leave for school at night to beat the early September heat. We would drive all night from Pennsylvania and make it to Charlottesville for breakfast. The dorms were scheduled to open at nine, and I was going to be the very first one to check in. At that moment, in the back seat of Dave's car, I had absolutely no idea why that had seemed so important. There was a slight chill in the air. I found myself shivering and I reached for my windbreaker.

It was a Saturday, the first one in September, and registration was scheduled to begin on Monday. My classes weren't going to start until the following Friday, so I would have six days to learn the ropes. I was nervous. All through high school, teachers had told the Class of 1967 how tough college would be. I didn't know what to expect. I never had much trouble making grades, but I wasn't a straight-A student, either.

My dad had always told me there were three important things a man should know to live a successful life. The first two were understanding his own limitations and knowing when he could exceed them. The third thing—the most important to my dad—was having a sense of honor and living by its precepts.

I had been a good student—half A's and half B's—but I worked hard for the grades I got. Dave, who had been a year ahead of me in high school, had gotten about the same kind of grades and had struggled to get a 2.2—barely a C average—in his first year at Virginia. "I should have worked a lot harder," he had told me. "If I can give you one piece of advice, that's what it would be. I got a little carried away partying, and it'll take me all of this year to get my GPA up to where I want it."

"I can't afford to screw around, Dave. I've got to get at least a 3.0 or I won't be able to get into law school. How come so many guys do so badly? Is it that tough to keep your mind on studying?"

Dave nodded. "Yeah, but there's more to it than that. They used to have something they called the 'Gentleman's C' at Virginia. The rich guys from the old families were happy to get C's and get their degrees. They considered it bad form to care about their grades."

"That's crazy."

"You'd be surprised how many of the guys in my fraternity are like that. They're always drinking, playing bridge, or making road trips."

I knew about road trips. Virginia wasn't coeducational in 1967.

The only women on the grounds—nobody called it the campus in those days without being corrected—were in the nursing and education schools. Most of them dated older guys, so first-year men wanting to meet girls had to travel to one of the women's colleges an hour or two to the east, south and west of Charlottesville. There wasn't much to the north, except Washington, D.C., 120 miles away. Richmond was half as far and twice as much fun for those Virginia students who couldn't live without a good-sized city. The only other options were "townies," the high school girls or the young working women of Charlottesville.

"Do guys make road trips during the week?"

Dave grinned. "Sure. Some guys will go anywhere to get laid."

"How about you?" I knew Dave had lost his virginity the previous summer, and I wondered if he had added any more experience. "How far would you go to get laid?"

"I've been on the road once or twice," my friend said with a sly smile.

Sex was still a mystery to me. I'd dated in high school, but I'd always chased what we used to call "nice girls." In 1967, we divided girls into two categories—nice and bad. The bad ones were the most fun, but you couldn't take them to CYO dances or introduce them to your mother. Once or twice, I'd reached the point where I might have had the chance to see what all the fuss was about. I'd always backed off. I was never sure quite why. It just hadn't seemed the right time to take that step.

We had a terrific breakfast—eggs, toast, hash browns, sausage and orange juice for less than two dollars each—and by the time we had finished eating and were ready to go, the sun had risen above the eastern horizon. Dave looked at his watch. "Damn, it's still only 7:15. You're not going to be able to check in for almost two more hours. I'd take you around and show you the city, but I'm almost out of gas."

Dave and I had known each other a long time, and if certain things didn't exactly go unsaid, they didn't have to be spelled out. "Why don't I buy you a couple of bucks worth?"

In those days, two dollars still paid for six gallons of gas, so my money bought Dave half a tank of Mobil regular and a clean windshield. Refueling completed, we toured the streets of town for more than an hour, finally driving all the way out to Monticello to see Thomas Jefferson's home.

Jefferson always had been one of my father's heroes. In recent years there's been all the revisionist stuff about him. Some people can't stand the thought of great men. They've got to bring everyone down to their own level. My dad died before the Sally Hemings revelations came out, but I don't think it would have changed anything. He had read most of Jefferson's writing, and he always was particularly impressed with the fact that this incredible man had asked to be remembered for three things. Jefferson's tombstone describes him not only as the author of the Declaration of Independence and the Virginia Statutes of Religious Freedom; it also names him as the founding father of the University of Virginia.

Not President. Not Governor of Virginia or Secretary of State or perhaps the greatest mind of the 18th century, a title CNN awarded him in its end of the millennium shows in 1999. Jefferson had wanted to be remembered for ideas, and that made him very special to my dad. Seeing Monticello touched me deeply. I thought of my grandfather and my father standing here as young men when they first arrived at the university; it was a bond across the years.

Dave drove me past the Rotunda and down Fraternity Row, showing me the Kappa Sigma Kappa fraternity house, where he was a brother. He had been trying to talk me into rushing there. I was pretty sure I wanted to pledge a fraternity. I knew the social life centered almost entirely on the fraternity houses and nearly half the first-year class pledged each year. Dave wanted me to follow him into KSK, but he knew I always had been interested in Sigma Phi Omicron, which had been my father and my grandfather's fraternity.

"SPO's a good house, but think about all the fun we could have together at KSK."

"I'll think about it, and anyway, bids don't go out until November. Isn't that what you told me?"

"Yeah. Just don't rush into anything."

I groaned at his pun.

By then it was almost nine, so Dave headed in the direction of the first-year dorms. It didn't surprise either of us that I was the first one in line at the housing office. "Name and hometown?" the older student behind the desk asked me in a bored tone.

"Robert Alan Miller Jr., Johnstown, Pa."

"Bob, Bobby or Robert?"

"Rob," I said. My friends and family always had called me Bobby, but I wanted to project a more mature image now that I was in college.

"Well, Rob, here's your key. You're in Kent House, Room 304. Your roommate hasn't checked in yet. Welcome to the university."

I hadn't brought much stuff. Two suitcases, my little portable stereo and a box of books and records. Even so, it took Dave and me two trips up the two flights of stairs to get my stuff into the room, a room that looked truly depressing.

For one thing, it was only a little larger than my bedroom at home. It looked a lot like a cell, with two shabby-looking metal beds that wouldn't have been out of place in an army barracks. The mattresses looked thin and uncomfortable, and I found myself longing for my bed from home. There was one metal dresser to the left of the door, with four drawers. At the other end of the room were two desks, each one next to the head of a bed. The furniture was an awful-looking shade of gray. There were no curtains or blinds on the windows, only a bare curtain rod across the top. The floor was covered with ugly brownish-green linoleum, and I knew it would be cold on winter mornings. I decided I'd better pick up a pair of slippers.

The walls were cinder blocks, painted a horrible shade of green that reminded me of the last time I'd had too much to drink. I mentally put posters at the top of my shopping list, planning to cover as much of the nauseating greenish paint as was humanly possible.

"Pretty grim, huh?" Dave asked. "The new dorms up on Alderman Road are better, but there aren't a whole lot of first-year men up there. Those dorms are mostly for second and third-year guys."

"This is really awful."

"Sure, but get a few posters and some other stuff and it won't look so bad. You'll only be living here first semester."

I shook my head. "I'll be here all year. My mom and I talked about it, and she doesn't think I should move into a fraternity house until next year. She says I need to get good grades both semesters, and it'll be easier if I stay in the dorms."

Dave shrugged. "She's right, but you'll wind up spending a lot of time wherever you pledge anyway."

Dave helped me hang my clothes in the closet, and then we set up my stereo on top of the dresser and put my books on the shelf over the desk on the side of the room I'd chosen. I hadn't brought many— just a few favorites. "Look Homeward Angel," "The Great Gatsby" and a couple of others. The personal touches helped, but the room still looked depressing. I hoped curtains and posters would make a difference, but I had my doubts.

2

When we had finished unpacking, we headed for The Corner, three short city blocks of shops and restaurants that made up the University's shopping district. "You can get almost anything here," Dave said. He pointed out Mincer's Pipe Shop, which had records, books and all sorts of university memorabilia, and the Rexall Drug Store, which had almost everything else.

There were two bookstores, several sandwich shops, two high-priced clothing stores and a few bars. We stopped at Sears and bought curtains and a good-sized throw rug for the room. Then we went to Mincer's and looked at the posters. I selected two and paid for them. "You should have waited till your roommate got here," Dave said. "You could have gotten him to pay half the cost for the rug and the curtains."

I shrugged. "It's no big deal. I made pretty good money working construction this summer, and I'd rather pay the whole thing myself and get stuff I like."

By the time we finished shopping, it was time for lunch. We went to the Virginian, a combination sandwich shop and beer bar. The sandwiches looked good, and I showed off some of my newfound independence by ordering a beer with my lunch. Back in those days, you could get 3.2 beer at age 18.

"You 18, kid?" the waitress asked me.

"Yeah." I reached for my wallet and my Pennsylvania driver's license to show proof of age. Before I had a chance, she walked off to get our order. Dave grinned. "Remember what I told you about the Honor System?"

"Sure. Gentlemen don't lie, cheat or steal or tolerate those who do."

"That's right. You just saw one of the benefits of it. Go into any bar near the campus, any bar where they know you're a student, and all you do is say you're 18. They'll take your word for it. You can cash checks anywhere, too. The merchants know no one from the school will write a bad check. It's an honor violation to bounce a check."

I had never seen anything like this. "And nobody takes advantage of that?"

"No way. There's a story going around that last year five first-year men were in here and they all ordered beers. They said they were old enough, but one guy wasn't. His friends turned him in for an honor violation and he was out of here."

"Just like that?"

"I've got my doubts about that story. It sounds like the kind of story someone made up to scare rookies."

I laughed at my friend, a rabid Pittsburgh Pirates fan who had been at Forbes Field as a 12-year-old in 1960 when Bill Mazeroski hit the home run that beat the hated New York Yankees and won the World Series. "I'm a rookie?"

He nodded. "Technically, you could have lied today, because you're not enrolled yet. Monday you'll go to an Honor System orientation, and then you'll sign a pledge. Then even if I was the one who caught you, I'd have to turn you in."

"Could you do that?"

"I'd have to. If I didn't, and someone else knew I knew you'd committed a violation, I'd be just as guilty. The way the code reads is that a gentleman will not lie, cheat or steal. Or tolerate those who do. I'm not worried about you anyway. You're the most honest guy I know." I tried to protest, but he ignored me. "I mean, the way the judge brought you up..."

From the time I had been old enough to understand, my father had stressed the importance of honor. It wasn't until that moment that I started to think maybe it had been his four years of college, back in the years just before the Second World War, that shaped him and made him what he was.

"I don't know, Dave. I know I'm not going to lie, cheat or steal, but I really don't know if I could turn someone else in. Seems to me I'd be ruining somebody's life if I did that."

"Well, the way the system describes it, you wouldn't be ruining anyone's life. They've already done that when they decided to lie, cheat or steal." Dave sighed. "That's the toughest part of the system. I hope you never have to find out."

3

Half of the guys who would be living on the third floor of Kent House had checked in by mid-afternoon Saturday, but not my roommate. I spent an hour hanging the curtains I'd bought and putting my posters on the wall. The two posters I'd purchased seemed unique, but I'd learn later they were two of the most popular posters of the late 1960s. One was of W.C. Fields playing poker, and the other was of Raquel Welch in that prehistoric movie, coming out of the water wearing a tattered bikini. I didn't know it then, but my room was a '60s cliché.

It was a time of antiheroes, and Fields was one of the best. "Trust everybody," he said. "But cut the cards." As for Raquel, that poster needed no explanation.

After I had the room in order, I was feeling tired. I wasn't sure how much sleep I'd gotten on the trip down. While I was putting my half of the room together, though, some guys dropped in and introduced themselves. Sleep would have to wait.

I've never been that great at names, so I tried to put as many names with faces as I could. I met Bruce Benson and Dick Simpson, two Texans sharing the room next door. I met Leo Mitchell from New

York, the closest thing we would have to a hippie, and Edward Lee Randolph IV, our link to the Old South.

Danny didn't show up at all on Saturday. We had been given two days to check in, so some guys wouldn't arrive until Sunday. There would be a total of 40 first-year men on our side of the third floor, and 12 of them hadn't arrived by Saturday evening. We were already starting to break up into groups, and six of us went to dinner together.

We walked past the new Alderman Road dorms to a pizza parlor just off campus, and we ordered three large pizzas and a couple of pitchers of beer. Our group was made up of the two Texans, Ed Randolph, Ricky Barton, Andy Lynch and me. Ricky was a scholarship football player from Baltimore, and Andy was a rich kid from St. Louis who had gone to Country Day School. We made up a fairly disparate group. Ed was the only Virginian among us, and I was the only one from the northern states.

I took a little ribbing at first about being a damn Yankee, but that ended when they learned that I was a third-generation Wahoo, the only one in our group fulfilling a family tradition. That seemed to outweigh whatever stigma was attached to growing up in a state where slavery nearly always had been illegal.

We started discussing fraternities, and everyone agreed that pledging was a necessity if you wanted to have any sort of a social life. We spent the next hour or so arguing the merits of various houses. Once we had exhausted that topic, we shifted to majors and learned that five of us were planning to study political science. That surprised me, but it shouldn't have. It was the trendy major. Ten years later we'd have been journalism students inspired by Watergate and 10 years after that we'd have been taking the first step toward our MBAs. The Sixties were days of activism, and all of us had grown up listening to John F. Kennedy exhort us to ask not what our country could do for us.

The sixth member of our group, Ricky Barton, had heard another call. He dreamed of playing professional football and would be a physical education major. "I'm mainly here for football. I was second-team all-state quarterback in Maryland last year. I'm on an athletic scholarship."

"How come you're not going to school someplace where they've got a good football team?" Dick asked. Even first-year men from Texas knew of Virginia's reputation as one of the doormats of the Atlantic Coast Conference.

Ricky grinned. "Hey, all-state in Maryland is nothing like all-state in Texas. This was the best offer I had, the only good school to give me a full ride."

The next topic on our unofficial agenda was an ever-popular one—girls. It was agreed that we would all make road trips as soon as possible, and that the barbaric rule of not allowing first-year men to have cars was a definite disadvantage in the never-ending quest for sexual fulfillment.

Dick Simpson, who hadn't done much talking up to this point, said he had heard there would be buses to take first-year men to mixers at Mary Washington and Sweet Briar the next weekend, and we all decided to make one trip or the other.

"I hear the best girls are at Hollins," Andy said. "That's about 110 miles from here." "What's so good about Hollins girls?" Ricky wanted to know.

"They're supposed to be nymphos. They're so far away they never get to see Virginia guys, so when they do they go nuts. You make it to Hollins, and you'll definitely score."

All of us solemnly considered the implications of that statement and decided separately that we would have to figure a way to get down to Hollins before the first snows fell.

The first party weekend would be Homecomings, in mid-October, but more important was Openings a month later. Not having a date for Homecomings would be bad, but Openings would be a disaster. Openings Weekend was the last party weekend before

fraternity bids were handed out and having a beautiful date would be one way to make a good impression.

When the waiter came around to tell us it was last call to order beer, I was surprised to realize it was past midnight. We had been talking for nearly five hours. We split two more pitchers and then staggered back to the dorms. I slept alone in my room for the first time. The bed was far from comfortable, but I've always been able to sleep anywhere. The dorm was noisy despite the late hour. It didn't bother me at all. I fell asleep within a minute or two after I got into bed, and I slept for nine hours.

4

My newly purchased curtains did their job and kept the sunlight out of the room on Sunday morning, so I wasn't awakened until my roommate arrived shortly after 10 o'clock. Daniel Aaron Jacobs opened the door with a bang, as if he wasn't expecting anyone else to be in the room. I would later see that Danny came into rooms that way a lot. It wasn't intentional rudeness. He just didn't think.

He looked to be about 5-foot-8. He had a dark complexion made even darker by his summer tan. He was maybe five pounds on the right side of skinny, although he didn't look muscular at all. He had brown eyes; curly brown hair and his features were slightly Semitic. He was wearing a golf shirt with the name of a country club over his left breast, tailored chino slacks and Bass Weejuns. Nicer clothes than I had in my closet.

As soon as he saw me in my bed, he quieted down quickly, but the damage was already done. "Sorry. You must be Robert Miller."

"Call me Rob," I said, sitting up in bed. "And you must be…"

"Danny Jacobs."

He extended his hand, and I shook it. "I didn't mean to wake you up. I'm sorry."

"No big deal," I said, looking at my alarm clock that I hadn't bothered to set. "I ought to be getting up anyway."

I was wearing only pajama bottoms, so I swung my legs off the bed and got up. I walked across the room and took a T-shirt out of the top drawer of my dresser. "So," I said. "You made it."

"Yeah. I wanted to come down yesterday, but my parents couldn't get away until this morning. They're downstairs, but my mom didn't want to come up until I checked to see if it was all right."

Five minutes later, wearing jeans instead of my pajamas, I met Irving and Yvette Jacobs. They were clearly Danny's parents, with a strong family resemblance. Irv was a heavyset middle-aged man, but Yvette looked too young to have a son who was a freshman in college.

Danny's dad was dressed similarly to his son, while his mother had on a dress that was what they call quietly elegant. Irv was balding, with only a fringe around his ears remaining. He probably could have stood to lose twenty pounds or so, but he seemed to have a certain strength about him.

Yvette's blonde hair was tastefully styled, and she didn't appear to be wearing much makeup. I knew from my own mother that all that meant was that she did a very good job of hiding it.

After the introductions, Danny's father surprised me with a question. "Excuse me for asking, Rob, but you don't appear to be ..."

"... Jewish? No, I'm not." I didn't tell them I was Catholic. "Why do you ask?"

Danny seemed almost embarrassed. "I think what my dad is trying to say is that my parents were expecting me to have a Jewish roommate."

I shook my head. "I don't think they do it that way here, sir. I think unless you specifically request someone, they try to mix people up."

"Well," Irv said. "I guess college is supposed to be a broadening experience."

Religion wasn't that big a deal to me. I had promised my mother I would go to Mass most Sundays, but we both knew there would be weeks I wouldn't make it. That was the way it had been for a couple of years now, and she had been good about it.

"Well, Rob," Yvette said. "I see you've already bought curtains and a rug for the room. They look very nice."

"Thanks, Mrs. Jacobs. I didn't know when Danny would get here, and I thought it would be a good idea to get it taken care of as soon as possible."

"How much do I owe you?" Danny asked.

"Don't worry about it. The stuff didn't cost that much."

"No, we want to pay half," Yvette said. I finally agreed to accept $10, and I helped Danny unpack his things. With everything settled, Irv and Yvette decided they wanted to take us to lunch. I wasn't all that excited about the idea, but I figured it would be easier than arguing, and anyway, it was a free meal.

We went to the University Cafeteria, the place where parents always took students. The Unicaf always advertised itself with some old McCall's magazine rating that had given it four stars, and its ads always had the four stars and the one word, "Outstanding."

Whenever I saw that, I thought of the cigarette advertisement, and I always wanted to add "and they are mild." It was kind of a bland, family-type restaurant, but parents loved it because it served vegetables and salads and didn't sell beer.

Danny's parents were planning to start for home after lunch, so I had to sit through their advice to their son. I wound up as an unwilling participant in their conversation. Every time Irv said something to Danny about how tough college was, or how to behave, or what to do and not to do, he punctuated it by asking me to agree with him. I didn't want to side with any kid's parents, so I usually pretended to concentrate on my food. I mumbled something like, "Oh, I don't know," and somehow managed to get through the meal without betraying my entire generation.

They must have thought I was strange to be so enthralled by roast beef and mashed potatoes. I offered to pay for my lunch, but Irv wouldn't let me. He settled the check, left a tip and offered to drive us back to the dorms.

"It's not that far, Mr. Jacobs. It's only about a five-minute walk, and maybe Danny would like to see some of the grounds before tomorrow."

"That sounds terrific," Danny said gratefully. "You don't mind, do you, dad?"

They said their goodbyes outside the restaurant, and Danny watched as his parents got into their two-year old Cadillac for the drive back to Annandale, Virginia, in the D.C. suburbs.

"If you're not in any hurry to get back, I thought I might do a little shopping. You know, some posters and stuff. You want to go along with me and show me where to go?"

"Sure," I said, figuring we should start getting to know each other. It would make things a lot easier if my roommate and I could be friends.

We shopped for a while, and he picked out two posters and a Playboy magazine. Then we walked back. I hadn't wanted to tell Danny's parents that I hadn't seen the Lawn myself yet, especially since I'd already been in town for a day and a half.

We walked along the Serpentine Wall, through the Colonnades and came out onto the Lawn. The buildings there were the oldest part of the school, dating back to the 1820s. Small rooms flanked the Lawn on both sides, and I knew from reading about them that they were the residences of the fourth-year men who ran the university. Important guys. Newspaper editors. Student body presidents. Top students and fraternity big wigs.

The rooms themselves were nothing special as I learned the first time I saw the inside of one. They were tiny and difficult to heat in the winter. They didn't have private bathroom facilities, so anyone living on the Lawn had to walk outdoors to get to the toilets and showers they shared with the other residents.

Each room did have a washbasin, and I later learned when the temperature dipped down toward zero in January, a lot of guys used their sinks for more than just washing their hands. It all sounded awful, but every year there were several hundred applications for the rooms. I knew if I ever had the chance to live on the Lawn, I'd jump at it. "It's really beautiful," I said as looked down toward Cabell Hall.

Danny grinned. "You act like you've never seen it before."

"I haven't, except in the catalog they sent me. I didn't make a visit in the spring. It was pretty far from home and I didn't have any long weekends. Anyway, I always knew this was where I wanted to go. My dad went here, and his dad before him."

"Oh? What does your dad do?"

"Not much. He's dead."

That certainly put a damper on the conversation. Danny looked stricken. "I'm sorry, Rob. I didn't know…"

"No problem. He's been dead for a couple of years now. I should have told you." I figured the best thing to do was quickly change the subject. "You've seen this before?"

"Yeah. We came down here for an afternoon in the spring. I was trying to decide between here and Michigan State. They recruited me. I was a National Merit Scholar, and they try to get as many National Merit Scholars as they can into their freshman class."

If his intention was to impress me, he had succeeded. "So you're a real brain? How come you're not living in Echols?" Echols was the honors house for the first-year class.

He shrugged. "My grades weren't good enough. I only had a B-plus average in high school. I just had great test scores."

"Hey, that's nothing to be ashamed of. Were those the only places you applied?"

"No, my dad wanted me to go to an Ivy League school. He made me apply at Columbia and Harvard. I told him I didn't have a chance, but he said to go ahead and try. I was right. They both rejected me. How about you?"

"Like I said, I always wanted to go to school here. I applied to Penn State as a safety valve, just in case they didn't take me here."

By this point in the conversation, we had made our way back to the dorm. Danny wanted to put his posters up right away, so I left to see if anyone else was hanging out. The hall was nearly deserted, but I found Bruce in his room, reading the same issue of Playboy Danny had purchased. I later learned that for a lot of guys, buying Playboy and reading it openly was their first defiant act of freedom as college students.

One guy in our dorm—he's a world-famous surgeon now, so I won't embarrass him by mentioning his name—couldn't quite deal with it. He bought the magazine but hid it inside Sports Illustrated when he read it and hid it under his mattress when he was finished.

"Hey, Rob," Bruce said as he looked up from his examination of the lovely Miss September. "Where the heck have you been? I was looking for you a while ago."

"My roommate got here. I went out to lunch with him and his parents." "What's he like?"

I shrugged. "It's hard to tell. He seems pretty young. Where did everybody else go?"

"Dick got a touch football game going with some guys from the second floor. I think they're on the field down the street. I'm not much of a jock, and I thought it might be nice to be alone for a little while. Dick's kind of a live wire, and it's always pretty wild when he's around."

We made plans to go to dinner later and I left him. I didn't feel like going back to my room, so I decided to do a little exploring. I walked over to the student union to see what I could find. Since it was Sunday afternoon, the bookstore was closed, but I found the reading and listening rooms upstairs. I couldn't check out any books or record albums because I didn't have my student identification card yet, so I walked back down to the Corner.

I had a beer by myself and then walked around. When I went back to the dorm at around 5:30, I was surprised to see that Danny had fallen asleep on his bed. I thought about awakening him to see if he wanted to go to dinner, but I decided to let him sleep. I went down to the bathroom and washed up, and then went next door to get Bruce. Dick had returned from the football game, and he invited himself along. The three of us walked down to the Corner for dinner. It was my third trip of the day, and I was starting to feel as if I could make it with my eyes closed.

We ate at Howard Johnson's and then decided to catch a movie. We didn't get back to the dorm until almost 10:30. Danny was still asleep, so I went across the hall. There were eight guys hanging out in Ed Randolph's room. I looked in on them, and somebody told me to come in and grab a seat. They had a wastebasket filled with ice and there were still a few cans of beer left. Ed tossed me one and I sat down on his roommate's bed. I hadn't met him, and he extended his hand. "Hi, I'm Joe Del Rio from Winchester."

"Rob Miller. Johnstown, Pa. What are you guys talking about?"

"Registration," Ed said. "We're trying to figure out which classes to take."

We talked for a couple of hours and decided that most of us were going to take biology as our required science. Since none of us were science majors, it looked as if that would be our toughest class. The thinking was that we could help each other study.

The conversation broke up after midnight, and I went back to my room to find that Danny was still asleep. I changed into my pajama bottoms in the dark and tiptoed out of the room to head down the hall to brush my teeth. I knew my alarm was set for eight, so I punched the button and jumped into bed. I was asleep before I had a chance to think about it.

5

Registration was pretty much what I had been warned to expect. I got most of the classes I wanted, but not all the sections. I got stuck with an eight o'clock three days a week. I wound up with American History, English Composition, Elementary Biology, Intermediate French and Calculus—a fairly standard schedule for first year. I managed to save some money by getting used books for three of my courses, but when I had all my books, I was out $65, and the texts completely filled the shelf above my desk. The history course looked as though it would be the one that required the most reading time, but it was also the only one that was anywhere close to my future major.

I was nervous about biology, calculus, and French. Dave had told me to be prepared to spend a lot of time hitting the books during the first semester. "Just remember, Rob. You can't screw around if you want to make grades. You've got to grind from Sunday night through Thursday night. Work hard all week and then raise hell on the weekends."

I figured I was ready, but it was obvious some of the other guys on the hall didn't have any idea what to expect. Danny was one of them.

From the way he'd been talking, I knew he'd never had to work too hard in high school to make grades. The impression I got was that he probably would have an easy time of it.

Classes started on Friday. I had everything except calculus and history on Mondays, Wednesdays and Fridays. French was a four-credit course and met Thursdays as well, and I had a three-hour biology lab on Monday afternoons. The other two classes were on Tuesdays, Thursdays and Saturdays. Back in those days, we still had Saturday classes, although they usually got canceled on the party weekends.

One class I had been warned about was English Composition. Dave had said the professors always assigned in-class themes the first day and they were legendary for grading them unmercifully. Anything better than a D on your first composition was supposed to mean you had a chance to become William Faulkner someday.

I wasn't thrilled about writing in class, partly because English was my eight o'clock class and I was a notoriously slow riser. After that, I had French at 9 and Biology at 11. Monday afternoons I'd be in the bio lab from two until five.

I dragged myself out of bed and put on a coat and tie. I tried to remember the last time I'd dressed up for school, and the best I could remember was the day they took our senior pictures. My mom had asked me to get a short haircut for those pictures. She wanted to order a lot of them and send them to all the aunts and uncles, and wallet-sized versions of the same photo would accompany my college applications. I had gone along with her request, and I had worn my best Sunday suit to school that day. It didn't work. She said the pictures looked great, but I thought they made me look like a convict. The only thing worse would have been if they'd been front and side view. I didn't wear my suit anywhere other than church for the rest of the year.

Here it was a tradition, though. Everyone dressed up for classes, no matter what day it was or what the weather was like. At first it seemed like a major pain, but as I headed to Cabell Hall for my first college class, I was already starting to like it. Several hundred dollars of the money I'd made working all summer had gone for clothes. Sport jackets, dress shirts, ties. I knew I didn't have the wardrobe that guys like Bruce, who came from serious Texas oil money, or Alan had brought with them. My clothes weren't as nice as Danny's, either, but it didn't bother me. I liked the stuff I had bought, and I thought I looked good.

There were 25 other first-year men in my English class. It was the first academic class I'd had that was all males, and it was the first one where I didn't know a soul. I'd lived in Johnstown all my life, and I knew half the kids in my class when I started first grade.

Dave Lyons and I had met on the playground the first day, and after the first week we were friends. It had been much the same with the kids in my class. We got to know each other quickly, and we all had gone through the school system together. This was different, though. These were guys from all over the country, and at least half of them were smarter than me. I hoped it was only half.

"All right, gentlemen, settle down." The teacher walked into the classroom right at 8 o'clock and looked around. "This is Section 17 of English Composition. It's a first-year class, unless you were unlucky enough to fail it last year."

That drew a nervous laugh from one or two guys. "My name is Mr. Chase, and I'm here to teach you to write semi-coherent compositions. Some of you may think you already know how to write, but I'll disabuse you of that notion very quickly." Another nervous laugh, this time from a guy over on the left side of the room. "You gentlemen may think I'm kidding, but I'm not. We'll take this first session to find out how much all of you need to improve. I'd like each of you to write me 500 words on the most influential person in your life."

He paused. "I want each of you to resist the temptation to write about your fathers ... or your ministers ... or athletic coaches." This time the guy on the left groaned. "You are welcome to turn in your papers and leave as soon as you're finished."

Twenty-six heads bent over 26 desks, and I could almost smell the fear. I figured everyone had heard the horror stories, and now they were face to face with the prospect of their first bad grade. For some it would be the first D they'd ever received.

I thought about my Cub Scout leader, and I thought about teachers I'd known. I decided those would be too predictable, exactly what the dreaded Mr. Chase would expect a scared first-year man to write. If I was in for a bad grade anyway, I thought I might as well have some fun with it. I'd always been a decent writer, and I had a good sense of humor. I decided to write about Buffalo Bob Smith and Howdy Doody.

Five hundred words came quickly. I wrote about the lessons of childhood, of learning to get along with others, of learning to share and be friendly. I had played on two varsity sports teams in high school, but I figured Mr. Chase had some kind of anti-athletic bias, so I wrote about sports not being the only way to learn the lessons of team play.

I was surprised to see that two or three guys took only 20 minutes to do their essays. I was finished with five minutes to go, but I spent the rest of the time looking back over what I had written to see if I could improve it. The essay wasn't half bad. I kind of liked it, but I still wasn't expecting anything more than a D. I knew the rules and I was ready to take my lumps. When the bell rang to end the class, I turned in my paper.

My other two classes were uneventful. My French teacher spent about half the period talking to us in French—I understood every other word or so—and then let us go for the day with a vocabulary assignment. All the biology teacher did was hand out a syllabus and tell us he'd give his first lecture on Monday. I was back in my room by 11:20. Danny wasn't there, but Ed Randolph stopped by and asked me if I wanted to go to lunch.

We approached our first meal at the student union cafeteria with some trepidation. Dave had told me all sorts of horror stories about cafeteria food, which was one reason I had only signed up to eat there for the first semester. It was cheap, though. My five-day a week meal plan worked out to about a dollar and a half a day, and there was nowhere else in town I could eat that cheaply. We loaded our trays with stuff that had a tenuous resemblance to food and found a table. "How'd your classes go?" Ed asked as he poked at his meat loaf.

"Not bad." I forked some blue lettuce into my mouth. "How about yours?"

"So-so. It's going to be tough to get used to eight o'clock classes, though." I nodded sympathetically. "I've got Calculus. In fact, your roommate is in my class. He seems weird. He's so nervous, so eager for everyone to like him. It's easy to see he's bright. He was one of the only guys in the class who understood what the professor was talking about, but he was obnoxious about it. He had his hand up the whole time."

I thought it would be a good time to change the subject. "Hey, are you going to one of those mixers this weekend? We're supposed to sign up for the buses by this afternoon."

Ed shook his head. "I just don't know if I want to spend the money for a bus trip. I'm on kind of a tight budget. I've got a girlfriend anyway. Her name's Elaine and she's at Lynchburg College. We dated through high school."

"Lynchburg. That's where you're from, isn't it?"

He nodded. "It's about an hour from here, down Route 29. If you want to go sometime, let me know and I'll have Elaine set you up with one of her friends. You're going to one of the mixers?"

"I thought I might. I've been having trouble deciding which one, so I thought I'd wait and see where some of the other guys on the hall were going."

"Bruce told me he and Dick are going to Sweet Briar, and I think Andy's going to Mary Washington to see some girl he knows from back home in St. Louis. I don't know about anybody else."

We discussed the relative merits of the various girls' schools for the rest of lunch, and we agreed that Hollins was the one place we wanted to see. At two hours away, it was the most distant of all the schools. Few of us made it there that year, and it wound up being sort of a Holy Grail of sexual liberation. I would later learn that the legend of unbridled nymphomania at Hollins was just that, a legend. It's amazing how reality so rarely lives up to our dreams.

There were a couple of girls from my high school attending Madison College, which was about 100 miles to the northwest on the edge of the Blue Ridge Mountains, so I figured I'd probably make a trip up there sometime soon.

My main social objective for September was getting a date for Homecomings, because by then I'd be rushing a fraternity. I hadn't dated much in high school. Neither had most of the guys I had hung out with. It hadn't been that big a deal. We'd all had girlfriends at one time or another, but where I came from, just hanging out with your buddies was more fun.

After signing up for the Sweet Briar trip, I spent the afternoon studying, trying to get a head start on my biology reading. I knew it and French would be my two toughest classes, and they were the ones I'd have to stay on top of every single day. I went to the union for dinner and was back at the books by early evening.

Danny was in and out of the room. He kept saying he was going to study, but he looked like he was having a hard time settling down and concentrating. He invited himself along with a bunch of guys who were going out to eat that evening. They asked me if I wanted to join them, but I begged off. I told them I'd already eaten. Besides, I knew I wouldn't get anything done for the next couple of days; giving up one Friday night to study wasn't going to kill me.

Dave had warned me that if I wanted to study in the dorms, I'd better buy earplugs or stereo headphones so that I could shut out the cacophony that always seemed part of the scene. Since it was the beginning of the semester, nobody had any big assignments coming due. All up and down the hall, stereos were cranked up and guys were singing along. I put a set of plugs into my ears and started working.

By 10 o'clock, three different guys had poked their heads into my room asking me if I wanted to get into a poker game down the hall and I had decided that trying to study any more was a lost cause. I sat in for an hour or so, winning a couple of pots and winding up a couple of bucks ahead. When I started getting bored, I begged off and went for a walk.

I stopped by the grill at the north end of the dorms. It was empty except for a couple of guys eating hamburgers and listening to the juke box, so I bought a Coke, poured it into a Dixie cup and took it with me. I went walking down the hill toward University Hall, the basketball arena on the north end of the grounds. I found myself wondering what Dave and his fraternity brothers over at KSK were doing. I knew rush was going to bring a hard choice for me. Assuming I didn't get blackballed, I was going to have to decide between my best friend's fraternity and my dad's.

For some guys, that probably wouldn't have been that tough a choice, especially since my dad wasn't even alive anymore. Tradition had always been big in the Miller family, though, and I knew I felt an obligation. I figured it would make it easier once I met the guys in Sigma Phi Omicron. If they were jerks, I wouldn't feel too bad about not joining. And if they were good guys, I'd find it easier to tell Dave I had decided not to pledge KSK.

Fraternities were on everyone's mind—even Danny had been talking about them, although I had to admit I didn't see him as the type. There were four different Jewish houses at the university, and he had gotten letters from three of them over the summer. He said he wanted to join one, so I assumed that was where he'd rush.

Suddenly, I felt a chill in the air, and I realized it must have been getting late. I had walked past University Hall without even noticing it, and I figured I was about a mile and a half from the dorms. It wasn't late—probably a little after 11—but with classes in the morning, I decided the smartest thing would be to go back and get some sleep.

Saturdays weren't too tough. I had two classes, at 10 o'clock and 11. The fall semester of 1967 was the last year before Virginia discontinued Saturday classes, and everyone was always moaning about what a pain it was to go to school six days a week. I didn't mind too much. I liked American History and I'd always been good at math. I figured these would be my two easiest courses, and since it was the first meeting for both, the teachers handed out assignments and let us go.

The weekend was about to begin.

6

The buses to Sweet Briar were scheduled to leave at 6:30, so we spent the afternoon preparing. I learned that a big part of those preparations involved getting one's hands on liquid refreshment with some sort of alcohol content. Except for 3.2 beer—we called it "near beer" back home—the drinking age in Virginia was 21 and the only place alcohol could be purchased was in state liquor stores.

With the Honor System in force, using a fake ID to buy booze was out of the question. The time-honored method in those days was to find a wino or some other lowlife willing to go inside and make the purchase. The fee was generally a dollar, which in those days still bought a good-sized bottle of cheap wine.

The salesclerks in the stores certainly knew what was happening when some scruffy-looking guy who smelled like Ripple or Boone's Farm wine would come in and solemnly purchase a fifth or two of expensive liquor. That's why the exchanges always took place a block from the stores.

Bourbon and rum were the two most popular choices, because they could be consumed straight or mixed with Coca-Cola. Nearly everyone who was going along on Saturday agreed that pints were the best purchase, since a flat pint of alcohol could be carried in the inner pocket of a sport coat.

Bruce and I were splitting a fifth of Rebel Yell ("Especially for the Deep South—Established 1849"), which Dave had assured me was good bourbon. Each of us had a plastic flask—99 cents plus state sales tax at Mincer's—and Dick had bought a pint of something called Colonel Lee for himself. "I never heard of Colonel Lee," Bruce said. "Is it even booze?"

Dick nodded. "I never heard of it either. I asked the guy to get me something good, but he bought this and kept the rest of my money. It was only $1.75."

"That's pretty cheap," I said. "I wonder if it's any good."

Dick grinned. "I'll let you know."

Bruce and I had two drinks each on the hour-long bus ride to Sweet Briar, but Dick already had put away more than half of his pint and was feeling good. "Gonna find me a woman tonight," he said. "Gonna dip my wick in some Sweet Briar poontang."

I figured if he could be that optimistic after half a pint of bourbon, I ought to have another drink. By the time we arrived at the mixer, all three of us were feeling extremely relaxed.

It was a good thing we had the alcohol along to liven things up, because the mixer was dull. Dave hadn't warned me about Sweet Briar, which turned out to be an Old South campus guarded by private Pinkerton security guards. The girls were the flower of upper crust southern womanhood. I danced with a few, but mostly I stood off at the side and talked to Bruce. He wasn't having much more fun than I was. The whole thing seemed more like a tea party than a mixer. By the time it ended, shortly after 1 a.m., both of us were more than ready to get on the bus back to Charlottesville.

Neither of us noticed that Dick wasn't around. In fact, we hadn't seen him for a couple of hours. The one time it had crossed my mind, I just figured he had been luckier than we had. He wasn't on the bus when it pulled out to take us back to school.

It was Sunday evening before we found out what had happened, and the story was amazing enough to make Dick the first legend of our hall. "Hey," Bruce said, poking his head through the doorway. "Dick just got back. You've got to hear his story."

It was apparently a pretty good one, because there were about a dozen guys gathered in the room by the time Dick Simpson started the second telling of his tale.

As it turned out, he had finished his pint of Colonel Lee shortly before it finished him. He had wandered away from the mixer and fallen asleep under a tree. At about 3 a.m., he had been awakened by one of the Pinkerton guards. "The asshole was kicking me. Not real hard, but kind of poking me in the side with his foot. When I woke up, he asked me what I was doing there. I told him I was waiting for a bus."

The room erupted in laughter. Showing a better sense of timing that I would have thought he had, Dick waited for it to quiet down and then continued with his story. The guard had escorted him to the edge of campus and pointed him north on Route 29. "I couldn't get anybody to stop and give me a ride. I guess I didn't look too fucking sober. I just started walking. It was about 3:30, and I walked for nearly three hours."

Shortly after sunrise, he had run out of energy. He came to a church by the side of the road and went inside. "I was just looking to see if I could get a drink of water or something. I couldn't find anything, so I decided to sit down in one of the back pews and rest my feet for a minute or two."

"Oh, no," someone groaned.

Dick winked at him. "Oh, yeah. I fell asleep in the pew. About three hours later, people started coming in for Sunday services, and they found me."

"They probably smelled you before they saw you," Bruce said. "They probably thought some animal crawled in there and died."

"They didn't want to let me sleep anymore and I wasn't in the mood for church services, so I was back on the road. I finally got a ride with a truck driver who dropped me off down the street."

"I came back from studying at the library and found him sleeping on the floor," Bruce said. "He still had all his clothes on, and he smelled like a brewery."

"You must have really been plowed," someone said.

"Hey," Dick said, chuckling. "The old Colonel really packs a kick."

Dick didn't know it, but he had just become the first person on our hall to get a nickname. For the rest of our first year, Richard Simpson was "Colonel Simpson," usually shortened to "Colonel," to all of us.

The group split up shortly after that. Most of the guys on the hall realized they had to study every night if there were classes the next day. There were a few who didn't think they had to start yet. Danny poked his head into the room to let me know he'd be down the hall playing cards. I thought about saying something, but I quickly decided it was none of my business. For all I knew, he was one of those guys who never had to study. I settled down to an hour and a half of memorizing French vocabulary.

7

I got into a comfortable routine easily over the next couple of weeks, dragging myself out of bed for classes and making sure I stayed awake through all of them. I'd never been much of a coffee drinker, but I forced myself to acquire the taste. It was either that or No-Doz, and the little white tablets always had made me sick to my stomach.

I occasionally took afternoon naps, but I studied at least four hours every evening, no matter what I had coming the next day.

My composition about Buffalo Bob had turned out to be a pleasant surprise. I didn't get the expected D, the grade almost everyone else in the class got. I got a C-plus, with a scribbled note from Mr. Chase. "This is interesting if a little bit rough, Mr. Miller. You've shown me some imagination. I'm looking forward to reading more of your work."

That scared me a little. I never thought of myself as a writer, and now I had something to live up to. Still, it was better than my first college grade being a D. I'd had D's before and they always made my stomach feel even worse than No-Doz.

The weekends were enjoyable. I spent one Saturday at Mary Washington and the next up at Madison, both times in hopes of finding a date for Homecoming weekend. The first weekend didn't work out, but one of the girls I had known from high school introduced me to her roommate at Madison.

Frannie Layton was from Norfolk, and she had the sexiest southern accent. She wasn't a classically pretty girl, but there was something about her that attracted me. She was about 5-foot-3 and a little on the buxom side, but she liked to dance close, which was a definite plus.

"You dance great," I whispered in her ear as she pressed tightly against me while the dance band in the Madison gym played a barely recognizable version of Otis Redding's "Try a Little Tenderness." It was the second time I'd been up to see her, and she had agreed to be my date for Homecomings.

We talked about the weekend. Bruce and I had rented a double room at the Downtowner Motor Inn, two blocks from the dorms. Dave had told me how quickly good motel rooms were snapped up for party weekends, so we left deposits to hold a room for Homecomings, Openings, Midwinters and Easters. We had agreed that if either one of us left school before the last of those, he'd forfeit his deposit unless the other guy could find someone else willing to take over his share. While the two of us were sharing the cost, Bruce's date would share the room with Frannie for Homecomings.

One thing most of us learned was that matchmaking for party weekends was a growth industry. Having a friend could lead to numerous setups, and for girls at the various women's colleges in those days, an invitation to a party weekend at the University of Virginia was usually worth risking an extended blind date with a friend of a friend.

Frannie and I agreed to talk the Monday before Homecomings, to decide when we would get together and to see if there was anything we could do to help our dateless friends. About two-thirds of the guys on the hall wound up finding dates on their own, and the rapidly developing grapevine managed to get blind dates for all but three more. I had asked Danny if he wanted me to set him up with someone, but he had a girl from home making the trip down. "You didn't tell me you had a girlfriend," I said, grinning.

He shook his head. "She's not my girlfriend. Her dad works with my dad, and we went out once this summer. She's still in high school."

I smiled. "And her parents are letting her come down for a wild weekend like this? I'm impressed, Danny. They must really trust you."

Danny shrugged. "Not completely. We made a deal. She's got some relatives down here—an aunt and uncle—and she's staying with them. They're going to let her stay out until 1 o'clock, so at least we'll get to go to the parties."

He knew as well as I did that the fraternities would be open for rush parties until 3 o'clock on Friday night and would shut down an hour earlier on Saturday. "Yeah," I said. "I guess that's not too bad."

"I've never really dated much, so this is new to me," Danny said. "Natalie's the first girl I'll ever have gone out with more than once."

I had work to do, so I nodded and picked up my biology book. It crossed my mind that I had just had one of the longest conversations with my roommate since the day we'd met. It certainly had been the most personal one.

Danny looked like he was going to study, too. That's a shock, I thought, figuring I could count on one hand the times I saw him with his nose in his books. I really envied him that. He was obviously a bright kid and didn't have to study much.

There's one lesson a lot of bright kids learn that Danny hadn't. He seemed to have a knack for annoying people by constantly letting them know how smart he was. Once in the first few weeks of school, I'd been in a group of guys talking about politics. Everybody seemed to think Richard Nixon would be running against President Johnson in 1968, and Joe Del Rio said Nixon had been governor of California before he was vice president.

Danny wasn't the only one who knew that was wrong. I knew Nixon had been a senator and not a governor, but I wasn't about to correct Joe in front of the group. My roommate didn't seem to have any problem doing that, though. Danny made it very clear that Nixon first had been a congressman and then a senator, that he'd never run for governor of California until after he lost the 1960 presidential election. He was right, but I don't think Joe was the only one annoyed when Danny told him how wrong he was.

I didn't spend a lot of time in bull sessions. I knew my own limitations. I had been putting in a solid four hours a night studying, and I was barely keeping up. Except for compositions in English, a couple of French quizzes and biology lab reports, there wouldn't be any graded work until the second week in November.

Dave had warned me about that. "It's going to seem easy. You're going to feel like you can take a night off any time you want because you don't have midterms until November. But forget about it. If you don't keep up, you'll wind up pulling all-nighters just to get C's and D's."

It had been good advice, and I was following it. I knew a lot of the other guys weren't. There was always at least one poker game, and there were some guys who didn't put in serious study time more than one or two evenings a week. I figured it was none of my business the way other guys spent their time. I had decided to make studying my top priority first semester, and the only other things I was going to do was pledge a fraternity and date occasionally.

Jack Mathews, our resident advisor, met with us the night before the first smokers to tell us what to expect. "How many of you want to pledge?" he asked the twenty-five or so first-year men who had crowded into his room. About two-thirds of us raised our hands. "What about the rest of you? Just haven't made up your minds?"

Most of them nodded. "Good. I admit I'm prejudiced on this score, but I think not belonging to a fraternity leaves you out in the cold socially. There's just one thing. My guess is that only half of you will get bids this semester."

Someone gasped. "How come? The pamphlet the Inter Fraternity Council sent around said there was a fraternity for every first-year man. Is that just a bunch of crap?"

"No," Jack said. "That's true, even though you've got to remember the IFC's main job is promoting the Greek system. I think there really is a fraternity out there for every one of you. But most of you are not going to find that fraternity, at least not this year. Tell me this, guys … how many of y'all are going to SAE or ATO tomorrow night?"

Almost everyone raised a hand. "That's what I mean. Last year's campus rankings had those two rated at the top of the list. They'll take twenty or twenty-five pledges each, and half of the first-year class will be going to their smokers."

"Yeah, but..."

"I'm serious. I'm an SAE, and our house and ATO can choose almost anybody we want, but I can think of at least five houses that won't even fill half of their quotas. Think about it. Some of y'all can save yourself a lot of heartache if you forget about the top houses and just try to find a house with guys you like."

It sounded like good advice, but I wasn't worried. The houses I was rushing were good but not great, and I had solid connections at both places. Despite that, I was a little nervous with smokers only one day away. Danny wasn't helping matters. I'd never seen him so antsy, so I asked him what was wrong.

"I'm just nervous," he said. "I really want to get into a good house."

"That shouldn't be a problem for you. You've got most of the Jewish houses after you, don't you?"

He shrugged. "Yeah, but I'm not sure I want to go that route. I'm Jewish, but we aren't the most observant family in the world. We're Conservative, but you've probably noticed I don't go to temple. I think I've been in a synagogue about five times in the last five years, and those times were for the High Holidays. But down here it's like I'm caught in between. To the Jewish guys, it's like I should automatically be one of them, and to everyone else it's like I have a big, hooked nose and I ought to be wearing a prayer shawl and fringes all the time."

I didn't think I was anti-Semitic, but I knew I'd been guilty of the stereotyping at one time or another. Back home, whenever one of my uncles bought a new car, he always told us proudly that he'd been able to "Jew the guy down" a little. I'd probably used the phrase once or twice myself, without ever thinking what it really meant. I never heard my dad say anything like that, though. He always brought me up to believe in equality.

There was a lot of turmoil when black people were fighting for civil rights in the 1960s, but my dad always stood foursquare on the right side of the issue. He said nothing was stupider than judging someone by the color of his skin or his religion or national origin. He told me the only measure of a man that meant anything at all was what was in his heart. I guess I had always taken tolerance for granted.

Hearing Danny talk about anti-Semitism was starting to make me feel uncomfortable, so I tried to change the subject. "So tell me, which smokers are you going to try?"

"I guess I'll probably go to the ones that invited me, but I want to go to some of the other ones, too."

"Then go. Nobody's stopping you."

He gave me an odd look. "Tell me, Rob. Do you think I really have any chance of getting into a non-Jewish fraternity?"

"Honestly?" He nodded. "I don't know, but I do know the reason there are four Jewish houses is that a lot of fraternities don't like to take Jewish guys. It's the same reason there are Negro fraternities at a lot of schools."

He sighed. "I guess I knew that, but I still want to try."

"Want some advice? Do whatever you want, but if you really want to pledge, don't forget the Jewish houses. Give yourself a safety valve."

It wasn't what he wanted to hear.

Both of us bent over our books. I was glad to see that Danny seemed to be taking his classes a little more seriously, even if he did give up on studying in a little less than an hour. He asked me if I wanted to go for a hamburger, but I told him I still had work to do.

"See you later." I nodded and was back into French grammar before he was out the door. I put in two more hours and felt confident I would be able to do well the next day. Danny still wasn't back when I finished, so I put the radio on and listened to some rock and roll on WUVA, the campus station, for a while before going to bed.

8

Bruce and I had decided we would start the evening together by hitting the KSK smoker. Jack had recommended that the guys who were interested in the same houses should go around together—"Safety in numbers," he called it—so we figured that was as good a place as any to start. He was going on to PIKA from there, and I was going over to the SPO house. I thought I could help Bruce by introducing him to Dave. He had told me Kappa Sigma Kappa was the house he really wanted. "It's one of only two fraternities that was founded right here at the University."

"You don't have to tell me. I told you my best friend has been trying to sell me on pledging there all summer. I think I probably know everything there is to know about KSK."

"So why don't you go for it? We could pledge together."

"I might, but my dad and my grandfather were in SPO. I think a lot of people in my family are expecting me to go that route."

Smoker Night turned out to be a long one. The parties had been scheduled to last until 2 a.m., and first-year men had been cautioned against drinking too much free beer. After all, the objective was to present yourself in a favorable light, and it's tough to make a good impression when you're puking all over your shoes. That's why I was a little surprised when Dave met the two of us at KSK with two Dixie cups full of beer. "There's plenty more where that came from, Bobby."

It was apparent that my friend and several of his brothers hadn't waited until the beginning of the smoker to start drinking.

I always was lousy at remembering names when I met a lot of people at once. Some people have that talent. I never did, no matter how hard I worked at it, but I tried my best that night to remember as many as I could. I met Rich, the editor of the Cavalier Daily, the school newspaper. He lived in one of the rooms on the Lawn, and we talked about how much he enjoyed it. I met Chuck and Eddie, two behemoths who played offensive tackle on the Virginia football team that was on its way to yet another losing season.

Bruce and I got separated quickly. I hoped he was meeting people because Dave was with me. "So, tell me," my friend said as he handed me another beer. "How do you like our house?"

"Seems really nice."

"Good. I've been talking you up to my brothers, and I think if you don't throw up or try to take your pants off over your head, you should get an invitation to meals."

Being invited for a week of meals was the first big hurdle of rush. Invitations did go out to Homecoming parties, a move that told would-be pledges if there was interest in them, but even without an invitation to the parties, anyone enrolled in school was still free to attend. Since the only real social life on the grounds was at the various fraternities, most houses opened their doors on the four major party weekends. Meals were by invitation only, though, and they marked the first real winnowing-out. The goal was to get at least two invitations to eat unless you already knew where you wanted to pledge.

I spent two hours at KSK, including thirty minutes of conversation with the chapter president. It was apparent that being Dave's best friend was helping me a lot, and I had the feeling that as long as I kept cool, I could probably pledge there if that was what I wanted. We talked about various things, and I realized they were really interested in me.

That was a good feeling, and it helped me get past the last of my nervousness. I saw Bruce once or twice, and he came by a little before 10 o'clock to tell me he was leaving. "You like it here?" I asked him.

He nodded. "Yeah, I do. And your friend Dave seems like a good guy, but I figure I'd better try to get over to PIKA. I'd hate to put all my eggs in one basket."

I left a few minutes later and walked across the quad to Sigma Phi Omicron. I decided that if I liked it there, I'd spend the rest of the evening there. After all, if I was going to go to only two houses, hitting the one where my best friend was a brother and the one where they had to take me because of my dad wasn't the worst idea I'd ever had.

When I got there, I was a little surprised to see Danny Jacobs coming out. "Hey, how are you doing?" I asked him. "Did you like it in there?"

He grinned. "Yeah, I did. They seemed like really good guys, and I think they liked me, too."

I wasn't quite sure what to say at the prospect of my roommate as a pledge brother. "So where are you going next?"

"Over to Phi Ep and the other Jewish houses. Like you said, I shouldn't burn those bridges the first night."

I watched him walk off, wondering what sort of an impression my roommate had made on my dad's fraternity. I knew I wouldn't ask, though. It wasn't any of my business, and anyway, I didn't want to know if he hadn't done as well as he'd thought. I figured he would find out one way or the other as soon as the next round of invitations went out.

After my first hour there, I knew I was in for a difficult choice. My best friend was a KSK brother, and I liked the house, but I had hit it off with the guys in SPO almost from the moment I walked through the door. Before I'd been there half an hour, I had been roped into a game of Thumper. It was the first I'd ever heard of the most popular drinking game at the University, a game I would play dozens of times over the next four years.

It was a complicated game involving hand signals and a keg of beer, and every mistake meant the one making the error had to take a swig of beer. Of course, every swig of beer led to more mistakes. The idea this time was to get the rushees drunk, to see who could hold his liquor and who couldn't. By midnight I was feeling no pain at all. I hadn't been a heavy drinker in high school, but I could hold my beer as well as most of these guys. Still, I was being cautious and drinking as little as I could each time I had to drink.

"Come on, Rob," one of the brothers said. "We can see what you're doing."

"Huh?" I tried to remember the name of the brother who had started ragging on me. I strained my memory a little harder and remembered it was Lonnie Edwards. "What do you mean, Lonnie?"

He laughed. "You think we haven't noticed you're trying not to drink? How are we going to find out if you can hold your liquor if you don't get drunk?"

I shrugged. My Dixie cup of beer was about two-thirds full, and I downed it as the guys at the table chanted, "Chug! Chug! Chug!" When I finished it, I slammed the cup down on the table, just as I'd seen the others do. That was good for a big cheer, and my loud belch was good for a second one.

An hour later, the game broke up. I was holding onto sobriety by the thinnest of margins when Lonnie took me aside. "I just thought I'd see if you had any questions about the house. I'm the rush chairman here, so it's my job to answer those questions."

I decided the best thing was just to listen, so I nodded and tried to look intelligent. I probably wasn't too successful, but Lonnie had drunk at least as much beer as I had. "Rob, you couldn't have known this, but we got a dozen different letters about you this summer. Our national sends letters around to alumni in various areas, asking them if they know of any promising young men we ought to get into the fraternity. There were more letters about you than anyone else in the first-year class."

"Who wrote you about me?"

"Brothers who were here when your dad was. Guys he kept in touch with. I don't have them with me, but someday maybe I can show them to you."

I nodded. The fraternity had meant a lot to my father, and he had told me many times about the close friendships he'd made in his four years as an undergraduate.

"I just want you to know that we want you to pledge here. We can't offer you a bid until just before Thanksgiving. You're a legacy, though, and everybody has been impressed with the way you handled yourself tonight. Unless you tell us you're not interested, you can count on getting a bid from us."

I don't think I'd had such strong feelings of emotion since we buried my dad. He and I always had been close, and I'd missed him a lot the last two years. When I'd walked into the SPO house and seen his graduating class picture in the dining room, I'd had to fight to hold back tears. I'd seen pictures of him from college before, but I don't think I'd ever realized how much I looked like he had at that age. And when I had hunted around for the Class of 1916 and had seen my grandfather's picture, I had known I really didn't have such a tough decision at all.

Dave would understand why I couldn't pledge Kappa Sigma Kappa, and I'd do my best to help Bruce get in there. "Thanks, Lonnie," I said, coming out of my reverie. "I've been impressed with you guys, too. I don't think I'll be rushing any other houses."

He grinned. "Thanks for that. I'll pass it along to the other guys. I think I'll get back to the party. You coming?"

I shook my head. "I think I'll just sit here and think for a few minutes."

Lonnie seemed to understand. "Sure, Rob, but one more thing. My dad was fourth year when your dad was first year. I was a legacy, too. That's why I took you aside to talk to you. We don't want you thinking the only reason you'll get a bid from us is because we have to give you one." I nodded. "I'll tell you this much. We do have to give bids to sons and grandsons of brothers, but if it's a guy we really don't think would fit in with the guys in the house, we don't exactly go out of our way to make him feel welcome."

Lonnie slapped me on the back and returned to the party. I noticed that it was getting late, and I was starting to feel tired. I thought about my Saturday classes. After pondering the situation for a minute or so, I decided I'd better get back to the dorms. I hadn't cut any classes yet and I didn't think this weekend would be a good time to start.

I was more than a little bit drunk. I felt pretty good, though. I felt as though I had managed to dispose of one of the biggest decisions of my first semester of college. It was a few minutes after 2 o'clock when I dragged myself into my room. The lights were off, and I noticed Danny was in his bed. He appeared to be asleep, so I didn't bother asking how the last part of his evening had gone. I figured it could wait.

9

By early October, something had started happening in our dormitory that happens anytime anyone puts a group of young males together.

Nicknames.

Dick Simpson had received the first one, courtesy of his legendary evening with the Colonel. The rest came less dramatically, mostly from Bruce and Dick. If every group of males winds up with nicknames, I suppose it follows that someone has to give them.

Someone once told me there were only two kinds of people in the world—those who give nicknames and those who receive them. On our hall, Bruce and Dick were the ones who gave out most of those nicknames. Some of them came more easily than others. Once Leo Mitchell's poor sanitary habits became evident, he got the nickname "Germ." Ricky Barton became "Johnny U," after his hometown football hero, and Andy Lynch, whose dad worked for Anheuser-Busch, became "Beer Man." It probably helped that he had a prodigious taste for it. Ed Randolph, the closest thing to a true southerner on our hall, somehow got the nickname "Robert E. Lee" after one of his distant relatives.

I wasn't worried. I didn't have any unfortunate habits, or any outstanding characteristics. I got along well with everybody, so I didn't think anyone on the hall would try to stick me with anything obnoxious. At least I didn't think I had any outstanding characteristics. I found out I was wrong. One thing I'd never paid a whole lot of attention to was the size of my friends' genitals, so I had never realized that I was a bit larger than average in that area.

Dick Simpson had been trying to think of a nickname for me for weeks and nothing had stuck. The first time he saw me in the shower, though, his problem was solved. I had my nickname. "The Root." I had no idea what I'd tell my mother if she ever heard it, and it was more than a little embarrassing. Still, I knew if I had to be known for something, there were probably worse things than people thinking I had a big cock.

Danny didn't have a nickname yet, at least not one people were calling him to his face. There were the usual anti-Semitic remarks from guys like Joe Del Rio and Dick Simpson, remarks I never really had noticed until I had a Jewish roommate.

If there was one thing that was obvious after a month or so, it was that my roommate wasn't really fitting in anywhere. He always seemed to be on the fringe of one group or another, but he never made any friends. I couldn't think of one guy he was hanging out with. The only time anyone ever came to our room to see him was when they needed a fourth for bridge or a fifth for poker. He was an enthusiastic card player, and on the rare occasions he managed to organize a game of his own, he brought the game to our room.

When that happened, I usually just shrugged, picked up my books and went across the street to the library to study. Hell, it was his room too.

Danny hadn't made a real great impression at the SPO house. When the invitations came out for Homecomings parties, the only one in our mailbox from Sigma Phi Omicron was addressed to me. I had one other one. Dave had made sure Kappa Sigma Kappa invited me, even though I'd tried to tell him I'd made up my mind. "Give us one more try. Come to our party on Friday night and then go to SPO Saturday night."

"I'll tell you what, Dave. How about if I come by for a couple of hours one of the nights?"

Dave shrugged. "We'll be glad to have you. By the way, I heard about your new nickname."

"You're kidding. Who told you?"

"Your buddy, Bruce Benson. Remember, he's rushing our house." I groaned. "Don't worry about it. That's not such a bad nickname. We've got guys in our house named Worm and Weasel for the same reason you're called Root. It's a lot better to be too big than too small in that area. I won't let it get around back home."

That was small consolation. I figured I had no choice but to get used to it. I wondered if there was some revenge I could take, but I knew I wasn't a vindictive guy.

Danny had received two invitations to Homecoming parties— AEPi and Phi Ep. That was as many as at least half the guys on the hall, but he seemed irritated by the fact that only the Jewish houses had invited him. "I didn't even make it to AEPi's smoker."

"Maybe they know that. Maybe they're giving you a second chance."

"I thought I told you I didn't want to pledge a Jewish house."

I didn't know what to say to that. I had already told Danny once that I didn't think a Jewish guy's chances of pledging a non-Jewish fraternity were that great. The few guys who had managed to do it usually had something else going for them. Bob Weckstein was a star defensive tackle for the football team, and that had been enough to get him into

Sigma Zoo, the legendary jock house. Danny didn't play sports, though, and it looked to me as if he could either pledge a Jewish fraternity or stay independent.

The rest of his life didn't appear to be going much better. His study habits were still erratic at best, and with midterms a month away, I was beginning to have serious doubts about how my roommate would do unless he really was a genius. I'd noticed something else, too. He was starting to cut classes occasionally. He couldn't do it too often. Cuts were still rigidly limited in those days, but some of our professors didn't take attendance. Especially in the huge lecture classes like biology, people could miss as often as they wanted, and it would go pretty much unnoticed. Twice in the week before Homecomings, Danny didn't bother getting up for early classes.

It was strange. I hadn't taken any psychology courses, so I didn't know much about the symptoms of depression. I took Psychology 101 as an elective my third year, but by then it was too late to do me much good.

Danny was staying up later at night and awakening later and later in the morning. He was a lot less talkative in October than he had been in September, but I was so wrapped up in my own studying that not having to make conversation was a welcome surprise. My classes were going well. I had a B average in English Comp, and I was borderline B-C after half a dozen French quizzes. There hadn't been much work yet in calculus or history, and I thought I might even have a shot at an A on my laboratory work in biology.

I was doing as well as almost anyone on the hall. I was working harder than I ever had in my life. It was a rare night that I studied fewer than five hours, and I even found myself spending some Saturday afternoons grinding in the library. That was the best time of the week to get real work done. Everybody else was either at the football game when the Wahoos were at home or listening on the radio when they were away.

I liked football, but I had grown up following real football teams, teams like Penn State, Pitt, and the Steelers. I really couldn't get excited about Atlantic Coast Conference football, so I took advantage of the empty library. I knew it would pay off later, and I was beginning to think I might have a chance at the B average I wanted so badly.

Even though I had established good study habits, it was tough to maintain them in the week before Homecomings. I had called Frannie long distance twice, and we matched two of her friends with guys on the hall who didn't have dates.

One of our matches had been a real chore. Rick Arbogast was the quintessential engineering student, or "Toolie," as we called them in those days. The movie "Revenge of the Nerds" was nearly a generation in the future, but Rick would have fit in perfectly, from his horn-rimmed glasses to his white shirt and pencil protector. He even had a slide rule hanging from his belt when he went to class over at the Tool School.

To further complicate things, he was without a doubt the ugliest guy in the first-year class. His face seemed to have more angles to it than a human face is supposed to have, and he was severely under-weight. The acne that covered his face, neck and upper back didn't help much either. Rick was the kind of guy who made you feel better about the way you looked, just by looking at him.

I wasn't thrilled when he came to me the Monday afternoon before Homecomings and asked if I could get him a date. "You've got somebody coming, don't you, Rob?" I nodded. "Does she have any friends?"

"I guess so." I wasn't making it any easier for him, and I knew I would help him out if he came right out and asked. I just didn't want to inflict this guy on any of Frannie's friends.

Rick took a deep breath. "Do you think you could ask your girl to get me a date? I know it's late, but everybody says the girls are all dying to come down here for a big weekend." He looked at me sadly, the mask slipping a little. "I'm sorry if I'm putting you on the spot, but you're my last chance. There's no way I'm going to get a date if you don't help me, and I don't want to spend the whole weekend in the lab."

I couldn't think of any good arguments, so I grabbed Frannie's phone number and headed for the pay phone at the end of the hall. It was in use. Joe Del Rio was talking to one of his buddies back home in Winchester, and it was fifteen minutes before he hung up and headed for the bathroom. I asked Rick for some change to make the call, and he obliged with a handful of quarters and dimes. Frannie was in. In fact, she was the one who answered the phone. We exchanged pleas-antries and then I got down to the point of the call. "I've got a guy here who's still looking for a date. His name is Rick Arbogast."

"What's he like?"

I decided to be diplomatic, especially since Rick was practically leaning over my shoulder. "Uh, he's about my height. A little thinner than me ..."

"He must be really thin, then. You're not exactly beefy. What does he look like?"

I looked at Rick, with his buzz haircut and his angular face. I couldn't lie, but I knew I had to sugarcoat the truth a little or Rick was in big trouble. "Well, I guess he looks studious." Rick punched my shoulder angrily. "Come on, man," I said, putting my hand over the mouthpiece. "Back off a little. I'm doing the best I can."

He nodded. "All right, but don't get me some pig. I don't want a pig for a date."

I resisted the temptation to ask him where he would be if his date were telling Frannie the same thing. "Relax, Rick."

"Are you still there, Rob?" Frannie asked.

"Sure. Do you have anybody in mind for Rick?"

"Well, there's one girl on the hall who thought she had to go home this weekend, but it turned out she's free after all. She put out the word she'd be willing to take a blind date. She's nice. Her name is Beth Erickson, and she's from your home state, from Scranton. I don't think there'll be any problem, but why don't you call me back tomorrow night just to make sure."

We exchanged goodbyes, and I headed back to my room to study. I figured I'd done my good deed for the month.

The rest of the week passed quickly. I'd called Frannie back the next night without Rick hanging over me. I'd learned that yes, Beth Erickson would be happy to come down for Homecomings and no, she wasn't expecting a whole lot of Rick. It was the first time I'd seen proof of what everyone was saying. Virginia party weekends were the biggest thing around, and there really were girls who were happy to come no matter who their dates were. Only three of the forty guys on the hall didn't have dates. Two had made plans to go home, and the other was going to spend the entire weekend in the library studying.

Even Danny was getting excited. He didn't know his date that well yet; she was someone he had wanted to date for a long time. "You think she'll be impressed?" he asked me Wednesday night.

"Sure. When you see how many college girls all over the state have been taking dates with almost anybody just to get the chance to come down here, I don't see how a high school girl could help but be impressed."

Danny nodded excitedly. "That's good, because I really like Natalie a lot. She's pretty, and bright, and she's got a great sense of humor."

"Well, I hope you two have a great time. Which parties are you going to hit? The two you got invited to?"

He shrugged. My question seemed to deflate his mood a little. "Yeah, but I thought we'd stop by a couple others as well. I thought I'd take another shot at the guys at SPO."

I didn't want to advise Danny too much. For one thing, my dad always had taught me that you couldn't keep people from making their own mistakes. Even if you told someone not to do something, once it didn't work out, he or she usually wound up resenting you for it. My dad's own philosophy about advice was that you gave someone advice about something once at most. If they didn't listen the first time, you let them make their own mistakes after that. I had already had one long talk with Danny about fraternity rush, so I wasn't going to say any more on the subject. I was surprised that he hadn't asked me to help him out with the brothers at SPO. That was what I had been dreading.

There was only one safe thing to say. "Well, I hope you have a great time."

On the Thursday night before the weekend, I finally broke my rule about studying on every school night. I had heard a lot about how the big party weekends really started on Thursdays, so I put my books away and went out drinking with three other guys from the dorm. We spent the evening putting away pitchers at the Virginian and we rolled in at about 2 o'clock in the morning. I made my classes the next morning, but I didn't do myself much good. It took every bit of energy I had just to stay awake.

I got back to the room by noon, totally exhausted. Frannie and her friends were due in at 5 o'clock, and it was going to be a late night. After wasting a few seconds cursing my poor judgment for going out on Thursday, and then a few more trying to convince myself I should have skipped my classes to get some sleep, I decided I would try to take a nap. I knew that putting a "Do Not Disturb" sign on the door would be tantamount to inviting everyone in the dorm to raise hell. All I could do was hope there wouldn't be much commotion. I pulled the curtains, turned off the lights and collapsed fully dressed onto my bed.

For once luck was with me. I wasn't bothered until Danny came into the room a little after three. After a moment or two of disorientation—I've never been a good daytime sleeper—I soon realized I had plenty of time to shower and get ready for the big weekend.

10

Frannie and I had agreed that we would meet in the lobby at the Downtowner. I was there a few minutes before five, and I wound up waiting nearly an hour before she breezed in with Beth Erickson in tow. She was quick with an apology, but it wasn't her fault. The girl who was driving hadn't been able to get away until about 3 o'clock, and the weather hadn't been great around Harrisonburg. What was normally a two-hour drive at worst had taken nearly three on rain-slickened roads. The weather finally had cleared about twenty miles west of Charlottesville, and that had lifted their spirits a little. "Did you wait long?" she asked me.

I shrugged. "A minute or two. Bruce and his date aren't here either, but why don't we see if we can get you checked in and then we'll go to dinner."

"Sounds like a good idea. By the way, this is Beth Erickson. Since you didn't say anything about a place for her to stay, I thought I'd let her sleep in the room with me."

I cursed Rick silently. He was turning out to be a real pain. Of course, Beth had turned out to be a terrific-looking blonde, and I felt a pang of guilt that I had saddled her with Rick. "Hi, Beth. I'm Rob. Your date isn't here. He said he would meet us at 6:30 or so."

Beth flashed a killer smile. "If he's anything like you, he's worth waiting for." Frannie giggled as she saw me blushing. "Beth's kind of a flirt."

"That's all right. I'm just not all that used to girls flirting with me."

Beth looked at me skeptically and affected a mock Southern accent. "Honey Chile, that dog simply will not hunt."

"I thought you were from Pennsylvania," I said.

Beth winked at me. The conversation wasn't going anywhere, so I asked them if they wanted to go up and change clothes before Rick came over.

"Sure," Beth said. "Are we all going to dinner together?"

I hadn't planned on having Rick and his date accompany us, and I was pretty sure Bruce wasn't going to be thrilled with the idea either. "We'll have to see. For all I know, Rick's got other plans."

I knew he wouldn't. Rick was so terrified by the prospect of a date—for all I knew, it was the first one he'd ever had with a living, breathing female, let alone one as lovely as Beth—that I knew he would jump at the chance to hang out with the rest of us. It probably would make it more comfortable for his date, too, to be able to stick around with her friend. That meant we would be stuck with Rick for at least part of the evening.

It didn't help when he showed up and found out how pretty his date was. Rick hadn't wanted an ugly pig, but I think he'd have been a lot happier with someone a little more average looking. What he had was the classic mismatch—Mr. Wizard meets the homecoming queen. To her credit, Beth didn't act at all uncomfortable.

Rick was incredibly nervous, but she kept doing her best to put him at ease. She asked him about his likes and dislikes, his hobbies, and interests. She tried, but it was obvious he was out of his league with a beautiful blonde who really had been the homecoming queen at her high school.

One other unforeseen problem was that Dick Simpson had

attached himself to our group. His date wasn't arriving until Saturday morning, so he was on the prowl. Bruce pulled me aside to tell me what Dick had on his mind. I couldn't believe it when I heard his plan. "You're kidding me. Dick's going to try and take Rick's date away from him?"

"Yeah," Bruce said. "It's easy to see she's not happy with Rick." I gave him a strange look, but he shrugged. "It's up to her. If she wants to party with the Colonel, she can. If not, she can stay with that toolie."

"What's Rick going to be doing through all of this?"

"The Colonel's going to get him drunk. He won't have any idea what's happening—or care—after he's had a few drinks."

That seemed like a horrible idea to me, but I figured it was none of my business. When I look back, I wish I had been different. I'm different now, but I had to grow into being the kind of person I am. Don't we all? I've probably asked myself that question ten thousand times since I was 18 years old.

Dick was sharing his fifth of bourbon, and Rick was halfway into the bag by the time we left for the parties. Frannie pulled me aside. "Does Rick always drink that much?"

I shrugged. "I don't really know the guy that well. I don't know how much he drinks."

I must have sounded annoyed because Frannie acted quickly to placate me. "I'm not mad at you. I was just getting a little worried for my friend."

I tried a smile. It's a good thing there weren't any mirrors around, because I don't think I could have stood the sight of how insincere I probably looked. "Don't worry, Frannie. Rick's a big boy. I'm sure he can take care of himself."

She didn't sound convinced. "Let's keep them with us."

We did, and Dick Simpson tagged along, too. He kept giving Rick more drinks, and Rick was so happy to be accepted as a drinking buddy by the popular, outgoing Texan that he was quick to drink them. We decided to go to the party at the ATO house first. It was a house I had no interest in, so I was glad to see this little drama played out somewhere it couldn't hurt my chances of pledging.

I hoped we'd be able to shake the rest of our little group before we went to SPO. No such luck. Rick was getting drunker and drunker, and more and more obnoxious. He had a basic hostility toward the fraternity system, so being drunk at a fraternity party wasn't the best thing in the world for him. By midnight Dick was trying to get him to go back to his room and sleep it off. Rick wasn't having any. Somehow he'd managed to remain upright enough to dance with Beth, and that seemed to be annoying the Colonel to no end.

I had seen enough. When Frannie and Beth went off to the ladies' room together, I pulled Dick aside. "Haven't you had enough of this, Simpson?"

He grinned. "What do you mean, Rooter?" He wasn't as far into the bag as Rick, but he had been drinking a lot and was feeling good.

"This little game of yours. Getting Rick drunk. Snaking his date."

"There's no way he can handle her. She's too much woman for the Slide Rule Kid. She needs about six inches of the old Colonel."

"If she's too much for him, that's his problem. It's not his fault your date couldn't get here till Saturday."

"Once I get this babe into bed, I might tell my date not to bother coming." "You're going to screw up three weekends. Not to mention mine and Frannie's."

Dick was too insensitive to listen to anything but his libido. "One more drink and he's history," Dick said, reaching for his flask. "Oh Rick, where are you?"

I didn't know what else I could do. I suppose if I had truly been concerned, I would have said something to Frannie or Beth, or maybe even warned Rick himself. That would have meant admitting that I had known about this from the beginning, though, and that was something I wasn't prepared to do. When Frannie returned, I asked her if she was ready to go to the SPO party. "Sure," she said. "I'll go get Beth and Rick."

The four of us—with Dick Simpson tagging along like a vulture—walked across the quad to the SPO house. Under any sort of normal circumstances, the others wouldn't have been able to get into a fraternity party at a house they weren't rushing. Big weekends weren't normal, though. Just my luck. Of course, Lonnie Edwards was the first guy we ran into as we showed up at the party, so of course everyone in the house knew that Rick was with me. I caught a couple of quizzical looks. Rick wasn't the type of guy who usually showed up at fraternity parties, but the brothers were glad to see me and they were making a fuss over Frannie.

She was really enjoying herself, and the band was great. In those days, all the houses had soul bands on big weekends. By the 1980's, they were calling that sort of music "Beach Music," and a friend of mine once defined it as music played by middle aged black men for drunken white kids. It may have been that, but it was great. The music was so damned evocative. Even a generation later, every time I hear "Double Shot of My Baby's Love" or "Expressway to Your Heart," I can almost see the guys I knew in college. I can almost smell the beer, poured from large kegs into big Dixie cups and sloshing over the sides.

Every time I hear Sam and Dave singing "Soul Man," or Otis cutting loose on "Try A Little Tenderness," I want to dance. I swear to God, the music takes me back. It makes me feel like I'm 18 again, and that's a wonderful feeling. Occasionally I even remember Home-comings 1967—even though I have done my best to forget it. What happened after we finally settled in at the SPO house was the biggest disaster I can remember in my four years in the fraternity.

Dick Simpson finally had run out of bourbon, so he made a beeline for the keg and filled a cup of beer for himself and another one for Rick. By then Beth was starting to realize something was wrong, and she tried to get Rick to stop drinking. He was too far gone, though, and he wanted to prove he could drink as much as the next guy. He downed the 16-ounce beer in three or four swallows, and then he dragged his beautiful date out onto the dance floor. It was a bad move. Rick was a horrible dancer. He moved like a mechanical man with a couple of parts missing, but he was too drunk to realize he was making an idiot out of himself. Dick stood off in the corner laughing. For the first time since I had known him, I wanted to punch his lights out.

Five minutes later, it happened. Rick started coughing. He couldn't stop, and for a minute I thought he was choking. I asked him if he was all right, and then I realized he was about to vomit. I looked around frantically, wondering if I could get him outside the house or into a bathroom in time. We were right in the middle of the dance floor, though, and the line for the bathroom had about a dozen people in varying degrees of need waiting. "Hold on, Rick," I said, trying to grab his arm and get him out of the main room.

He shook his head, as if to tell me he wasn't going anywhere. Then I heard a rumbling noise deep in his stomach and it started. He didn't just vomit, either. He projectile vomited, what we later would call booting. I saw it coming and I jumped off to the left, just in time to escape getting Rick's lunch and dinner all over my sport coat. Dick Simpson wasn't so lucky. He'd been on his way over with another beer for Rick, hoping this would be the one to get him to pass out, and he took it right in the middle of his chest.

"You asshole!" He dropped the beer to go after Rick, and I wasn't lucky enough to get out of the way a second time. My pants were drenched with beer. I looked at Dick's shirt and knew I had gotten the better of the exchange.

Rick wasn't through. He was careening around like he didn't know where he was, and the second wave of vomit went in an entirely different direction. It hit a gorgeous redhead who happened to be the date of the president of the fraternity. She started screaming, and that turned everything up a notch or two emotionally. The third wave mostly landed on the couch, and by the time the fourth came up, Rick was doubled over on the floor. The fourth wave landed all over Frannie's shoes.

Three brothers came running up to see what was happening. "Get that guy out of here," the irate president hissed, trying to comfort his screaming date at the same time. One of the bigger guys in the house started to grab Rick. I tried to restrain him, and the guy sloughed off my arm without even a glance. His elbow caught me in the mouth, and I could feel my lip starting to bleed.

Two burly brothers took Rick by the arms, frog-marched him to the front door and half-pushed, half-threw him outside onto the lawn. He just lay there in the yard, looking like an idiot. "Get the fuck out of here, and don't ever come back to this house again or you won't get off this easy."

Lonnie came over and confronted me. "How well do you know that guy, Rob?" I shrugged. "He came with you, didn't he?"

"Yeah." I sighed. "He lives on my hall, and he asked me to get him a blind date for the weekend; his date is a friend of my date. The girls wanted to stay together, so we all came here."

"Rob, don't try to explain. It's too late for that. Just do us all a favor and get your buddy back to the dorms before he tries to come back inside."

I wanted to tell him that Rick wasn't my buddy, but I just nodded as Lonnie turned and walked back to the party. I still couldn't see Frannie, but Beth was out on the lawn with Rick, trying to help him to his feet. I hurried down the steps and went over to see if there was anything I could do. Rick was so drunk he didn't even know where he was. "Wanna party some more," he said, pawing at Beth. She cringed, and I stepped between them.

"Rick, calm down." I wanted to shake him a little, but I was afraid he'd start vomiting. "We've got to get out of here."

He shook his head drunkenly, as if trying to figure something out. "Gonna take my date back to the motel. Gonna get some pussy tonight."

"Rick," I said, keeping my voice as low as I could. "You're not being cool." "Don't wanna be cool. Wanna get me some pussy."

The president of the fraternity came out onto the porch. "Are you going to get that guy out of here or...?"

I racked my brain trying to remember the guy's name, but I was drawing a complete blank. "Yeah, yeah," I said. "We're leaving."

I managed to convince Rick we had to continue our conversation somewhere else. I still didn't see Frannie, and I hated to leave without her. I didn't have any idea how upset she was, or whether she blamed me for what had happened, but as fired up as Rick was, I couldn't very well leave it to Beth to take him anywhere.

"Beth, can you find Frannie?" I looked at Rick, who had fallen to his knees again. "Do you think you two can get back to the motel without any trouble?"

That brought a smile to her face, although it didn't look like a happy smile. "I think you're the one who's got the tough job, trying to get him home."

"Yeah," I said, sighing heavily. "Somehow I think I deserve it, though."

Beth didn't understand, but she wasn't all that concerned with my problems right now. "Should I tell Frannie you'll call her in the morning?"

"Yeah, if you think she'll want to hear from me after this."

Beth actually laughed at that one. "I guess we'll have to see," she said, looking sadly at her date in a heap at my feet. Then she turned and walked into the house.

It took me the better part of an hour to get him back to the dorms. Rick kept falling, and he threw up three more times. By the third time, it was little more than dry heaves, and it sounded like he was turning himself inside out. The next to last time, when there was still some substance to it, some of the vomit finally landed on me. I felt as though I'd been punished at last for my complicity in the plot to get Rick drunk. Of course, I thought my punishment was far worse than just a little vomit on my clothes.

I thought I'd ruined my weekend with Frannie and my chances of getting into SPO all at the same time, so I wasn't in any mood to sympathize with Rick. Still, I couldn't just put him to bed all covered with vomit. I helped him down the hall to the bathroom and got him out of his clothes and into a cold shower.

I didn't know what to do with his clothes. They smelled to high heaven, but I for all I knew, this was his best suit. I put the clothes in a heap at the foot of his bed. "Do you have any pajamas around here, Rick?" I asked him as he started nodding off. I didn't get an answer, and I couldn't find anything. Finally, I located a T-shirt and put that on him. He collapsed on the bed, and I pulled his blanket up over him.

Even though it was a little before 3 o'clock in the morning, the dorm was almost empty. Most of the guys were still out with their dates, and the ones who didn't have dates had gone home for the weekend. There was a light on in my room, though. Danny was sitting on his bed reading.

"I thought I heard you come in," he said. "Is something wrong?"

"Don't ask. You really don't want to know. How did your date go?"

"Not bad. It ended early. I had to have her back at her uncle's house by one, remember?"

I didn't want to tell him I had forgotten, so I just nodded. "Aren't you going to bed?" "Soon. I'm kind of keyed up."

I smiled a little. "Well, I'm exhausted, so I think I'd better get some sleep, or I'll never get up for my Saturday classes." I was asleep within five minutes. I dreamed about the fiasco at the SPO house. In the dream, Rick's first outburst hit me squarely in the face.

11

By the time I dragged myself out of bed Saturday morning, Danny was already gone. Somehow, I stayed awake through my two classes, and when the second one ended at 11, I hurried to a phone and dialed the Downtowner.

The switchboard operator put the call through, and Beth answered. "This is Rob Miller. Is Frannie there?"

"She's in the shower."

I wasn't sure what I would say to Rick's date, but I figured maybe I could find out a little about what the mood was like. "I guess you two got back all right last night."

"Sure" She sounded noncommittal.

"Have you heard from Rick yet?"

"He called a few minutes ago. He's really embarrassed. He was sure I'd never want to see him again. He was practically crying. Rob, there's something you ought to know. Last night, before we left the fraternity party, Dick Simpson made a very crude pass at me. When I turned him down, I guess he was drunk enough and proud enough of himself that he told me what he had been trying to do to Rick. Frannie knows about it, too."

This was trouble. I tried quickly to collect my thoughts, wondering what I would say if she asked me the question I knew she was going to ask next. "Rob? Did you know anything about that? Did you know that he was trying to get Rick drunk so I would go off with him instead? Did you?"

I wanted to lie. God, I wanted to lie. I knew it would make her feel better if I let her believe Dick had done all that on his own, without anyone else knowing about it. I have never been able to lie, though. Especially to save my own skin. "Yes, Beth. I knew."

It wasn't the answer she expected. "Were you helping him?" she asked incredulously.

"No, I wasn't," I said quickly. "I tried to get him to stop. I told him it was stupid, and I told him he was being an ass. I really tried to get him to stop. He wouldn't."

"Why didn't you tell us about it? Why didn't you warn Rick?"

Because I'm chicken, I thought. Because Dick is cool and Rick isn't, and I didn't want to take Rick's part against Dick. "I don't know," I said miserably. "I'm sorry."

"You ought to be. You really ought to be ashamed of yourself." She sighed. "Rick was so humiliated this morning. He told me he didn't even remember what had happened when he first woke up, but when he saw his clothes on the floor, all covered with, you know, that brought it all back to him. He asked me if I wanted to call off the weekend."

"Did you?"

"You don't understand at all, do you?" she asked angrily. "That poor guy got trashed by two guys he trusted, and you're acting like it was his fault. Of course, I didn't call off the rest of the weekend. He's picking me up in an hour."

Good for you, I wanted to say. That's great. I wanted to say a lot. I wanted to tell her how special she must be, but I stood there holding the receiver and didn't say a thing.

"Frannie's out of the shower now. I'll put her on."

I talked with my date for a few minutes, and she didn't blame me as much as Beth did. But what had happened had taken the excitement out of the weekend. Having someone vomit on your shoes can do that, I guess. She didn't cancel, but we went through the motions. We sat together at the football game, and we went to dinner and a concert together. We went to a party over at KSK—I couldn't bring myself to go back to Sigma Phi Omicron. We danced until about two, and then I took her back to her hotel room. We stood at the door outside her room, and it was clear the situation had become awkward.

I knew something, even if neither one of us would say it. I knew that whatever had been happening between Frannie Layton and me wasn't happening anymore, and I knew if I called to ask her out again, she would either let me down gently or shoot me down fast. It wasn't that anything had really gone all that wrong between us. It was more like we were mutual survivors of the same disaster and seeing me again would only remind her of the awful evening when someone threw up on her at a fraternity party.

"Do you want to get up for breakfast tomorrow?" I asked her. There wasn't really anything else happening on Sunday, but most of the girls who came for the weekend stayed at least till mid-afternoon before heading back to their various colleges.

She shook her head. "We've got to get an early start back. I've got a couple of tests next week and I really need to study."

"Hey," I said, smiling gamely. "Have a nice life."

"You too." Then she turned and opened the door to her room.

12

I spent Sunday of Homecomings studying in Alderman Library and was a lot better prepared for my Monday classes than I had expected to be. Danny had been out with his date most of the day Sunday, and when he came back to the room after dinner, he was in a better mood than I had seen in a long time.

Tuesday afternoon I learned that I hadn't blown my chances with the fraternity. Invitations to meals had been sent out the day before; I opened my mailbox to find invitations from Kappa Sigma Kappa and from SPO. When I called Lonnie to find out what was going on, he told me nobody blamed me for what had happened. "Stuff like that happens all the time on party weekends. That's what happens when you have to let the GDI's come to your parties."

I knew from two weeks of rush and six weeks of school that GDI stood for Gamma Delta Iota, or more accurately, for God Damned Independents. Guys who weren't fraternity material. I guess that's how those of us who were saw it. "Don't worry, Rob. We still want you. Just don't bring that other guy back ... ever."

Just as my mood was getting better, Danny's went right into the dumps. The two invitations I'd received to meals were the only two in our mailbox. He hadn't gotten any from the fraternities he'd been pursuing, and since he hadn't shown any interest in the Jewish houses, they had finally given up on him. "I think I messed up," he said, sighing.

I shrugged. What else could I tell him that I hadn't said before? I wanted to say something that would make him feel better, but I really couldn't think of anything. I knew how badly I wanted to pledge, and how upset I had been when I thought I had blown it with the SPOs. I knew how relieved I had felt to see the two invitations with my name on them. I had traced my fingers across the embossed, raised lettering on the envelopes almost as if I were trying to convince myself they were real.

Fraternity rush was a real downer for most of the guys I knew. Nearly everyone had been special in high school in one way or another. Six guys on our hall had been class presidents their senior year in high school and at least that many others had been newspaper editors, or football quarterbacks, or big shots in their graduating classes. Now, after six weeks of college, some of us were being told we weren't good enough to survive the first real cut for the fraternities we wanted. Some took it well. Some vowed to make a better impression in winter rush, or to buckle down and concentrate on grades.

Some took our resident advisor's advice and lowered their sights, deciding to go after lesser houses the next time around. Some others didn't react as well. Some guys cursed the system and said they would never try again. They started drinking more, or missing classes. My roommate fell into the second group.

Most houses had given out two or three times as many meal invitations as they had spaces in their pledge class. That meant there was at least one more serious winnowing yet to come. Meals would provide a lot of the material for that process. The invitations were for five lunches and five dinners at the house. Would-be pledges would be assigned to sit with different brothers at each meal, giving the fraternity members the opportunity to learn as much about rushees as they could.

A week after meals, there would be a second set of smokers, and the following week would be more meals. The final functions of rush would be the Openings Weekend parties in mid-November, with bids due to be given the Thursday before Thanksgiving. Most of us knew the rush schedule as well our own class schedules. It was a grueling process designed to favor the houses. Anyone who was a serious candidate would likely wind up visiting a fraternity between fifteen and twenty times.

Only a few kids really had the system beat. They were the top athletes, or the rich guys from old families. They were the ones houses were falling all over themselves to get. I knew two first-year men who got three bids at the end of rush. One was a scholarship athlete, and the other one's father was the majority stockholder in a tobacco company.

The rest of us—the ones lucky enough not to get weeded out early—had to decide on one house by the midway point of the rush process. Then we had to hope we hadn't eliminated the one that really wanted us. It was an emotionally debilitating process, and we probably spent as much time discussing the fraternity system in that fall of 1967 as we did arguing the morality of the war in Vietnam or the civil rights movement.

Call us shallow. Call us insular. Both of those criticisms would certainly have been true, but people always get the most excited about things that affect them personally. For most of us that fall, pledging a good house meant more than anything except getting good grades did. To some, it mattered more.

I knew I would have to budget my time more effectively during meals week. I usually didn't eat lunch, using that hour to get a head start on my studying while I ate a sandwich. Midterms were scheduled for the second week in November, and in at least two of my classes what I did on the midterm would determine nearly half of my final grade.

In addition, I didn't have a date for Openings, the first of the three major weekends. I had thought Homecomings was a big deal, but Openings was even bigger. The organizers had the Four Tops coming in for a concert on Saturday night, and Martha and the Vandellas were the headliners for a dance in the gym Friday night.

I wasn't too worried. I knew I could clear at least one Saturday to make a road trip. I wasn't alone in that problem. Apparently at least half of the guys I had spoken with weren't planning to bring the same dates back for Openings. For some it was because they hadn't hit it off as well as they'd expected, while others had asked and been turned down. I wasn't too surprised to hear that Rick Arbogast had called Beth early to ask her if she wanted to come back for Openings. I wasn't surprised that she had said she couldn't, either.

"What did she tell you?" I asked when Rick came into my room to tell me the news. "That she has to wash her hair that weekend?"

"She just said she thought it would be better if we didn't go out again."

"I guess she must have been kind of embarrassed by what happened Friday night," I said as tactfully as I could.

He shrugged. "I suppose. It's not really that big a deal. Most girls don't usually go out with me more than once. I thought after Friday night she wouldn't even want to see me again, but we got together Saturday and had a pretty good time. We went to the football game, and to the concert. Then instead of going to the frat parties, we went back to her hotel room and just watched television together."

I didn't think that sounded massively exciting, but I didn't want to put Rick down after being a silent partner in his humiliation over the weekend. "Did anything happen?"

"Yeah. After a while, I got up my nerve enough to kiss her, and she really liked it. We ended up kissing a lot and fooling around for about an hour. That's why I was kind of surprised when she said she wouldn't come back for Openings."

That conversation stayed with me for a week or so. I had been impressed by the fact that Beth Erickson had stood by Rick instead of walking out on him in the middle of the weekend and stunned that he wound up having a lot more physical contact with his date than I did with mine.

I still felt bad about what had happened. I didn't know what I could do, short of talking to Rick and apologizing to him, and I didn't want to do that. I thought Rick should have known better. Just because someone was trying to get him drunk didn't mean he had to do it. I didn't go so far as to blame him for what happened. Maybe I was trying too hard not to blame myself. I did feel sorry for Beth. Aside from the fact that her date getting sick didn't make her first party weekend one for the scrapbooks, the Colonel had been treating her as if she were just a piece of meat.

I wasn't as conscious of feminism in those days. The university wasn't exactly a bastion of liberal thought. Hell, I knew guys on our hall who regretted that women had been given the right to vote. Still, what had happened wasn't right.

I decided to write Beth a letter. I sat down at my desk and tried to compose what I wanted to say. After about fifteen minutes of thinking it over, I composed a short note.

Dear Beth,

I know you'll probably be surprised to hear from me after what happened at Homecomings, but I just wanted to write and apologize.

Not only wasn't what happened fair to Rick Arbogast, it wasn't fair to you either to be treated like someone who could be passed from one guy to another. I'm sorry. I wasn't an active part of Dick's plan. I wasn't even in favor of it. I told him it was a bad idea, but you were right. I should have warned Rick.

You probably know from talking with Frannie that our weekend wasn't pleasant after that and that we won't be seeing each other anymore. I suppose I got what I deserved.

I just want you to know I was very impressed by you. I thought you were a bright, pretty girl and you deserved better than what you got down here in Charlottesville. You don't have to reply to this letter.

Sincerely,

Rob Miller

I looked the letter over a couple of times. I even held onto it for a day and a half before I mailed it. Mea culpas really weren't my thing, and I hated admitting I'd been wrong. One thing I learned from my dad is that you've got to do the right thing even when it hurts. I haven't always followed that advice, but I have usually managed to remember it.

I mailed the letter. I figured since I had said I wasn't expecting a reply, there wouldn't be one. I was wrong, though. A week later I came back from Biology lab in the afternoon to find a letter from Beth Erickson propped up against my desk lamp.

I wasn't sure what to expect. My first thought was that it would be a nasty letter, asking me if I thought apologizing could make something like that better. That would have been the most logical reply, and the one I still felt I deserved. Unless I opened it, I knew I would never find out what was in the letter, so I took a deep breath, crimped the back of the envelope, and tore the flap off. The letter was on two small pages.

Dear Rob,

Thank you for writing. I was quite surprised and a little touched to get your nice note. I think I can honestly say you were the very last person I expected to hear from this week.

I don't blame you for what happened over Homecomings. I have two older brothers, so I know how boys can be with each other. When I thought about it, I realized that expecting you to tell Frannie or me what Dick was trying to do would have been out of character for most guys.

I suppose what I was most disappointed by was just being in the situation I was in. A blind date with someone I didn't even know, a guy who obviously wasn't comfortable around girls.

Back home, I was always popular, and I never had a problem getting dates. Then to find myself taking a date with a guy I wouldn't ordinarily have gone out with just to go to a party weekend in Charlottesville, well, that made me feel cheap.

One thing I learned is that I'm not going to accept any more blind dates to come down there. If I ever go to a party weekend again, it'll be because a guy I want to spend time with wants to spend time with me.

So don't worry, Rob. I forgive you. You're a nice guy and it was nice of you to write to me. If you ever find yourself in Harrisonburg and you'd like to look me up, it would be nice to see you.

Yours truly,
Beth Erickson

That made me feel a little better, and by the end of October I felt like I was finally getting past any guilt I felt for my passive role in Dick Simpson's idiotic plan.

To be honest, I was too busy to give it that much thought. With midterms closing in, I was studying every chance I got. Biology was getting to be a real killer, and I was afraid a poor grade in that one course could really drag my average down. I was juggling my time like mad. Rush was heating up, and I had finally told Dave I had decided I wanted to pledge SPO, and I couldn't spend any more time over at the Kappa Sigma Kappa house. I had been a little nervous about it, because I didn't want to hurt my best friend's feelings. "Are you all right with this?"

"Sure, Bobby. I think we could have had a lot of fun together, but I knew all along you wanted to pledge the house your dad and your granddad did."

I nodded. "If the SPOs hadn't turned out to be a good bunch of guys, I probably still would have ended up over at your house. We're still going to be friends, aren't we?"

"Come on, Bobby. We've known each other since I was in the second grade. Do you really have to ask that question?"

I grinned, shaking my head. "Just wanted to make sure."

13

By the beginning of November, I was beginning to feel like I was getting the hang of college. I had settled into a routine that seemed to fit me comfortably. One thing I had learned was that I could study more effectively early in the morning. I knew Alderman Library opened at 7 o'clock, so I got up at six, showered and dressed and headed over there most mornings to get in a quick hour of work before classes.

That wasn't easy. I've never been a morning person, and it's tough to get to bed much before midnight when you're living in a college dorm. The one thing I was losing out on was sleep, but I got into the habit of catnapping in the late afternoon. That helped a lot.

Midterms were getting closer, and you could almost smell the panic. Guys who had spent the first two months screwing around in the evenings were glued to their books. Even Danny seemed to be buckling down. He would sit down at his desk and stay there for most of the evening. When I finally turned off my light at midnight, he would still be studying.

I wondered if it would work, if two months of neglect could be overcome by a week of hard work. I knew Danny was quicker than I was, so I supposed there was a chance he could come out of midterms with decent grades. I was pretty sure I would resent it if he got better grades than I did. The only people on the hall who might have out-worked me were a couple of the toolies. I knew Rick Arbogast studied all the time, so I thought he might do better. I didn't think anyone else would. At least I hoped my diligence would be rewarded.

My four midterms—in every class except English Composition—were crammed into a three-day period in early November. The week would start with a French exam on Monday morning and my history and calculus midterms were scheduled for Tuesday. The biggest one, the one everyone on the hall was dreading, was biology on Wednesday. Four of us had decided to study together starting Tuesday afternoon, starting with page one of the textbook and sticking with it until we had all the material covered.

By Wednesday night, the pressure would be off for all but a few unlucky guys. Openings would start Friday, but the consensus was that Thursday was looking like a night to really cut loose and let off some steam.

With one week to go before midterms, and less than two before the party weekend, I still didn't have a date. I hadn't gotten away for any mixers, and the last thing I wanted to do was ask someone else to set me up. I thought about trying once more with Frannie. Then I thought about the girls I had dated in high school, back in Johnstown. I wondered if there was anyone I really wanted to invite. There wasn't.

Strangely enough, I wasn't that worried. Maybe it was because I was so wrapped up in other things. Maybe it was because I've always felt that things work out if you play fair and give them half a chance. Maybe I was just being naive.

The Thursday before midterms, I had an idea. At first it seemed like a good one, but then I shot it down as being ridiculous. It wouldn't go away, though, and I found myself considering it all day. What if I asked Beth Erickson?

First, I told myself, she probably wouldn't say yes. I had been part of what had happened, and even if she didn't blame me, that didn't mean she wanted to date me. I read and reread the letter she'd written me. She had said to call her if I was ever up there, but I thought that might be nothing more than politeness.

Finally, around the middle of the evening on Thursday, I decided to take the plunge. I got five dollars worth of quarters and headed for the pay phone. Joe Del Rio was on it again, talking with one of his buddies. I stood and waited, trying not to look impatient, as he wrapped up the conversation. "It's all yours, Rob," he said after ten minutes or so.

I remembered the number from the times I had called Frannie, so when the operator came on the line, I gave it to her. She told me to deposit six quarters for the first three minutes and I did. I knew there was a chance Frannie might be the one to answer the phone, but I hoped my luck would hold up long enough for that not to happen.

"Third floor." Good. It was a voice I didn't recognize.

"May I speak to Beth Erickson?"

"Hold on. I'll go get her." A minute or two later, Beth came to the phone.

"Beth, this is Rob Miller. I'm sure you're busy studying for midterms, so I won't keep you too long. I'll get right to the point of the call."

I told her how nice her letter had been, and how glad I was that she didn't blame me for what had happened. I told her how nice I thought she was. Then I took the plunge. "I know you said in your letter that you wouldn't come back down here unless it was with someone who really wanted to be with you, and I know this is short notice, but I was wondering if you would like to be my date for Openings Weekend."

At first, she didn't say anything. I guessed I had surprised her. I hadn't gotten a laugh or an immediate refusal, but when the silence stretched past five seconds, I started getting concerned. "Beth? Are you still there? Did you faint ... or die from the shock?"

She laughed. "No, I'm still here, but I do have to admit you've surprised me again." "Does that mean yes?"

"Right now, I don't exactly know what it means. You've taken me by surprise. Would it be all right if I took a day or so to think about it?"

"Sure. Does that mean you might say yes? You don't have any plans?"

"No, I don't. And yes, I might say yes. Give me a day or so to think about it. I'll give you my answer if you call me back tomorrow night."

"That's fine. I'll call you around ... is seven all right?"

"That's fine. And Rob? Thank you for asking me. I'm flattered."

When I hung up the phone, I felt a sense of relief. I knew I would be nervous until I got her answer, but I also knew I had to get some work done. I studied until about 2 o'clock and then collapsed into my bed, exhausted. For some reason, though, I was having a little more trouble than usual getting to sleep. I tossed and turned for a little while and then finally told myself the only way I'd sleep was to remain motionless. After about five minutes, I was still awake. My roommate must have thought I had gone to sleep, though, because I heard the springs of his bed creaking.

At first, I couldn't figure out exactly what was happening. Then I realized he was masturbating. My first reaction was embarrassment. I felt as if I had intruded on something I had no desire to know anything about. It wasn't as if I had never done it before. I mean, what kid doesn't? There's the old joke that 98 percent do it and the other two percent lie about it. I had heard that, so I knew it was normal.

Growing up Catholic, though, I had had it hammered into me time and again that it was a sin, that hair surely would grow on my palms and my vision would fade to the point of blindness. I didn't believe any of that, but I was Catholic enough and guilt-ridden enough that I didn't masturbate very often, and I was incredibly embarrassed to be in the same room while my roommate was doing it.

I don't know how long it took him. It probably wasn't more than a few minutes, but it seemed like forever. I found myself wondering how often he did this. After all, I was a sound sleeper. Finally, the bedsprings stopped creaking and he started breathing easier. A few minutes after that, I fell asleep.

I slept through my alarm Friday morning, missing my early study hour over at Alderman and scrambling just to get to my composition class on time. I was relieved to see that Danny already had left the room by the time I got up. I certainly didn't want to face him. I thought maybe I could talk to Dave about it, to see if he knew anyone who had run into that sort of thing the year before.

When I reached Dave at noon, he didn't want to talk at first. "You know it's against the rush rules, Bobby. We're not supposed to have any contact outside of official house functions until rush is over."

"Come on, Dave. I'm not rushing your house anymore."

He thought for a minute. "All right. I'll tell you what. Be in front of the dorms in fifteen minutes and I'll drive up there and pick you up. We can go someplace off the grounds and talk. You can buy me lunch."

It was half an hour before he drove up in his Corvair. I got in and he drove to a pizzeria three miles south of the grounds. "Hey," I said. "It's good to see you."

He grinned. "Yeah, we really haven't been seeing each other much since you decided not to pledge our house. So, what's up?"

"How hard is it to change roommates?" He looked shocked. "How tough would it be to switch roommates at this time of year?"

"Real tough. They frown on it unless two guys are practically ripping each other's throats out. Literally. What's wrong? I know you're not that fond of your roommate, but I didn't think it was that bad."

I shrugged. "I don't know. Maybe I'm overreacting." I told him the whole story. He was a little surprised at first, but not much. He didn't laugh, but he did seem a little amused by the fact I was upset. "So, what do you think I should do?"

"First try and remember this. There's at least one kid on every hall that gets caught playing with himself. He's usually the guy who's the butt of all the jokes, and he's usually unhappy. We had one on our hall last year. His name was Edgar Davidson. He was a real fuckup. He stopped going to classes and skipped half his exams. I think he got about a 1.0 GPA first semester and then dropped out in the middle of winter. He just couldn't take it. He didn't fit in here at all, and once people started ragging on him, he was through."

I thought for a minute. "I'm not sure Danny fits in all that well either. I don't think he's made any close friends, and he messed up rush badly. A couple of the Jewish houses seemed interested in him, but he had his heart set on joining one of the regular fraternities. I kept telling him he shouldn't burn his bridges, but by the time he realized he wasn't getting anywhere, he'd stopped getting invitations from AEPi and Phi Ep."

"Didn't you tell him most of the houses won't take Jewish guys?" I nodded. "It isn't even an official thing, but in our house, it only takes two negative votes to eliminate someone. We've got at least five guys who say they'd never vote to let a Jewish kid into the house and twice that many who'd never vote for a Negro."

"That's pretty rotten."

"Yeah, it is." I was glad to hear my friend say that. "It isn't right, but one basic thing about the fraternity system is that you get to choose your brothers, and guys just seem to want other guys like themselves around."

"Anyway, ever since Danny realized he wasn't going to get a bid, he's been kind of depressed. Then last night I find out he's over in his bed jerking off."

Dave shook his head. "That's definitely not cool. Even though I'll bet every guy on your hall has done it at one time or another since he's been down here."

I hadn't, but I didn't say anything. "What should I say to him?"

"Jeez, that's a tough one. I sure don't know what to tell you. It would be tough to say anything without embarrassing him, but now that you know about it, it'll probably be bugging you. Give me a couple of days to think about that one."

I nodded. "Hey," he said. "It could have been worse. You should hear what happened in the dorms two years ago. I think it was in Dabney House. This guy woke up one morning and found his roommate in bed with him. The guy's roommate was snuggled up against him and kissing him and..."

I held up my hand. "You're not going to tell me all the details, are you?"

Dave laughed. "Well, not if you don't want to hear them. It turned out the guy's roommate had fallen in love with him and couldn't control himself anymore."

"You mean he was..."

"Uh huh." Dave nodded. "Homosexual."

"What happened to him?"

"You mean after he got out of the hospital?" My jaw must have dropped because Dave laughed. "He made a big mistake. The guy he climbed into bed with outweighed him by fifty pounds and could bench-press 400 pounds. He was a tackle on the football team."

I grinned. "I guess if you look at it that way, what happened with Danny wasn't that bad. Thanks for putting it into perspective for me, Dave."

By then our pizza had arrived. I had missed breakfast and I was hungry. For the next few minutes, we ate and made small talk. He told me Bruce was doing well and probably would get a bid to pledge KSK. "You can't tell him, though. It'll be better for him to find out along with the rest of the pledges. I suppose you're in like Flynn over at SPO. Hey, who are you bringing down for Openings?"

"I'm not sure yet."

"You'd better get sure fast. It's a week from today. How are you going to get a motel room at this late date?"

"Oh, that's no problem. Bruce and I reserved that same room at the Downtowner for all four party weekends this year. All I need is a date, and I'll find out tonight if I have one." I told him about Beth, and how I'd be calling her in about six hours to get her answer.

"Isn't she the girl you set that toolie up with? The guy who blew chow over at SPO?" I nodded. "What's up with that?"

I wasn't sure I could explain it, but Dave was my best friend. I told him about how bad I had felt about what had happened, and how I had written to Beth to apologize. I told him about the nice letter I had gotten back. I told him that I had been thinking about her, and I told him I had basically made the call on the spur of the moment. "Do you like her?" he asked me.

"Yeah, I think I do. She really showed a lot of class the way she handled things with Rick. She's pretty and bright and..."

"You think she'll say yes?" At this moment I honestly didn't know, and that's what I told him. I didn't have any feel for the situation at all. "You never do," he said. "You could have gone out with so many girls back home, but you always enjoyed hanging out more."

I shrugged. "Well, I'm going to give you some good advice," he said. "Then I'm going to do you a big favor. If you like this girl and you want her to come down, you need to sweep her off her feet. You're supposed to call her at seven, right?" I nodded. "Well, it's a little past one now, and Harrisonburg is a two-hour drive from here. What you need to do is buy some flowers, drive up there and tell her you came up to get her answer in person."

I smiled. It sounded good, but Dave always had been a lot more successful with girls than I had. "I like it, but there's just one problem. No car." Dave waved his keys. "You're kidding. You're going to lend me your car?"

"Yeah, on one condition. I'm broke. Lend me twenty bucks for the weekend and leave the gas tank full when you bring it back."

"Sure. I'll cash a check. No problem at all. And thanks. You've been a big help."

14

It took me a couple of hours to get everything squared away, but I was on the road west by a little after four. I had gone back to the dorm to change clothes. Danny was there but was engrossed in his biology book. I wasn't about to make idle talk, so I changed clothes quickly and left the room without saying a word.

I stopped by the florist on the way out of town and bought a dozen roses. I was incredibly nervous about what I was doing—Dave was far more adventuresome than I was in those days—but I was at least a little eager to try something different.

The traffic wasn't heavy, and I made it to Staunton in less than an hour. The interstate heading north was just east of town, and I got on with two hours still to go. I was still making good time when I arrived in Harrisonburg. I had forty-five minutes to spare, so

I stopped at McDonald's and had a burger and a coke to try and pick up my energy level and calm myself down at the same time.

I knew where Beth's dorm was located from the time I had met Frannie up here. I found myself hoping I wouldn't run into her. In fact,

I was hoping I could get into the dorm without seeing anyone I knew. I was lucky. The girl sitting behind the front desk was a stranger. I walked up to her at three minutes till seven, roses in hand. The girl smiled at me. "Who are you here for?"

"Beth Erickson."

I stood there nervously while she rang Beth's hall. Since it was almost exactly 7 o'clock, I found myself hoping she would be eagerly awaiting a phone call.

"Beth Erickson?" A pause. "Your date is here." Another pause. "He's standing right in front of me." She lowered her voice, but I could still hear. "He's really cute, and he brought flowers. Why don't you come down? Maybe you forgot."

The girl hung up the phone. "It's really strange. She must have forgotten about your date. She said she wasn't expecting anybody, but she would be down to talk to you in five minutes. You can sit over there and wait."

Suddenly, I felt completely panicked. I wanted to leave, to run out to the car and not stop running until I was safely back at school. This may have been the kind of thing Dave would do, but I had never had Dave's confidence with girls. I fought the feeling, I told myself there was nothing to do but gut it out. I knew deep down this had been a good idea, so I took slow, deep breaths until I felt myself starting to relax. Right about when I had things under control, Beth came down the stairs.

She looked terrific and I found myself very glad I was here. She didn't see me at first, or maybe it was just that she didn't know what she was looking for. That gave me a chance to look her over a little, and she was every bit as pretty as I'd remembered. Her blonde hair was a little bit mussed, and she wasn't wearing a lot of makeup.

She was about 5-foot-7, a little on the tall side for a girl, but still nearly five inches shorter than I was. She had a figure that was good if not spectacular and she seemed to light up the room as she entered it. Since she hadn't been expecting a guest, she was wearing a Penn State T-shirt and a pair of faded blue jeans. She looked great and I stood up to get her attention right about the time her eyes found me. "Beth, hi," I said, extending my arm and handing her the dozen roses I'd brought.

"Rob?" Her expression was mostly confused, although I hoped I detected some pleasant surprise in there as well. "What are you doing here?"

"I was in the neighborhood, and..."

She laughed. "You're crazy. You know that, don't you?"

I grinned at her. "I guess my secret is out. I just figured I would get your answer about next weekend in person. Have you eaten dinner yet?"

She shook her head. "I've been so busy studying that I hadn't had time to get away. When Linda called up and told me I had a date waiting for me, I panicked. I haven't been going out with anyone lately, so I couldn't imagine who it could be. I must look awful."

If she was fishing for a compliment, I knew I was going to oblige. "Not at all. You're as lovely as I remember you from Homecomings."

She winced. "Thanks, but that's not my favorite memory."

"Oops, sorry."

"That's all right," she said, smiling. "Did you say something about dinner?" I nodded. "Just let me put these in some water. I'll get my coat and be right back down."

Suddenly, I felt great. She hadn't given me my answer about Openings, but somehow, I had a feeling that when she did, I would like what she had to say. When she came back down the stairs five minutes later, she was still wearing the jeans. She had changed from the T-shirt into a nice blouse, though, and her hair was combed perfectly. "There. Now I'm ready."

"I don't know the restaurants here, so you choose one."

She took my arm. "Anything's fine. I'm just so surprised to see you up here."

"I hope it's a pleasant surprise," I said, looking into her eyes. The nod was almost imperceptible, but it was there. "Good."

We went to a little Italian restaurant in the downtown area a mile or two away from the campus. It had great spaghetti and even better atmosphere. I still wasn't bringing up the subject of Openings. It was funny, but I didn't care. I found myself liking this girl from my home state, and I knew that even if she didn't want to come down to Charlottesville again so soon, I still wanted to pursue her.

We talked about the various classes we were taking, and we found that four of our five classes were the same subjects. The only one different was that she was taking Spanish instead of French. "I hate foreign languages," she said. "And everybody said Spanish was the easiest one."

"I guess. I took three years of French in high school, though, so it was easier for me to stick with it. How are you doing in your classes?"

"Not too bad. I got pretty good grades in high school, mostly A's, but I think I'd be happy to come out of this semester with a B average."

"Me too. I've got to get at least a 3.0 if I want to go to law school, but everybody says your grades are lower your first semester."

"Sure. You've got to get used to all the freedom."

I laughed. "Yeah. Although I think all this so-called freedom is highly overrated. What did you say you were doing when I got there tonight?" She looked at me quizzically. "Studying, right?" She nodded. "All right, then. Tell me how many times you spent Friday nights studying when you were in high school."

She understood immediately. "God, never. I was always out on Friday night. If I didn't have a boyfriend, I was out with my girlfriends or at somebody's house for a party." I spread my palms in triumph, but Beth shook her head. "That's too easy. Just because you and I study doesn't mean the freedom isn't there. Tell me how many times you went out during the week when you were in high school."

"Never. Well, hardly ever."

"That's right. I didn't either, but there are girls on my hall who go out and get drunk four or five nights a week. Freedom is in the eye of the beholder. And there's going to come a time when the bills will come due for those girls."

We kept talking about a variety of subjects and time passed quickly. I learned about her family—she had two older brothers and two older sisters. She told me her father was a heart surgeon and she learned about my relationship with my dad. "You miss him, don't you?"

"Yeah. I miss him a lot. I thought he would be around for at least another twenty years. I thought he would get to see my kids growing up."

She looked at me in mock horror. "You've got kids?"

I knew what she was doing. I had been getting a little morose talking about my dad, and she was lightening things up. I decided to play along. "A boy and a girl. They haven't started school yet."

"Oh, that's all right. I thought you had a big family. I can handle two kids."

I grinned at her. "You're a terrific girl, Beth." That was good for a bright, full-wattage smile. It was the first time I had seen her smile that brightly, and I knew it was a smile I could really learn to love.

For the first time in hours, I looked at the clock over behind the cash register. We had been in the restaurant for better than three hours. I had thought it was more like one hour. I had been enjoying myself so much I hadn't noticed the passage of time at all. "I feel terrible. I ruined your study night. You're going to hate me when you have to take your midterms."

"No problem. I probably shouldn't tell you, but I wasn't getting anything done. I was reading the same page over and over again, waiting for it to be 7 o'clock so you'd call."

"Little did you know I'd show up on your doorstep."

I tossed a dollar on the table for a tip and paid our six-dollar tab—things really were a lot cheaper in 1967—at the cash register. I helped Beth into her coat, and we left the restaurant. The car was parked a block away, and the wind coming out of the Shenandoah Mountains had gotten cold.

It was only early November, but it smelled as if a snowstorm was on its way. Winter came early that year, as I recall. On that night, it felt as though it already had arrived. We walked slowly, as if we didn't want to get to the car. Neither one of us said much of anything. I wanted to put my arm around her, but I was afraid to be too forward. When we arrived at Dave's Corvair, I reached down to unlock the passenger door. She put her hand on top of mine as if to stop me for a moment. "Rob?"

"Yes?"

"This has been a really nice evening. And you know what one of the nicest things was? We've been together nearly four hours and you still haven't asked me about next weekend." I shrugged. "I told you I had been waiting for your call, but one of the reasons I was having trouble concentrating was that I really hadn't made up my mind whether I was going to say yes or no.

"It isn't that I didn't like you. It's just that you called so late that I couldn't tell whether you really wanted to spend the weekend with me or if you had just gotten to the point where you needed a date, and I was the only one you could think of."

"I understand."

"I know you do. But when you showed up here tonight with those flowers, and now that we've spent such a nice evening together, well, you've made me believe that you like me and that you really want to get to know me better."

I nodded. "I do. And even if you don't want to come down for Openings, I still want to go out with you again."

"I hope that's true. Because I like you too."

I figured it was time to get up my nerve enough to kiss her, so I leaned in and touched my lips to hers. She didn't pull back at all. It wasn't a passionate kiss, but it was a soft, pleasant one that lasted longer than I'd expected. Beth finally broke the kiss, reaching up and gently stroking my cheek with her right hand as she pulled away. "That was nice, but could we get into the car? I'm freezing."

I laughed and opened her door. When I finally was seated on the other side of the front seat, she snuggled close for another kiss before I started the engine. This time I could feel some passion. I held her tightly. I wasn't going to try anything more. The last thing I wanted to do was go too fast, so this time I was the one to break the kiss. "You're a terrific kisser," I said.

She giggled. "You're not so bad yourself."

Without the heater running, the inside of the car wasn't much warmer than the street. Beth was obviously still cold, and I was beginning to feel the chill myself, so I started the engine. In a few minutes, it had warmed up enough so that we could make the drive back to campus.

"I wish you could stay longer," she said. "But I know you've got that long drive."

"Uh huh, and it's starting to feel like it's going to snow tonight. I want to get started before that happens."

After parking the car across the street, I got out and walked her to her dorm. We stood in the doorway and shared a goodnight kiss, and then I said I'd better be going.

"Good night, Rob," she said softly.

"Good night, beautiful."

I got the smile again for that one, and I could swear it almost warmed the frigid air. I looked at her again, trying to memorize her features for the drive back. "Well, got to go."

She turned to walk into the building, and I practically flew across the street to the car. Just as I was about to get in and close the door, she seemed to remember something. "Rob?" she called to me from fifty feet away. "The answer is yes."

This time I grinned. I had almost forgotten the purpose of my trip. "Really? Yes?" She nodded, blowing me a kiss. "Call me and we'll work out the details."

15

The weekend passed in a blur after that. I got back to town a little before two and fell right into bed. This time I didn't have any trouble getting to sleep, and if my roommate did anything in his bed that night, I didn't know it.

I went directly from my Saturday classes to the library, and except for a meal break in late afternoon, I spent the next twelve hours studying for my midterms. The time went by quickly. I had the occasional problem concentrating, mostly when my mental picture of Beth's face came into sharp focus, but mostly I worked.

I called Beth on Sunday. Both of us were too busy to talk long, but we shared enough of a conversation to get rid of any doubts that our Friday evening together had just been a pleasant dream. She told me she'd be down by around 5 o'clock on Friday, and I told her I was looking forward to it. We talked until the operator came on and told me I was out of time. We swapped endearments and got back to our studying.

It was getting to the point where you could feel the panic on our hall. Guys who hadn't been studying all semester now were glued to their desk chairs. Most of them didn't even want to break long enough to go out somewhere for a meal, so the vending machines in the basement had been cleaned out completely.

Our biology study group broke up at about 10, and Bruce asked me if I wanted to get out for a while. "I haven't eaten all day," he said. "I'm going out for a hamburger, and I wondered if you wanted to go along."

"Sure. I've still got a little more I want to do before I turn in, but I think I'm just about ready for my French test."

We walked down to the little grill at the end of the dormitory complex. It was open until midnight, but it was nearly deserted. We ordered sandwiches and sat down waiting for them to come. "You in good shape?" he asked me.

I shrugged. "I guess so. I've been working hard all along, so I ought to be. I just wish I knew what to expect from some of these professors."

"I know. We've been hearing all along about how tough the exams are, and this week we start finding out. Biology is the one that scares me. There's just so much stuff we're supposed to have memorized."

"I know. I can't see myself getting better than a C in that class and I'm worried about it dragging down my average."

"Better than a C?" he asked incredulously. "God, Rooter. I would be thrilled to get a C."

At that point our sandwiches came, and we stopped talking for a while as we ate. Bruce was the one to kick-start the conversation a few minutes later. "Rob, did you ever get a date? If you didn't, I can probably find somebody who'll take your half of the room."

"No problem. I'm all set."

"Since when? You told me Thursday you didn't have anything going." I just smiled. "Come on, Rooter. Give me the scoop."

I told him about calling Beth and asking her, and about driving up the next day and seeing her. I told him about the evening we spent together and how well we hit it off.

"That sounds great. But where did you say you met this girl?"

"At Homecomings."

"Wait a minute. I knew that name sounded familiar. Wasn't she the good-looking blonde with Arbogast?" I nodded. "Well, she was definitely too much woman for Super Toolie to handle."

That was the first time I heard Rick's new nickname. Like I said, Bruce and Dick were the ones who had given out the nicknames. Dick had been calling Rick a fucking geek since the night he had vomited on him, and somehow, I thought Rick would hate this a little less. Hell, I thought. Knowing the way toolies are, Rick will probably like this one.

"Well," I said. "I better get back to French vocabulary."

I studied for another hour and a half before going to bed. When I fell asleep, Danny's light was still on. I dreamed about Beth and woke up at six feeling refreshed. I thought about skipping my composition class to get in a little more studying, but I knew I was ready for my French midterm. At least I knew I was as ready as I would ever be.

Mr. Chase wound up giving us an in-class assignment, so I forced my thoughts back to the English language and wrote five hundred words on some inane subject I couldn't remember two hours later. I finished five minutes early and went into Cabell Hall for a cup of coffee to get myself perking for my French test.

It was tough. I had known it would be, and foreign languages never had been my strength. I had worked hard, though, and there wasn't anything on the test that surprised me. I had told myself all along I'd be happy with a B in French, and when I walked out of the classroom, I felt confident that I had managed at least that much.

Mondays were tough for me that fall. After English at eight and French at nine, I had a one-hour break before biology. I had known all along I wouldn't be able to get a lot done on Monday, so I had done the bulk of my studying for my Tuesday exams earlier. I still had the evening, but I knew I'd be spending at least half of that working toward the dreaded biology exam.

The days were starting to pass more and more quickly. I had been in Charlottesville more than two months and things were starting to happen. Not only were midterms finally here, but Openings Weekend was only four days away and with it the final functions of rush. After that, bids would come out and there would be one more week until

Thanksgiving. I was excited about that, because it would be my first trip home since I had been away.

Dave and I were leaving after our Wednesday classes and driving straight through. We would have three days at home with our families before driving back on Sunday. The letters I had been getting from my mother made me eager to see her. This was the longest I had ever been away from home, and I missed her a lot.

Tuesday's exams went smoothly. History was an essay test, so it was hard to figure how it would be graded. I felt good about the work I had done, though, and I thought I would probably do no worse than a B. I felt the same way about calculus. Nothing at all on the test had surprised me, and I had finished early. I knew I had gotten either an A or a B.

By noon that day, I was three-fourths of the way through my exams. Only biology still loomed ahead, standing in front of me like that giant monolith in "2001: A Space Odyssey" that we would all spend the next summer arguing the meaning of. Our study group had made plans to spend as much time as we needed, starting at two in the afternoon. We went through the text and our lecture notes, page by page, going over every item we came across, no matter how insignificant. It was the first serious study group I had ever been involved with. In law school that became a way of life, but this was the first time I had done this, and it seemed odd to share my work with three other guys.

We worked through the afternoon and took a half-hour break for dinner. We picked it up again at seven and kept going until nearly midnight. Finally, when we started repeating ourselves, Bruce spoke up. "I think we're as ready as we're going to be."

Joe Del Rio wasn't so sure. "I still don't understand that stuff in Chapter Five." "Man, we've been over that and over that," Ed Randolph said.

I agreed. "I think we've reached the point where we're just going to drive ourselves crazy if we keep going."

Joe made one last pitch for help, and Bruce said he would spend a few more minutes with him. Ed and I called it quits and headed for our rooms. "What do you think?" he asked me.

"I don't know. I'm still scared to death, but I don't think there's anything we could have studied that we didn't."

I slept the sleep of the just that night, and I didn't even bother getting up early to cram. I knew I was as ready as I could be. That didn't mean I was going to get an A. It just meant that whatever I did get, I would know I couldn't have done much better.

We got our compositions back in English, and I had another B. I was surprised when I crossed the quad for French to see that Monday's midterm grades already had been posted. About eight of the guys in the class were crowded around the classroom door, trying to see how they'd done. When a space opened, I pushed my way forward. The grade lists had the names cut off and the marks were posted by Social Security numbers. Once I figured out which line I was on, I glanced across to the right.

I couldn't believe it. I saw the 88 across from my number and suddenly it was a great day. We were graded on a 10-point scale—90 for an A, 80 for a B and so forth—so my 88 meant I'd gotten a solid B-plus on my French midterm.

It was a good start. The day became even better when I saw that French class had been cancelled for the day. That gave me two hours to kill before the biology exam. I decided to make sure the things I had memorized were still hanging around within easy recall. Two hours passed quickly, and I walked into the lecture hall with as much dread as I had felt at any time since coming to the university.

I felt myself starting to panic, but I fought the feeling down. I knew I was ready. I knew there was no rational reason to be worried. The proctors came around and handed out the exam booklets and answer sheets and 200 heads bent over 200 booklets and began to regurgitate what biology we had learned over the last two months. It was the toughest test I had ever taken in my life. Knowing the facts wasn't enough. We were supposed to be able to apply them and draw conclusions, and I wasn't sure I understood the subject well enough to do that.

I worked slowly, pondering each question as long as I could without falling behind. There were fifty questions to be answered in fifty minutes, so it wasn't that difficult to keep track of time. I skipped one or two, figuring I could come back to them at the end.

As it turned out, I didn't have time to go back and finish them.

When the professor called for our papers, I had answered only forty-seven of the fifty questions. Oh well, I thought. I'd be happy with a 94. Real happy.

Once the papers had been handed in, it was as if a giant sigh of relief had hit our part of the first-year class. For most of us, midterms were finished. Our first real encounter with college work had been completed. It would take a week or so to find out who had prospered, who had just survived and who was in danger of falling by the wayside. The university issued advisory grades after midterms for the first-year class, with one copy sent home and the other sent to the student.

Each teacher put down the grade each student would have if the semester ended at that point. The idea was to show students if they needed to work harder, but most of us knew our strengths and deficiencies without seeing them in print.

I felt good. I seriously doubted I had much of a chance to earn the 3.3 average required for the Dean's List, at least not this semester, but I knew I would come away with at least a B-minus average. I figured I had made a successful transition to college work.

Half of the guys on the hall still had tests Thursday, so things were quiet Wednesday evening. I knew Beth had finished her midterms at about the same time I had, so I gave her a call to ask how she had done. We talked for about fifteen minutes about nothing in particular. There was still a lot to talk about. She hadn't heard any of my best stories and I still wanted to find out everything I could about her. I somehow knew we would keep hitting it off, and with midterms out of the way, I was really looking forward to the weekend.

There were a few guys just sitting quietly in Andy Lynch's room talking, and Andy motioned for me to come in and join them. "We were just talking about that song they've been playing on WUVA lately," Andy said. "The one by Procol Harum. You know, A Whiter Shade of Pale."

"It's pretty strange," Ed Randolph said. "Like nothing I've ever heard before."

"It sure isn't like most of the stuff we hear down here," I said. "It's getting so I'm surprised any time I hear anything that isn't soul music."

"What do you think of Whiter Shade of Pale?" Ed asked.

"I like it," I said slowly. "I don't think I've figured it out yet, but it's got a great sound." "What do you think the title means?" Andy asked me.

"I don't know. What do you guys think?"

"Ghosts," Ed said.

Andy shook his head. "Where do you get ghosts out of those lyrics? They don't say anything about ghosts."

Ed was adamant. "What else could be a whiter shade of pale but ghosts?" "Rob?" Andy asked.

"Well, this might sound silly, but I don't think Ed is that far off when he says ghosts. When I heard the title, I thought of death and terror. You know, like in a horror movie. Being frightened to death."

Andy looked at me skeptically. "A horror movie?"

"Not exactly. Have you ever seen a dead body?"

"No way," Andy said. "We didn't have a whole lot of corpses at prep school."

"Didn't you ever go to a funeral?" He shook his head and I continued. "If you'd ever been to a funeral, you'd know what I'm talking about. My dad died two years ago, and when I went to the funeral home to view his body, he looked so pale. He looked like he wasn't even there, like he'd never been there."

I always felt emotional when I talked about my dad's death, so I paused for a moment. "I wondered where he was. I'm Catholic, and I believe in eternal life, but when I saw my dad's body, all of a sudden, I had a real feeling of terror. I wondered what if I was wrong. What if my dad was in some horrible place, or even worse, what if he was just— nowhere? Anyway, that's what I thought of the first time I heard that song."

"Wow," Ed said. "That's pretty serious."

I laughed. "Hell, I don't know if that's what it's about. I mean, where does the mirror telling its tale fit in?"

No one could explain that, and since no one had any conclusive proof of the real meaning of the song, that made it a great topic. I must have sat in on four discussions that eventually got around to talking about "A Whiter Shade of Pale" that year. I learned a lot more later. I even learned I'd been hearing some of the lyrics wrong, but that little piece of information was three years in coming.

We talked for a while longer, and then I went to bed.

The calculus grades were posted Thursday, and I had gotten an 85. I hadn't dared to hope for anything better, and it meant I was pretty certain of B's in three subjects—calculus, French and English Comp— for my midterm grades. I was pretty sure I wouldn't have any worse than that in history, so if I got at least a C on my Biology test, I'd be within reaching distance of my 3.0 holy grail heading into the second half of the semester.

16

By Thursday afternoon, the dorm was starting to resemble a zoo without the keeper. Our resident advisor was over at his fraternity house, so there wasn't any semblance of authority around. Guys were filling their wastebaskets with ice and then with six-packs of beer, getting ready to blow off a major amount of steam. Most of us had classes Friday, but the first day of Openings Weekend was always the worst attended day of the fall semester.

Dick Simpson was trying to organize a game of thumper, and the only problem was that too many guys wanted to play. Six different guys on our hall had stereos, and every one of them was cranked up to full volume. At one end of the hall, the Beatles were singing about lovely Rita the meter maid, and at the other end the Four Tops were belting out their desire for Bernadette.

The scene was almost bacchanalian, and it wasn't until that moment I fully realized exactly how tense things had been for the last week or so. Half the guys probably wouldn't finish the semester with 2.0 averages, but on this night at least, everyone was cutting loose as if they'd just made the Dean's List.

The only guy I didn't see was Danny. I knew he didn't drink. I knew he was only 17 and wouldn't be 18 until March, and he didn't fit in with most of these guys. We had talked about it before. The only advice I'd been able to come up with was that he should try to go along to get along.

"Jeez, Danny. It's one thing not to drink, but every time somebody offers you a beer, you act like you're proud of the fact you've never had any alcohol. How do you think that makes them feel? I know two different guys who swear they're going to get you falling-down drunk before the year is out."

Danny knew he was uptight. He knew he tried too hard. He asked me for advice several times, but I never came up with anything. I've never been Mister Popularity or anything close, but I've never had trouble making friends.

"You want advice?" He nodded. "Well, I don't know if you do this on purpose, but I've heard guys call you a snob. They say you think you're better than the rest of us because you're so bright."

He shook his head. "I know I'm bright. I can't help that, but I don't think I'm better than anyone else."

"Then relax. And stop correcting people. The way you do it, it's like you're coming right out and telling them they're idiots." He gave me a stricken look and I shrugged. "I'm just telling you what it sounds like."

He had seemed to be trying lately, and I didn't think it was a big deal that he wasn't cutting loose with the rest of us. A few minutes later, I stopped by our room and saw that he was in there with three other guys who hadn't felt like getting wild. Joe Del Rio, Rick Arbogast and Steve Madden—a quiet guy from Richmond I have all but forgotten—were in the room with him, and the four of them were playing cards.

"What's up, you guys?" I asked.

"Just playing a little bridge," Steve said.

"Don't let me stop you." I grabbed my wallet and headed back to the party in Dick's room. There had been talk of sending out for pizza, so I wanted my money with me in case the time came for me to chip in.

"Where's your roommate, Rooter?" Dick asked me drunkenly. "Where's that fucking kosher asshole?"

"Hey, Colonel," Bruce told his fellow Texan. "Cool it."

"Where the fuck is Jewboy Jacobs?"

"Danny's next door. He and some guys are playing cards."

I wish I hadn't told him. Dick had been Danny's main antagonist, and neither one of them had much use for the other. "Whass the matter? Is Jacobs too good to drink with us?"

"Calm down, Dick. Just because Danny doesn't drink..."

The Colonel was about four beers past calming down. "Danny's a pussy. A fucking Jewboy Yankee pussy." I didn't think anything would really happen. I thought Dick was just blowing off steam, posturing to impress the rest of us. "I'm gonna take him a beer. I want to see that little fuck drink a beer."

No one stopped him as he pulled a can of Budweiser out of the wastebasket and headed for the door. Bruce and I followed him to make sure things didn't get out of control, but we didn't notice Dick shaking the can as he headed into Danny's and my room. We were standing right behind Dick when he walked through the door, and we watched frozen as he popped the can with the opener in his other hand and started spraying Budweiser all over the four guys sitting there quietly playing cards. "Wake up, Jacobs! It's time to be a man. Time to party with the big boys."

I was a little surprised to see Danny laugh. He looked at Dick and seemed to sneer. "Well, guys," he said, pointing at his antagonist. "Here's a perfect example of how people with tiny little peckers try to get your attention."

The other card players laughed, and it was easy to see Dick didn't take well to being ridiculed. "Yeah? Well, at least I'm not a fucking Jewboy Yankee pussy, Jacobs."

This time he had pushed the right button. Danny was up like a shot, his face contorted in anger. I knew there had been a lot of frustration building in him, but I didn't expect to see him throw a punch. As drunk as he was, Dick reacted quickly. He slipped the punch, which barely grazed his face. As Danny kept coming, he turned and ran out the door and down the hall. Danny shouldered his way past me and took off in pursuit.

"Wow!" Bruce said. "We'd better go after them and make sure

nobody gets hurt."

I agreed, and the two of us started running toward the door Danny had just gone through. Two or three other guys on the hall quickly got wind that something had happened and started following us. The Beatles were telling us all we needed was love, but love was the last thing on Danny's mind right now. It was going to be interesting to see what happened if he caught up with Dick. Neither of them was particularly big or strong, and neither could be called the physical type.

I thought that with Dick drunk and Danny furious, my roommate might have the advantage, and I kind of felt as if it was payback time. Dick probably had this coming to him after all the taunting he'd been doing for the last month or so.

Danny chased Dick and we chased Danny for five minutes before it finally ended in the basement post office in Emmett House. Danny had been gaining steadily, and he caught Dick with a flying tackle in front of the mailboxes. Bruce and I came through the door right as Dick hit the floor, and we watched for a minute as Danny quickly jumped on top of him and pinned him. Dick tried to cover his face with his arms, but Danny punched through them, hitting him four or five times in the head and shoulder area.

It was clear that he had the upper hand, and that Dick didn't have much of a chance to defend himself, so Bruce and I moved in and broke up the fight. Danny struggled against us as we pulled him off his antagonist, and he managed to throw one last punch that hit Dick in the mouth and split his lip. "Get him off me." Dick moaned.

"Fuck you, Simpson," Danny hissed. "You keep away from me or next time I swear I'll put you in the hospital."

I expected Dick to retaliate verbally, but for once he showed some good sense. Bruce pulled a handkerchief out of his pocket and handed it to his roommate, who swabbed his bleeding lip with it. "Come on, Colonel. Let's get out of here before you get the rest of the shit kicked out of you."

I supposed that left me responsible for my roommate, and I released Danny when he seemed to have calmed down a little. "Damn it, Rob. Why did you stop me?"

"Jeez, Danny. I had no idea you were such a tiger. Why did we stop you? Well, I was afraid you might kill Dick. Even if he deserved it, you probably would have regretted it sooner or later. Wouldn't you?"

Danny was still real angry, and I was guessed he had a lot of adrenaline pumping through his system. He took two or three deep breaths and then sighed. "I don't know. It felt so good to hit him. He's been all over me for so long."

Dick had deserved it, but I wasn't sure how this fight would affect Danny's status on the hall. It couldn't hurt if people knew he had fought back and won a fight. On the other hand, though, Dick was a dangerous enemy, and I didn't think it would be easy to patch things up between the two of them. "You all right now?"

He laughed. "Me? Sure. I'm fine. I never got hit. I just got some beer on me, and I think maybe I bruised my knuckles when I punched him in the teeth."

The clock on the wall of the post office said it was nearly ten. It seemed a lot later, but I knew the party had started early on this last night before Openings Weekend. I didn't feel like going back to Dick's room for the thumper game. I was pretty sure Danny wasn't going to go back and play cards. "You want to go get a hamburger?" he asked me.

"Sure. It might not be a bad idea to get out for a while."

We went back upstairs and got our coats and decided to walk down to the Corner instead of going to the grill in the dorms. It took us about ten minutes to get to the Virginian, and we went inside and ordered steak sandwiches. He tore into his as if he hadn't eaten for days. He finished it and ordered another one. I was barely halfway through the only sandwich I was going to eat. "God. I was hungrier than I thought."

I didn't say much. I waited to see if he wanted to talk. Finally, he finished his sandwich and his coke and sat back in the booth. "How'd you do on your midterms, Rob?"

I smiled. "I think I did pretty well. The two I got back so far were B's, and I'm pretty sure I didn't get worse than a C in anything. Even biology. How'd you do?"

He shook his head. "Lousy. I knew I hadn't been studying enough, but I just couldn't seem to do anything about it. So far I've got a C in English and D's in math and Spanish."

"How do you think you did on the bio test?"

"Shit." It sounded funny hearing him curse. "That's the only one I'm not worried about. I've always been good in science, and I'll be really disappointed if I didn't ace it."

"No kidding?" I couldn't imagine anyone getting an A in that class. "That's great, Danny."

"I'd trade it in a minute for B's in Spanish and math."

"Hey, these are just midterms. You can still bring your grades up on your finals. All you've got to do is work harder."

"My parents are going to kill me. When they see those advisories next week, they're going to go nuts."

"Just tell them they're not real grades. Tell them you had some trouble adjusting but you're starting to get the hang of it."

He thought about that for a minute. "That might work."

"It ought to be worth a try. Hey, have you got anyone coming down for Openings?"

He shook his head. "Natalie's parents wouldn't let her come down again so soon. Besides, I didn't feel like going to the fraternity parties now that they've told me they don't want me. I'm leaving after classes and going home for the weekend."

He didn't ask anything about my date, and I didn't volunteer any information. We had just had an intimate conversation, but I still didn't find myself liking Danny much more than before. He was too desperate to have people like him, and I was still wondering what I should do about the fact that I had heard him masturbating in the next bed. That was a problem that would have to be discussed. I hoped he would just stop, and I wouldn't have to embarrass both of us by confronting him with it. It all seemed really complicated but I never expected college to be simple.

17

Half the guys in the dorm didn't get up for Friday classes that morning, including my roommate. I found myself getting more than a little irritated, but I knew I wouldn't say anything to him. I knotted my tie, put on my sport jacket, and headed for Cabell Hall. It wasn't as though there was anything important I'd miss today. I was going because I knew it was too easy to get into the habit of cutting classes, and because I was hoping to see my other two midterm grades.

After my first two classes, I went by the history department to see if the grades had been posted. They had, and I was pleased to see that I had gotten another 88. That meant I had two B's and two B-pluses, with biology still to go. I did a little quick figuring and realized if I got at least a C-plus in bio, my average would be a shade under 3.0. Even if I only got a C, I'd have nearly a 2.9. As tough as things had been, and the way some of the other guys' grades seemed to be shaping up, that would leave me with one of the best grade point averages on our hall for midterm advisories.

I hurried over to the biology building to find my grade, and I knew they had been posted when I saw about fifty guys crowding up

110

to see theirs. Most of them were coming away disappointed, some with shocked looks on their faces. Most were guys I didn't know, so I had no idea how hard they'd worked. Still, I couldn't help being worried. The crowd moved quickly, and it was my turn after about ten minutes. I noticed there were a lot of failing grades, with more than a few scores down in the forties and fifties. Then I settled in and searched for my number somewhere near the middle of the list. When I found it, I closed my eyes and offered up a quick prayer to the Blessed Virgin.

I looked at my score and felt relieved. I had gotten an 80. I could hardly believe it. A B-minus. True, the lowest B-minus possible, and a C-plus if I had missed one more question. I figured my GPA quickly in my head and realized I was a shade over 3.0 at the halfway point of the semester. Two B-pluses, two B's and one B-minus. I had kicked ass. I tried hard not to show any reaction, because I knew most of the guys who were looking at their biology grades didn't have much reason to smile.

I held it in until I got out of sight of the building, and then I let out with a giant whoop. I stopped by my room to drop off my books and see if Danny was awake. He wasn't, and that surprised me. It was nearly 10:30 and he was still sound asleep. I left the books, grabbed my biology notebook, and headed back across the street to go to class.

A day that had started with great news got even better when Beth arrived at 5 o'clock. I was tired, but I'd been too euphoric all after-noon to sleep. I was hoping that feeling would carry me through the night until I got the chance to get some sleep. Beth looked even better than I remembered, and I knew it would be very easy to fall for this girl. She was wearing her blonde hair down over her shoulders, and her blue eyes seemed brighter than usual.

"How'd you get to be so beautiful?" I asked her as we waited to pick up her room key at the front desk at the Downtowner.

She looked pleasantly surprised at the compliment, and she linked her arm through mine and whispered in my ear. "You smooth talker. You know exactly what to say to a girl, don't you?"

My ego wasn't the only thing swelling at that point. I had been looking forward to this all week, and between liking this girl and feeling terrific about the grades I had gotten on my midterms, I had a feeling it was going to be a wonderful weekend.

Beth said she didn't need to change clothes or freshen up, so we headed over to the Virginian to have a beer before dinner. We sat and talked for about an hour, basking in the enjoyment of each other's company. She already had told me she had grown up in a big family, with two older brothers and two older sisters. "I'm the baby. Both of my brothers and one of my sisters are already married. How about your family?"

"Well, you know I'm an only child." She nodded. "And I told you my dad was a judge, and he died a couple of years ago. My mom went back to work when my dad died. She's working now as a receptionist for a real estate firm, and she's been studying to get her license. She likes it, and it gives her something to do."

"Are you two close?"

"Sure. I'm all she's got. Are you real close with your family?"

"Yeah," she said, grinning. "We're one of those big, friendly old Scandinavian families. The only thing I can't figure out is how we wound up in Scranton. All the other Ericksons, all of the aunts and uncles, live in Minnesota."

We finished our second mugs of beer and I looked at my watch. "We probably ought to get going if we're going to meet Bruce and his date for dinner. Besides, if I drink too much more, I might fall asleep."

I suppose I was still naive in those days because I hadn't thought of my date with Beth in sexual terms at all. I hadn't been plotting a way to get her alone in the motel room, or off in the back seat of Dave's car. It wasn't that I wasn't interested in her that way. All we had done was kiss, but the touch of her lips against mine had excited me tremendously. Somewhere in the back of my mind I knew I wanted to do more with her, but back then things were still more relaxed.

Back then people didn't fall into bed on the first date unless it was also going to be the last date. If you liked a girl, if you wanted more than just sex, you took things slowly. When I was in high school, the general rule of thumb—at least from the stories I had heard—was that most nice girls would let you have sex with them once you dated them for at least a year. I figured the reason I was still a virgin was that I'd never gone out with anyone for more than two or three months.

I always thought there was time. My dad never talked to me about saving myself for marriage the way Father Cepicki did when he addressed our youth group at Holy Name Church, but he did say each year of my life would only be lived once, and that I was never going to be young again. He told me I would be able to do adult things my whole life, but that I would only be able to do kid things when I was a kid. Sex wasn't a kid thing to my dad. He told me he trusted me to do the right thing, and that he would always stand by me no matter what I did, but I had to remember actions had consequences.

He said if I got a girl pregnant, there wouldn't be any abortions or adoptions. He would call his friend Bob Torrance down at the steel mill and get me a job on the graveyard shift. There wouldn't be any college or law school. He would see to it that I could support my family, but if I was going to act like a man, he wanted me to be a man.

It had impressed me tremendously, much more than the stuff about the sanctity of Catholic marriage. I learned my father's lesson very early on—actions have consequences. It was that simple to me, and I knew I would never be trapped by any consequences of actions I didn't take.

Bruce's date was the same girl he'd brought down for Homecomings, a redhead named Nancy from Mary Washington, so she already knew Beth. After all, my date had been a last-minute addition to the room at the Downtowner with Nancy and Frannie the last time around when she was with Rick. "It'll be nice to have only two of us in the room this time, won't it?" Beth asked her.

"Absolutely," Nancy said. "You guys should have seen it. The three of us kept elbowing each other out of the way when we were trying to put on our makeup."

It was a little strange to hear that and remember that the third girl, the one who wouldn't be in the room, had been my date. I had been sorry at the time that things hadn't worked out with Frannie, but now I felt like the only purpose in dating her had been as a step along the way to meeting Beth.

I sat back and let the other three carry most of the conversation at dinner. I was feeling a little bit tired, and my second wind hadn't kicked in yet. The dance over at the gym with Martha and the Vandellas was supposed to start at nine and run until one, but we'd only go for an hour or two before we left for our various fraternity parties.

I knew from Dave that KSK was almost certain to give Bruce a bid and hearing him talk at dinner about how he hoped things were working out there almost made me want to tell him. I remembered my promise, though, and kept my mouth shut. My own plan was to stop by KSK for an hour or so. I knew Dave wanted to meet Beth, so we'd go there for a while and probably end up over at the SPO house around midnight.

The parties were supposed to run until 3 o'clock. I had serious doubts I would be able to keep it going that long, and I felt extremely lucky that both of my Saturday classes had been cancelled for the post-midterms weekend.

I looked over at Beth, who was telling a story about one of her professors. Her face looked animated, and her eyes were flashing as she got to the punch line. Both Bruce and Nancy started laughing, and even though I hadn't heard a word of it, I tried to laugh, too. I must not have done a real good job of it, because all three of them looked at me strangely. "Are you all right, Rob?" Beth asked me.

Nancy laughed. "You sounded like my dad does when he knows he's supposed to laugh but doesn't think something is funny. Like one of his boss's jokes."

I was trapped. "Well, then I'd better tell the truth before my date starts to think I don't find her jokes funny. The truth is I was kind of off somewhere mentally."

Bruce jumped in and saved me. "What he isn't telling you is that he was falling asleep. This guy has been studying so hard that he's way short on sleep."

"Is that it?" Beth asked sympathetically.

I was embarrassed, but I admitted it. "I suppose so."

She smiled, snuggled close and put her head on my shoulder. Shortly after that, I felt as if I finally was starting to get my second wind.

Friday night was wonderful. We went to the gym and danced every dance for two hours. I still remember all those great Martha and the Vandellas songs, songs like "Heat Wave," "Jimmy Mack," "Dancin' in the Streets." We heard them all that night and we danced to every single one. I hadn't noticed it in October, but Beth was a terrific dancer. She moved around with a lot of reckless abandon, and when she was in my arms for the occasional slow dance, she pressed against me just enough to make it interesting.

The fraternity parties were more of the same, and I could tell she made a big impression on Dave when we dropped in on the KSK party. "So, this is the lovely Beth Erickson," he said. "You're the one I lost my car on a Friday night for."

I had told her the story of how Dave had loaned me his Corvair so that I could come up and see her, and she had thought it was romantic. "I think we'll just have to call you Cupid," she told my friend a little teasingly.

"I don't know," I said. "I think Dave would look pretty strange in a diaper."

Dave laughed. "Take good care of this guy. Bobby's been my best friend almost since we really were wearing diapers."

I looked around the Kappa Sigma Kappa house while we danced to the soul band they had in the living room, and I realized I had met most of the brothers at one time or another. Even though Dave had known all along that I was pretty set on SPO, he had kept inviting me and kept after me long enough that I had become well acquainted with his fraternity. If something went wrong and I changed my mind, he would probably be able to get me a bid second semester. It was nice to have options.

After about an hour, a little after midnight, I told Beth we probably ought to get going over to the other party. I knew she was a little apprehensive about going to SPO. After all, that was where we had been in October when Rick had lost his dinner, lunch, and breakfast. She had told me she was concerned that people would remember she had been his date and would hold it against her. I said it didn't work that way. "And if it does, if anybody treats you badly, we'll leave. We'll come back here."

"Really? You'd do that for me?"

"Of course. I don't want to do anything that would make you uncomfortable."

We walked arm in arm across the quad, and Beth hugged me

from time to time. I wasn't as concerned as she was, because I had talked to three or four of the brothers about exactly that. I had told Lonnie Edwards that Beth's only connection to Rick was as a blind date. "What's the problem?" he had asked me.

"Nothing, I hope."

"Rob, if she's your date, she's welcome in our house. That's all there is to it. Just don't bring that guy back."

"Don't worry. I think Homecomings was Rick's only contact with the fraternity system."

Lonnie met us at the door, and he welcomed Beth warmly. "Rob's told us so much about you." I hadn't, but it sounded good. "Rob, why don't you go get a beer for yourself and your beautiful date while I take her around and introduce her to some of the brothers."

I looked at Beth, who seemed to have relaxed almost instantly. "Sure," she said. "I could use a beer."

I found the keg without too much trouble, shaking hands with two or three pain-free brothers along the way. Bart Kondracki, one of the biggest brothers at 6-foot-4 and 260 pounds, was manning the keg. Bart had played varsity football until he'd torn up his knee the year before, and he was one of the stalwarts of the SPO flag football team. It took three guys to block him on defense, and I had come to see he was practically an offensive line in himself when his team had the ball. "Hey, Miller," he said. "How's it going?"

"Not too bad, Bart. You the beer man here?"

"Yeah." He stifled a belch. "How many brews you need?" I held up two fingers. "Where's your date?"

"Lonnie's introducing her around."

"Hey," he said as he handed me the first of the two Dixie cups filled with beer. "You'd better learn quick not to leave your date with Lonnie. He's a hound. Give him fifteen minutes and he'll have her up in his room. Give him twenty and he'll have her clothes off. Give him thirty and she'll be having his child." I must have looked panicked because he laughed. "Just kidding, kid. Lonnie's a real stud with the ladies, but he'd never snake a date from anyone in the house."

Bart handed me the second beer and I thanked him. "No sweat, kid. Hey, do you play football?"

I shrugged. "I've played a little. Varsity in high school, but I sat on the bench most of the time. Nothing more than that, and I wasn't that good."

"What position?"

"Mostly tailback."

"Great. We can always use more guys who can run the ball. You're going to be here Thursday night, aren't you?"

Thursday night was bid night. "That's up to you guys."

Bart winked at me. "See you Thursday, Rob."

A friend of mine from back home once told me that he thought there were a handful of really perfect days in your life, days when everything felt good. The secret was to recognize them when they came. I hadn't known at the time whether I believed him, but this was starting to look suspiciously like one of those perfect days. I only hoped it would last through the weekend.

We stayed out late Friday night, and I dropped Beth off at the motel a little before four and staggered home to my bed. With Danny away for the weekend, I had the room to myself, and I slept like the dead until my alarm awakened me a little before 11 o'clock. We had planned it so we would have just enough time to have lunch and get over to Scott Stadium for the football game, and it worked out just that way. Beth looked terrific. I was starting to realize I wanted her to be my girl and I wanted to see her for a lot more than just party weekends.

We sat with a group from our hall at the game. Bruce and Nancy, Dick and his date from Mary Baldwin College and Ricky Barton and his girlfriend from back home in Baltimore. The NCAA still didn't allow freshmen to play in those days, so Ricky was watching the hapless varsity with the rest of us. "They need you out there today, Johnny U," Dick said drunkenly as Virginia fell behind North Carolina by another touchdown.

"Maybe next year," Ricky said, trying to concentrate on the action on the field.

Beth and I were watching sort of half-heartedly. Mostly we were talking with each other, still learning about each other. We knew we both liked the Beatles, hated James Bond movies, and didn't watch much television. By early in the fourth quarter, the game was out of reach and the crowd had started leaving to change for dinner and the concert. Bruce and I had made dinner reservations at the Boar's Head Inn outside of town. It was the nicest restaurant in Charlottesville and was on the expensive side, but this was the biggest weekend of the fall and both of us wanted to impress our dates.

The four of us shared a taxi out there and had the best meal any of us had eaten since leaving home for college. Then we took another cab back to the grounds and walked over to University Hall for the concert.

The Four Tops were at the peak of their popularity in those days. By 1967 we were starting to see that not all the good soul music was being made in Detroit, that the rawer Memphis sound of Otis Redding, Wilson Pickett and Sam & Dave was probably a lot better than the slick stuff coming out of Detroit. All of us had grown up with Motown, though. All of us had listened when the Supremes told us to stop in the name of love, or when the Temptations said they weren't too proud to beg.

The Four Tops were special, too. I still think their first two big hits, "I Can't Help Myself" and "It's the Same Old Song," were two of the best songs to come out of the sixties, and every time I hear them, I remember that night and the luminescent smile on Beth's face. I remember Bruce and his date dancing in the aisle when Levi Stubbs was singing "Baby, I Need Your Lovin,'" and I remember a lightness in my soul that was rarely there after my first year of college.

I was happy. I was going to be nineteen in a little less than a month and I thought I had everything I'd ever wanted. Good friends. A great girl. Good grades. How could life possibly be better?

The concert lasted about two hours, and we went straight from there to the parties. This time Beth and I didn't bother party-hopping. We just went straight to the SPO house. This was the last contact rushees would have with the brothers before bids were issued Thursday, and everybody who was on the fence wanted to make that one last impression. Enough guys in the house had made it clear to me that I'd be getting a bid that I could just relax and enjoy myself.

So, I did. Beth and I danced and talked and drank beer and

danced some more. We held each other close during the slow dances and kissed as they ended. "God, Beth," I mumbled as she stroked my cheek during one of those kisses. "You're driving me crazy."

Beth hugged me tightly. "I'm having such a good time this weekend, Rob. I'm so glad you asked me down."

The dance was over, but we were still standing there in each other's arms. Nobody thought that was particularly strange. By this time of night, a lot of people were feeling quite warm toward each other. "Beth? Can we go outside and sit on the porch and talk for a few minutes? It's quieter out there."

"Isn't it kind of cold outside?" I shrugged. "All right. As long as you promise to keep me warm if I start to freeze."

I agreed, and we adjourned to the big porch of the house. It was a little quieter out here, and we sat down together in a love seat. She snuggled against me, and we kissed again. "That's so nice," she said. "It's so easy to be with you like this."

I had never been as smooth with girls as my friend Dave had, so I probably fumbled a little more than necessary to get the words out. "Beth, I want you to know that I really like you."

She kissed me again. "I really like you too, Rob." She kept kissing me and I lost my train of thought for a minute. "You don't have to say anything, baby."

"I just ... Well, it's just that a lot of guys here don't date anybody all that regularly. They just get dates for big weekends or take road trips." She nodded, encouraging me to continue. "I guess what I'm trying to say is that I think I'd like to have something more than that with you."

She understood. "You want me to be your girlfriend."

I looked at her a little apprehensively. "I know that sounds crazy. I know this is only the second time we've gone out, but I really like you."

She smiled sweetly and kissed me again. "It's not crazy, Rob. I like you too, and I would love to be your girl. I'd love to have you come up and see me on weekends, and just hang out together sometimes and not even do anything special. I want to keep on getting to know you, too. As long as we can take it slow in one respect."

"What do you mean?" I asked, although I thought I knew.

"I know a lot of people at these parties are going to end up in bed with each other tonight. The times I've been alone with Nancy this weekend, she's been telling me how much she likes Bruce and how she wonders if she can hold out much longer." I nodded. "Well, Rob. I really like you a lot, and I'm not going to lie to you. I wonder what it would be like to be alone with you in bed, with all our clothes off and..."

I moaned. "I hope you know what that's doing to me."

Beth giggled. "Yeah, I think I do. Anyway, I do wonder. That isn't the way I was brought up, though."

"Me either. I've told you about my dad. One thing I got from him was a pretty good sense of morals, and I decided a long time ago I wasn't going to make love with someone unless it meant something."

"Are you a virgin?" she asked softly. I nodded. "So am I." She blushed a little at such an intimate revelation. "I don't think I'm a prude, and I don't know if I want to stay a virgin until I get married, but I do know I want my first time to be with someone I love and who loves me more than anything else in the world."

We kissed for a while. I wanted to tell her she didn't kiss like a virgin, that she was driving me crazy, but I figured it might embarrass her. I just enjoyed it. We left the party a little after two and walked back to the motel. Bruce hadn't brought Nancy back yet, so Beth and I had the room to ourselves. "Do you want to come in for a while?"

I must have looked a little apprehensive. "Don't worry, Rob," she said, giggling a little. "I won't attack you."

I stayed for about an hour, and we stretched out on the bed and kissed a lot more. It was all innocent. No clothes came off, although she let me get away with a lot of interesting caresses outside her blouse. Both of us were excited by the time we heard the key in the lock. We broke apart as if it were our parents coming in, and when we realized what we had done, we both laughed. We were sitting up on the bed when Bruce and Nancy walked into the room. "Shit," Bruce said softly.

I laughed. "I guess you were hoping you'd beaten us back here, weren't you?"

Nancy blushed, but Bruce nodded. "I thought you'd be staying out a lot later. You did last night."

Nancy smiled. "Sorry, lover," she said to Bruce. "I guess you guys will just have to go back to the dorm. After all, it is pretty late."

Bruce and I walked back together, swapping stories about what had happened at the parties we'd attended. We didn't talk much about Beth or Nancy. We weren't close friends yet, more like acquaintances on their way to friendship, and each of us liked his date enough to lift her out of the category of locker-room gossip. "Hell of a weekend, wasn't it?" he said.

"It isn't over yet. Beth isn't leaving till late afternoon."

He looked glum. "Nancy's ride is leaving around lunchtime."

Sunday was a quiet day, with nothing planned. The party weekend had ended with the fraternity blasts Saturday night, so Beth and I just kind of hung out. She still hadn't seen "Bonnie and Clyde," so we walked over to the University Theatre after lunch and caught a matinee. Once the show had let out, there wasn't really a lot more time. We went back to the motel and checked her out. Then we sat out in front and held hands while we waited for her ride to come by and get her.

"Rob, this was the nicest weekend I've ever had. It was certainly a lot more fun than the last time I was down here. You're so nice, and you did so many things to make this special for me. Can I tell you something?" I nodded. "I just wanted to tell you that last time, when I was down here with Rick and you were with Frannie, when we were all out together on Friday night, I really thought you were cute. I kept wishing you were my date instead of Rick. That's why I could hardly believe it when you wrote to me."

I started to say something, but she kept talking. "That was so wonderful of you. I can't think of too many guys I know who would have apologized for what happened. You're a great guy, and I'm really happy you want me to be your girl."

I kissed her. "You're the one who's special. I'm a lucky guy." Before we had a chance to say anything more, her ride arrived. "I'll call you in the next day or two," I said. "We'll figure out when we can get together again."

"Good. I hope it's soon."

18

The last week of school before Thanksgiving was going to be interesting.

First was the challenge of getting back into the routine of classes. Everyone had been studying at a fever pitch. Some had been rewarded and others had learned that cramming at the end wasn't good enough to give them the grades they wanted. Midterm grade advisories would be in our mailboxes Monday afternoon, and copies would be mailed to everyone's parents. I knew my mom would be pleased to see how well I'd done. The tough part now would be not letting down, even for a week or two. I knew if I wanted these same grades at the end of the semester, I'd have to work every bit as hard.

Second was the fact that fraternity rush was finally finished. Over the next three days, the 36 houses would decide who would get bids. At 6 o'clock Thursday evening, representatives would be allowed into the post office to distribute bids. Two hours after that, the first-year class would be allowed into the mailroom to get the news, good or bad.

Anyone accepting a bid would put on a jacket and tie and go directly to the house that wanted him. Some of the ones who had been left out would head down to the Corner to drown their sorrows at the Virginian or somewhere else.

It promised to be a very interesting week.

Danny got back late Sunday night, after I had gone to bed. I wasn't asleep yet, but I pretended I was. I was too tired for a long conversation. I figured if he wanted to talk, we could talk in a day or two. I slept for eight hours and dreamed about Beth.

I woke up Monday with an interesting idea, and I used the free hour between my French and biology classes to hustle down to the Corner to the florist's shop I had visited the week before Openings. I ordered a dozen roses to be sent to Beth at her dorm. "What's the message?" the gum-chewing girl behind the counter asked me. "You're supposed to send a message with them."

I thought for a minute. "Just say they're from the happiest guy in Charlottesville."

The girl looked at me strangely for a second, and I realized she probably thought I was sending them because I had gotten laid. I thought about explaining, but figured there was no point to it. "How much is it?"

She added up a few figures. "It's $17.25."

I wrote her a check and then hustled across the Lawn to make it to biology on time.

The next few days passed uneventfully. My advisory grades were exactly what I had expected, and I knew my 3.04 average would please my mom and show her I was taking college seriously. Beth called to thank me for the flowers, and we talked for about twenty minutes. I told her I would try to get up to Harrisonburg that weekend, but I didn't know what responsibilities I would have during my first weekend as a fraternity pledge. I promised to call her on Friday. Danny seemed depressed, but he didn't go out of his way to talk to me. I wasn't about to inject myself into his personal life without an invitation, so I let it ride.

There was a story sweeping the dorms Monday night. Supposedly a kid in one of the other first-year dorms had been kicked out of school for cheating. Nobody seemed to know exactly who it was, or what the class had been. I heard three different stories Monday night, and I didn't know whether to believe any of them or not.

The rumor became reality Tuesday when I saw that day's issue of the Cavalier Daily. In a small, black-bordered box on an inside page, there was a simple notice. A student had been expelled from the university for an honor violation—cheating.

By that evening, the facts had started making the rounds. The kid had been a first-year man named Alex Kendrick who lived up on Alderman Road. He had been caught cheating on a Spanish midterm, copying answers off the paper of the guy sitting to his left. The guy sitting behind him had turned him in, and he hadn't bothered to contest the charge. He had left school over the weekend and would never be allowed to return.

A group of us talked for three hours about what had happened. It was the first time the Honor System ever had really hit home, even though none of us had known Alex Kendrick. I told Bruce I didn't know if I would have been able to turn the kid in if I was the one who caught him.

"I'd do it," he said. "In a heartbeat."

"So would I," Dick Simpson said.

Ed Randolph and Andy Lynch agreed with Bruce, and only Ricky Barton said he wasn't sure he could do it. I was in the minority on this one.

"Why couldn't you turn him in, Rob?" Ed asked me. "The guy knew the rules. They make it very clear exactly what the Honor System is when they accept us. Everybody goes through the lecture and orientation before registration. Every one of us has to sign the honor pledge or they won't let us register."

I shook my head. "Guys, this is serious. I don't know this guy, and I couldn't care less why he cheated. All I know is sometimes people do desperate things. Think about this. The guy might not have been planning to cheat. He might have studied his ass off and then found out he didn't study enough. Maybe he didn't even mean to cheat at first."

"So what?" Dick asked. "He cheated. He got caught. He's out. Fuck him."

"Look," I argued. "The guy messed up. He made a mistake, but it's not like he killed somebody. Wouldn't it be a better system if there were a little mercy? The guy didn't have to get the death penalty for his first offense, did he?"

No one agreed with me on that one, even Ricky. The consensus was that the only reason the system worked as well as it did was that the single sanction was effective. "So, we're scared into being honest. Is that it?"

That wasn't it, as far as they were concerned. "Rob, you're either honest or you're not," Bruce said. "Once you start cheating, you've shown you don't have any honor."

"Bruce, that's not true at all. What about giving people a second chance? Everybody makes mistakes."

"Not in the Honor System," Ed said somberly.

I was relentless. "Maybe that's the problem. And if you want to know something else, that's not even the biggest problem I have. I don't like the idea of them forcing us to turn each other in. I'm not going to lie, cheat or steal, but I resent the hell out of being told that I've got to be a policeman and be responsible for the honor of everyone else."

"Who do you want to be responsible?" Bruce asked.

"At most colleges, the professors watch their classes, or they have proctors doing it. All we're doing is saving them work, and frankly, I don't spend a whole lot of my time looking for ways to save professors work."

"But we've got to enforce it," Ed said. "It's our system."

"That's total bullshit. It's not our system. It's a system some old guys put together back in the nineteenth century. We weren't even born then."

"It works," Bruce said.

"Damn right," Dick agreed. "And we don't need some Yankee trying to tear down all our traditions."

"Our traditions?" I lifted an eyebrow and glanced at Dick. I didn't like him one bit, and I wasn't going to take that from him. "I don't remember your father and grandfather going to school here, Colonel."

I was surprised when Dick backed down. He usually didn't stop arguing so quickly, but maybe this was too serious a subject for him. We all talked a while longer about the kid who had left school, and we wondered what would happen to him.

"I'd kill myself if I got kicked out for an honor violation," Andy said.

"Seriously?" I asked.

He shrugged. "Well, maybe not. My dad would do it for me."

That effectively ended the discussion, but it didn't stop me from thinking about the subject. I remembered my conversation with Dave back in September, and I hoped once again I would never come into close contact with the enforcement part of the Honor System. Wednesday night the topic of conversation was equally serious, but in a different way. A bunch of us got together and talked about fraternity bids.

Only five or six guys on the hall were confident. Another five or six were hoping their optimism wasn't unwarranted and the rest of the ones who had been rushing were sort of hoping against hope at this point.

When 6 o'clock Thursday evening came around, I was out on the quad playing football. I could see representatives of the different fraternities heading into the post office, but I tried to put it out of my mind. I didn't want to just sit and wait, and I was too keyed up to study. I had decided I could afford to take one weeknight off.

It was dark by 6:30, but most of us stayed out until we couldn't even see the ball. I went back upstairs at 7:30; knowing I still had half an hour to kill before the mailroom would be open to the horde of those waiting to learn their fate. Danny was studying. I had noticed that he had really been working hard in the three days since he had returned from home. I wondered if his parents had given him a bad time about his midterm grades and decided they were probably the type of folks who really expected a lot from their son.

I picked up my history book and tried to concentrate on manifest destiny. I knew American History was my best bet for an A this semester. I had only missed by two points on the midterm, and with a paper and a final exam accounting for seventy percent of the grade, I felt pretty good about my chances.

Not tonight, though. All I could think about was the bid in my mailbox. I knew it was crazy to be so tense. After all, I had been told more than a month ago that I would be getting it. I couldn't help wondering how, if I was this tense over a sure thing, some of the guys who really didn't know were reacting.

Five minutes later, Bruce knocked on my door. "Three minutes till eight. Want to start down?"

I snapped the book shut. "Why not?"

Bruce glanced at Danny. "You want to come with us?"

Danny laughed, but it was a humorless sound. "I think I'll pass. Bring my bid back up to me, would you?"

"Sure," I said, getting up quickly and leaving the room.

"What's that about?" Bruce asked me as we walked down the hall.

"Danny hasn't been getting any invitations since the second week of rush."

"Oh. I thought he still was rushing one of the Jewish houses. I wouldn't have said anything if I'd known."

The crowd outside the mailroom was huge. There must have been five hundred guys waiting to get in. Our resident advisors were blocking the entrances, and when the little hand on the clock reached the top of the hour, Jack Mathews stepped away from the door. "Good luck, gentlemen."

I wasn't about to trample anyone, and I certainly didn't want to get trampled. I stayed back toward the rear of the crowd and waited until some of it cleared out. I could see my mailbox from where I was standing and it was apparent that there was an envelope inside, so I felt pretty good.

Bruce came out of the horde after taking about five minutes to fight his way to the front. He looked like he was wearing clothes that had come straight out of the hamper, and his usually neat hair was pretty badly mussed. He was grinning, though, and he had an envelope in his hand. "I got it. KSK."

"Anything for the Colonel?"

Bruce shook his head. "The only place Dick was rushing was ATO, and they were only going to take twenty pledges. He'll get in somewhere next semester if he lowers his sights a little. You get yours yet?"

I shook my head. "I thought I'd wait until things calmed down a little. I didn't want to come out of there looking like you."

"It must be nice to know you're getting a bid." I shrugged. "I'll tell you what. I'll stick around until you get brave enough to go in there." That was good for a laugh, and after about five more minutes, the crowd was small enough for me to walk across the room and open my mailbox. I was shocked to see that there were two envelopes inside.

Damn, I thought before reaching in and taking them out. Maybe one of the Jewish houses went ahead and gave Danny a bid. When I looked at the names on the front of the envelopes, though, I saw that both were addressed to me. I knew right away what had happened. I opened the first envelope and saw that it was the bid I'd been expecting from SPO. Then I opened the other one. It had the same message— from KSK. I couldn't help but feel a twinge of pride to know that a house I didn't really want to join would offer me a bid. I knew it was Dave's doing, and I was glad that he was my friend.

"Did you get it?" Bruce had come up behind me without my hearing him.

I nodded. "I got two bids."

It didn't surprise him. "SPO and KSK, right?" I nodded. "Any doubt which one you'll take?" I shook my head. "I didn't think there was, but it would have been nice to pledge together."

All pledges were expected to arrive at their new houses by 10 o'clock, with the understanding that the ceremonies would be finished before midnight. All of us had classes on Friday, and none of the houses wanted to get their newest members in trouble academically.

Before I went over to Sigma Phi Omicron, I called Dave to let him know how much I appreciated what he had done. "Bobby, you might not believe this, but it wasn't even my idea. When your name was brought up, I told them what you told me, that you weren't going to accept a bid from us. Some of the other guys really liked you, though, and they said we ought to go ahead and bid you in case something had happened to sour you on SPO this last week or so."

I didn't know what to say.

"You impressed a lot of guys with those midterm grades. We don't have one guy in the second-year class who did that well last year. You keep it up, hear?"

I heard. I told him to thank his brothers for the bid and to tell them I thought they had a terrific house. "Hell, we all know that, and I told them if your dad had been a KSK brother, you'd be pledging with us. Hey, hadn't you better get going?"

I realized it was a quarter of ten and I'd have to hustle. "Thanks again, Dave."

Sigma Phi Omicron had given out twenty-two bids. By 10:15, which was the deadline for showing up or calling to accept, twenty-one first-year men were standing in the party room in the basement of the house. I looked around at my new pledge brothers and realized I didn't know any of them. I thought I recognized one guy from my American History class, and I was sure some of them must be in our huge biology lecture section.

Aside from that, all of them were strangers. I knew these guys would become my closest friends over the next four years. Most of us would live together right here in the house and I would wind up knowing more about some of them than I ever wanted to know. For now, though, it felt strange. It felt almost like first grade again.

We all stood there, waiting anxiously. Most of us had heard wild stories about the hazing fraternities put their pledges through. We'd heard of pledges being forced to strip naked and sit on large cubes of ice, of having to pick olives off the floor using only their butt cheeks. We'd heard the stories of pledges being dumped out in the country in their underwear, and of the guys who'd been tied up and put on trains heading to Tennessee.

I figured some of the stories were apocryphal, but I knew a lot of those things happened. I remembered asking Dave over the summer what he had gone through. He just grinned and wouldn't tell me anything. "You think I'm going to spoil it for you, Bobby? It's different at different houses, anyway. You'll find out soon enough."

The one brother most of us had dealt with was Lonnie Edwards as rush chairman. He was the one who walked into the room and welcomed us. "We're pleased to have you all here. We got one call turning down our bid, and that gentleman told us his midterm grades had been too low. We invited him to rush next semester when he had his priorities more in order, and he said he might."

Lonnie looked around, scanning us for any signs of fear. Then he grinned. "Gentlemen, my job as rush chairman is complete. I now turn you over to your pledge trainer, Brother Kondracki."

Bart Kondracki walked into the room, looking bigger than he ever had. I thought it was a little ominous that the biggest, toughest guy in the house was going to be our trainer and I wondered again what he would put us through. He stared hard at us, and I thought I heard one of the guys in line moan. I know I heard someone giggle, but he choked it off as quickly as he could. Then Bart broke into a big grin. "Hi, guys."

Twenty-one first-year pledges gave a sigh of relief. Whatever was going to happen, it wouldn't happen on our first night.

Bart explained to us what our responsibilities would be as members of the pledge class. We would be pledges until early April, when those of us who finished the course would be initiated as full brothers. Those who didn't complete the requirements, or who finished the first semester with less than a 2.0 grade point average, would be given the option of quitting or continuing as pledges for another semester.

Until we were brothers, we would be responsible for most of the work around the house. Kitchen duty, weekend cleaning, yard work. We would be required to attend group study halls two hours every night, and we would have to memorize most of the information in our pledge manual. We would have to carry spiral notebooks around, and over the course of our pledge period, we would fill the notebook with the name, home address, birthday, major and girlfriend's name of every brother in the house.

We would always carry a pack of chewing gum in case a brother wanted some. If we were ever without our gum or our spiral notebook, any brother could demand twenty pushups from us.

"There may be other ... surprises," Bart said. "Everything you do will be a part of the ultimate objective of forming the members of the SPO graduating class of 1971 into a tight-knit brotherhood. You guys need to look out for each other. You're pledge brothers now."

Then he went down the line and told each pledge to give his

name and his hometown. I knew I would never remember half the names, but I did my best to put faces and names together. There was one other guy from Pennsylvania, a kid named Stu Sanders. I hadn't seen him before, but he was from Philadelphia, and he had been one of the very best basketball players in the state. I had heard he was down here on an athletic scholarship, and I was impressed that a guy who would be playing varsity basketball next year would be one of my brothers.

One of the other guys, a blonde-haired kid named Randy Metcalf, was from southern California. He looked like he had grown up on the beach with a surfboard under his arm, and I wondered what he was doing so far from home and why someone who was accustomed to eternal sun and sunshine would want to live through Virginia winters.

I heard two of the guys give Chicago as their hometown. I figured they were friends who had gone through rush together, but I couldn't be certain. After all, the Windy City was the second largest in the United States back then.

Most of my pledge brothers were from the south, with more than half from various towns and cities in Virginia. Only two came from the Deep South, one from Mississippi and another from Georgia.

"Get to know each other over the next couple of weeks," Bart told us. "When you come back from Christmas break, we're going to ask you to elect a pledge class president. Those of you who aren't on the meal plan can start eating your meals here on Monday. The rest of you will be asked to start eating here second semester." He looked around and smiled at us. "Gentlemen, we are going to administer the oath to you, and that will make you official members of the pledge class. You've got the weekend to buy your notebooks and chewing gum, and your pledge duties will begin on Monday. We'll need your checks for the pledge fee and your first month's dues at that time."

I was pleased to hear that I wouldn't have any fraternity responsibilities until the following week. With midterms out of the way and my weekend free, if I could get Dave to lend me his car, I could go up to Madison and see Beth on Saturday.

19

Dave drove a hard bargain. He told me the only way I could use the car was if he went along, too. "Ask Beth to get me a date. We'll double."

"I thought you were going out with that girl from Sweet Briar. Lynn?"

Dave shrugged. "It wasn't going anywhere. I think I'm ready to start looking again."

"She dumped you, huh?"

"I can't understand it."

I told my friend I would see what I could do, and when I called Beth on Friday evening, I laid it out for her. I said I really wanted to see her, but it would require a quid pro quo. She said she would see what she could do, and she promised to call me back in an hour. I went back to my room to wait, and it was closer to an hour and a half before Joe Del Rio came down the hall to tell me I had a call. "Thanks, Joe."

"Can you make it quick? I've got to call one of my buddies back home."

I knew this guy must have been spending all his extra money on phone calls. His phone habits had earned him the nickname "Mr. Watson," as in Alexander Graham Bell, but that was his business. "I'll keep it short."

Beth told me it hadn't been a problem; she knew four or five girls who didn't have dates and would be glad to go out. She had known it was for my best friend, so she tried to be a little more selective. "I think he'll like the date I got for him. Her name is Marianne, and she's this beautiful redhead. She was a cheerleader in high school, and she just broke up with the guy who asked her down for Openings."

"Did you tell her about Dave?"

"Sure. I told her how nice he was. She's eager to meet him."

We talked about our week for a little while and would have talked longer except that I saw Joe poking his head out the door of his room to see if the phone was free. I told Beth I had better cut it short and that I'd see her tomorrow.

It turned out to be an interesting weekend. Dave and Marianne hit it off, and Beth and I were getting to know each other better. The evening wasn't anything spectacular, typical dinner-and-a-movie stuff, but no matter what I did, I was enjoying it if it was with Beth. Dave and I wound up splitting the cost of a cheap motel room so we could stay over and see the girls again on Sunday.

We had brunch with them and returned to school in early afternoon. I wasn't sure when Dave and Marianne would be seeing each other again, but Beth asked me if I could come up the second weekend in December to take her to their Christmas formal.

"Formal?" I asked skeptically. "Does that mean I'd have to wear a tuxedo?" I knew I'd say yes, but I teased her for a little while about my reluctance to dress up.

When we got back to Charlottesville late Sunday afternoon, I knew I had a lot of work to do. I studied until half past midnight and then went to bed. For some reason, I was having trouble sleeping again. I kept thinking about Beth, and how much I liked her. I certainly had had crushes before, but I knew I had never been in love. I found my-self wondering if she would be my first lover, and I thought about how badly I wanted to take her to bed.

That made me restless, and I considered taking a cold shower. That was always Father Cepicki's remedy, and it had worked for me on more than one occasion. I didn't want to get out of bed, though, and I decided I'd give it five more minutes. It didn't take that long. I fell asleep and slept soundly through the night.

Nothing much happened over the three days before Thanksgiving break. We paid our pledge fees and dues at the house, and we had our first meeting as a pledge class. Classes seemed longer than usual, and no one got much done. The Thanksgiving break was only four days, but it was the first real break in the schedule since the beginning of September and it seemed as though even the professors were eager to have some time off. My only concern was if an expected early winter storm would screw up the roads. Snow was falling in Indiana and heading east by Tuesday night, and Dave wanted to leave early so we could make it home before the storm got to western Pennsylvania.

He talked me into skipping biology—the only time all year I missed that class—so we could be on the road by 10:30 in the morning. I called my mom and told her if the roads were clear, I should be home in time for dinner. She told me she'd fix something special. It had been nearly three months since I had seen her, and I had been missing her a lot.

I was feeling very grown-up after nearly three months of college, but I was really looking forward to being home. If Dave hadn't suggested skipping class, I probably would have come up with the idea myself.

Danny was in the room when I came by for my suitcase. He was packed, and his ride was leaving a little after eleven. I told him I hoped he would have a good Thanksgiving, and I wished him a safe trip. He did the same and said he would see me Sunday.

We had known each other for nearly three months, but I didn't think we were any closer than we had been the day we met. The best friend I had in the dorms was Bruce, and I had thought about asking him home for Thanksgiving. I knew he wouldn't go all the way to Texas for what amounted to a long weekend, but when I had broached the subject of his plans, he told me Dick had an uncle in New York and the two of them were going up there on the train.

I was glad he wouldn't be stuck in town. I couldn't imagine anything more depressing than eating Thanksgiving dinner in the cafeteria or down at the Corner. I knew the kitchen at the SPO house would be closed, so I wondered what some of my new pledge brothers would do. If I had known them better, I would have inquired. It was still early, though. I still had one foot in college life and the other in my home-town.

When I asked Dave if he had felt that way, he told me he didn't get over it until he went home for summer vacation after his first year. "I was bored out of my mind," he said. "When you're just home for short breaks, you visit your buddies and go around to your old haunts. But when you're stuck at home for three months after being away at school for a year, you go nuts."

I thought he might be right, but that wouldn't be a problem until next summer. At least this time, I had more things to do than time to do them. In addition to a big Thanksgiving dinner and local visits, I was hoping to drive to Pittsburgh on Friday to see my grandparents.

I was taking my books along. I didn't want to go five days without doing schoolwork, and I hoped I could find the time at least to study French and biology. As it turned out, I had plenty of time. We made it to Johnstown just ahead of the first storm of winter. Then the storm hit hard and dumped eight inches of snow on us. We had a white Thanksgiving. The weather turned cold, and the roads got icy, so I didn't go anywhere outside of town. I spent time with my mom, and I studied. I phoned Beth in Scranton to see how she was enjoying her vacation and we talked for about ten minutes. I told her I would call her when I got back to school Sunday night.

I tried watching television. I even went to the movies once. It was odd, though. Movies and television had been a regular part of my life before, but they almost had vanished from my personal routine. The only time I went to movies was with friends or dates, and I never watched television. My life was changing a lot from what it had been.

I listened to the radio, rock and roll out of Pittsburgh in the daytime and WKBW from Buffalo at night. They were just starting to play a lot of the songs I had been hearing for weeks on WUVA, so I closed my eyes and pretended I was back at school.

"You've changed, Bobby," my mom told me. "You seem more mature. You're quieter than you were last year, and you seem more, I don't know, focused." I smiled. "How do you like school?"

"It's strange, mom. You know me. I don't think I ever was a real gung-ho student. I got good enough grades, but I always felt like I had to force myself to study. Now it's like I want to study even when I don't really have anything specific to do. Now it's like I get angry with myself when I don't work hard enough."

She nodded. "You're growing up."

We talked about college life. She hadn't been surprised to learn I was pledging Sigma Phi Omicron. Tradition and all. She was glad I was enjoying myself and she was especially interested when I mentioned Beth. I told her how we had met. I didn't gloss over my passive role in what had happened to Rick. She frowned a little at that, but she smiled when I told her about the letter I wrote to apologize. "I'm proud of you."

"Really? I thought you would be disappointed."

My mother shook her head. "Bobby, your dad and I never had to be that tough on you. Whenever you did anything wrong, you always wound up punishing yourself a lot worse than we ever could have."

I didn't understand. "What do you mean?"

"Remember last summer when you borrowed the car to play golf with Dave?" I nodded. "I told you it was all right, but I needed it back by 3 o'clock because I had a doctor's appointment."

I remembered. Dave and I had played our best golf of the summer, and we had finished the round tied. He suggested we play another round to break the tie—four more hours on the links. I had completely forgotten my mother needed the car. When I didn't show up to drive her to the doctor, she had spent twelve dollars on a cab. I came home tired and excited, and as soon as I saw her, I remembered what I had forgotten.

Before she even had a chance to ask what had happened, I started apologizing. Before she could even suggest the punishment she had in mind -- not letting me use the car for a week—I had decided I shouldn't be allowed to use it for the rest of the summer.

"I was disappointed when you forgot to come for me, but I didn't think it was the most horrible thing in the world."

I still felt bad about it. "I was pretty irresponsible."

She smiled. "You forgot, and you were ready to give yourself the death penalty for a very minor offense. I suppose part of that comes from growing up as the son of a judge." I laughed. "Well, I don't think your dad would have wanted me to punish you any more severely than what I had in mind."

I had a hard time comprehending that. After all, I remembered sitting in my dad's courtroom and watching him sternly sentence criminals to terms in the state penitentiary.

My mother explained. "I don't think you can be a judge, and you certainly can't be a parent, without understanding mercy. That was the first time you were irresponsible. If it had been the second time, I would have made the punishment tougher. And if it had been the third time, maybe then I would have said you couldn't use the car for the whole summer."

I changed the subject. She laughed when I explained how Dave had talked me into borrowing his car and driving up to see Beth. I told her how nervous I had been and how glad I had been that it all had worked out. "Do you really like her, Bobby?"

I nodded. "Sure, mom. She's great. The only problem is that we're a hundred miles apart and it's tough to see each other as often as we'd like."

She didn't have much to say to that. She knew me well enough to know I wouldn't let anything interfere with my classes. "I was really pleased when I saw your grades."

"Thanks. I just hope I can keep all of them at least that high through finals."

My mother smiled. "Maybe you could use a little extra incentive. I didn't tell you this before you went down to school, because I knew you were worried about whether you could do the work and I didn't want to put any more pressure on you." I nodded. "But now that you've proved to yourself you can do it, I'll tell you. Your dad put a little extra money aside a few years ago. It was money he got when your grandfather died. We talked about it some, and he said that one of the toughest things about going to school in Charlottesville was the fact that the girls were all so far away."

I nearly laughed. I never pictured my dad as a ladies' man, and for the first time I realized that he probably had made a lot of the same road trips I had made before meeting my mom in Pittsburgh the summer between his third and fourth years of college.

My mother was still talking. "Anyway, he said the one thing he always wished he had when he was at school was a car. Of course, it was the Depression then, so there was no money for anything like that. But when he got this money, we decided to put it aside and buy you a car if you got good grades your first year of school."

I was speechless. My second year seemed so far away, but the thought of having my own car at school made me feel great. Then the rest of the thought kicked in, the realization that I would have a car because my dad had made plans three years ago to get me one. "I miss him so much, mom."

"I know, sweetheart. So do I. But he'd be so proud of you."

She told me he had put $500 into a savings account in 1964, and she had been adding five dollars here and there. With the extras, and the interest, she said there would be something like $650 for me to buy a car the next summer. "You can buy it no matter what, but the only way you can take it to school is if you've got that 3.0 average you keep telling me you need for law school."

I knew my second year would be great. I would be living in the fraternity house, and I would be finished with my pledge period. I would have a little more flexibility in my course selection, with many of my required courses out of the way. I would be one year away from upper division, from taking courses in my major. And I would have a car.

Dave and I went by the community center Friday night. With school out for Thanksgiving, I figured I would see some of my friends who had been a year behind me. They asked me all kinds of questions about college, and I answered them while Dave stood around acting like a world-weary adult until I reminded him he had done exactly the same thing the year before when it was me asking and him answering.

"Yeah, Bobby. We all grow up, but you'll always be around to remind me where I came from. I'll never be able to get away with anything as long as you're around."

It was getting late, and with the snow the streets were almost deserted. He drove me home and we talked. He said he liked Marianne, and that she had asked him to go to their Christmas formal. He said he had accepted, and I laughed. "What's so funny?"

"Oh, nothing. It's just funny how things work out. I was trying to get up my nerve to ask you if I could borrow your car to go up there for that same dance."

"That's funny. And you know you can borrow it any time I'm not using it."

I thanked him. Dave and I had been best friends for most of our lives, ever since we had gotten into a fight in elementary school. It had been an argument in a football game, with Dave in second grade and me in first. We wound up on the ground, punching wildly at each other. When one of the teachers broke it up, we both had bloody noses. The teacher marched us to the infirmary and turned us over to the nurse. She told us to keep our heads up so the blood wouldn't drip all over our shirts, and she wiped our faces clean.

Then she made us hold compresses to each other's noses to stop the bleeding. We had started talking while waiting for the flow to halt, and we'd been friends within a few minutes. We had joked about that first day ever since, and one of our running arguments was over who had won the fight. I knew in my heart I had beaten him, and he was equally certain I was the one on the bottom of the pile. The question would never be resolved. If we had been able to settle it, it would have cost us one of our favorite topics of conversation. That fight had been a jumping-off point for almost continuous competition between us. We had been battling good-naturedly for twelve years to prove which one was tougher.

It had started on the playground, in heated games of kick-ball and Red Rover. Both of us played Little League baseball and Pop Warner football, and each of us had done well. Dave wrestled in junior high, while I played football and baseball. When we got to high school, he warmed the bench for two years in high school as practice opposition for a kid who won a state wrestling title, and I got into three games that had already been long decided in varsity football.

Maybe the most surprising thing is that we never competed for girls. Part of that stemmed from the fact that we liked different types. I was attracted to athletic blondes like Beth, and Dave liked flashier girls. Marianne with the flame-red hair certainly fit into that category. After all these years, he and I were closer than most brothers.

He never treated me condescendingly because I was a year younger, either. In fact, we hung out together so often in high school that one of my teachers said she thought we were twins. I wanted to tell her that we didn't look anything like each other, but I understood she was just being nice, and I learned real early you don't get anywhere by contradicting your teachers.

The toughest thing about college had been not being able to spend time with my best friend. The rush rules had kept us apart. Of course, it had been good for me, too. If I had gone to school and hung out with Dave all the time, I probably wouldn't have made any new friends. I might have been in the same situation as Danny in the dorms.

I didn't think I would have been an outcast. People bring a lot of that on themselves. There weren't any overwhelming reasons people didn't like Danny. He wasn't strange looking, and he certainly wasn't stupid. Most of it was the way he carried himself. He was usually a little aloof, except for what I was beginning to think of as his Mr. Hyde mood. That was when he seemed almost desperate to be included.

I knew his parents were very demanding. I could tell from the one time I met Irv and Yvette that Danny hadn't had a whole lot of freedom. I figured part of that came from being a year younger than most of the kids in his class. He had told me—maybe a little too proudly— that he had skipped one grade in elementary school and could easily have skipped another one if he'd wanted. I don't know what reaction he had expected from me. My initial reaction, which I didn't tell him, was that I would have hated being a year or two younger than everyone else in my class. I had read a story somewhere about one of those prodigies who finished college at the age of 12, and all I could think about was how lonely that kid must have been.

Where I grew up, street smarts were a lot more important than book smarts. It wasn't as though we were idiots. We had our share of National Merit Scholars, and two kids in our graduating class wound up in Ivy League schools. We probably even had our share of Danny Jacobses, but they weren't the kids I knew.

The worst part of it for Danny was that he wasn't happy with who he was—a bright kid who hated being bright. What Danny wanted more than anything else was to be one of the guys, even though I think he realized his intellect set him apart.

Also, Danny was clearly on the verge of having a big problem with Dick Simpson. Dick hadn't been in his face since the night of the fight in the mailroom. I think he was shocked that Danny had beaten him, and he resented it. His anti-Semitic remarks were getting worse, and I knew Danny hadn't had his final showdown with the Colonel.

After a long weekend at home, I was eager to get back to school. We left after Mass on Sunday morning and drove straight through. Most of the roads had been cleared, and by the time we got out of Pennsylvania there wasn't much snow anyway. The trip passed really fast the rest of the way. We stopped for an early dinner in Culpeper, an hour north of Charlottesville, and relaxed for a while. Dave dropped me off at the dorms a little after seven. It was strange, but I felt as if I were home.

20

When I think back on my first year of college, I remember there wasn't a great sense of urgency that December. Finals were after Christmas back then, and I think we all figured we had plenty of time over Christmas break to catch up. I know I fell victim to the December blahs more years than just that first one.

Beth's Christmas formal up at Madison was wonderful. I remember how incredible she looked in the baby blue dress she wore that night, and I knew I was starting to fall in love with her. It took me longer to get around to telling her.

Danny seemed to be getting more depressed. Twice in the last week before we went home for Christmas, I heard him masturbating when he must have thought I was asleep. I still thought I should say something to him about it, but I decided to wait until after Christmas.

I saw Beth once more before going home. The university let out for Christmas on a Thursday that year. Dave and I decided to go home by way of Harrisonburg, and we took Beth and Marianne out to dinner Thursday night. "I'm going to be so bored at home for three weeks," Beth said as we sat and talked after dinner.

"Hey," I said, laughing. "You'll be too busy fighting off all your old boyfriends to be bored."

She hit me playfully. "I don't have old boyfriends. Just one stupid new one who's going to be all the way across the state."

I kissed her and then things got a little more serious. "Are you going to be at home the whole time?"

"Yeah. How about you?"

"Well, I thought I might fly to Paris for New Year's Eve."

She laughed. "Why don't you drive over to Scranton instead? It'll be a lot cheaper, and I've been telling my mom about you." I must have reacted with a look of alarm. "Don't look so frightened, Rob. I talk to her about everything. We're close. Do you mean to tell me you haven't said anything to your mother about me?"

"Hey, baby," I said, clowning a little. "I don't kiss and tell." She frowned. "Yeah, I've told her about you. She said you sound really nice."

"I am really nice. This conversation is stupid."

I thought for a minute about going over to Scranton to see Beth during Christmas break, and I liked the idea. If I didn't go visit her, it probably would be a month before we saw each other again. We only had one car, though, and I didn't think my mom would be excited about me taking it to go more than two hundred miles in the middle of winter to visit my girlfriend. "I don't know if I can get the car."

Beth shrugged. "Then take the bus. We can use one of our cars to get around."

"Where would I stay?" I leered at her. "In your room?"

She looked shocked. "Rob! My daddy would kill you if he knew what you wanted to do to his baby daughter."

I leered at her. "We'll have to be sneaky, won't we?"

"You're not getting anywhere near my room. I'll lock my door. We have a guest room downstairs. That's where you'd stay."

"Oh," I said, feigning disappointment. "Will you sneak down to my room, then?"

Beth was still acting shocked, but I knew the thought of me visiting her at home and staying overnight had her at least a little excited.

I knew nothing would happen, other than a little innocent necking, but that didn't stop me from flirting with her.

"So how about it?" she asked. "Do you want to come and visit us? I told my mom I might ask you, and she said it was a good idea. My parents have always met my boyfriends, and it would probably make them feel better about you if they knew you."

"It might make them feel worse," I said, trying to sound a little dangerous.

She wasn't going to let me get away with that one. "Yeah, sure. You're the type of boyfriend that every girl's parents love. Like those old Andy Hardy movies our folks used to watch back during the war."

I told her I would check with my mother to see if she had made any plans, but I would love to come if she said it was all right. We decided I could come over on the 30th and go home three days later. "That'll give my dad and my brothers a chance to check you out. You can watch football with them on New Year's Day."

My mother said she wished she could let me use the car, but she needed it. Since I would be home for two weeks before I went to see Beth, and nearly a week after I got back, my mom said it was up to me if I wanted to take the bus to Scranton. I called Trailways for times, and then I called Beth to tell her I would be there for dinner on Dec. 30th.

"That's great. My folks are looking forward to meeting you."

It turned out to be the highlight of Christmas break. I spent most of the time I was home studying, getting ready for my fall semester finals. I went out with Dave a few times in the evenings, and I went to a Christmas party hosted by a girl I had gone to high school with. Everyone seemed different. All of us had been changed, either by the schools we were attending or the fact we hadn't gone to college. Two guys at the party had enlisted in the Marines and were awaiting orders to Vietnam. I realized how little the events of the world were touching me in Charlottesville.

All that would change within a couple of years when protests would reach even the conservative colleges. In 1967, though, the budding antiwar movement hadn't really gained a foothold at the university. I tried to explain it to someone a decade or so later, when they asked me what it had been like to be a college student in the late sixties. I said

I wasn't part of that scene; the first large protests I had seen had been during law school at Penn State.

Virginia in the late sixties—in the final years before coeducation—was more like the 1950s or even the 1940s in some respects. We hung onto our traditions with a death grip, somehow afraid that losing them would sweep us into some uncharted territory. I'd look at my friends with their close-cropped hair and Brooks Brothers wardrobes and wonder if we were characters in an old movie. We were so sheltered. We talked of honor, and we danced to sweet soul music, and we hoped with all our hearts it would never end. I think we knew we were already anachronisms.

Beth was right. Bringing home a clean-cut boyfriend who wore a tie would be something her parents would love. I didn't think of myself as Andy Hardy, but I knew I would never try to sneak into Beth's room. I spent four days with the Ericksons, and I didn't get to spend much of it alone with Beth. There were more people there than Beth had expected, so I didn't even get the guest room. I wound up sleeping on a sofa in the den.

It was my first real experience with a family that big. There were fourteen Ericksons—including spouses and small children—and one Miller at their big dining room table. Beth's older sisters both made a fuss over me, and I felt like part of the family.

We went to a New Year's Eve party that some of her friends from high school were hosting, and we had a great time. We danced until midnight, and then we all stood around while someone counted down the seconds to 1968. I found myself thinking back on the year that was ending. A year ago, I had been awaiting my SAT scores and my acceptance at Virginia. My biggest concern then was whether I'd be able to beat out Tommy Carpenter for starting shortstop on the varsity baseball team in the spring.

A lot happened in 1967. The Vietnam War heated up, and the Summer of Love transformed San Francisco. The Boston Red Sox won the American League pennant in their "Impossible Dream" season. Later we all would look back on 1967 as one of the last innocent years. All the events that were about to unfold would change society forever. Of course, I didn't know any of it was coming as I listened to the countdown on New Year's Eve. "Three ... two ... one ... Happy New Year!"

Suddenly Beth was in my arms and we were kissing. "Happy New Year, Rob. I think it's going to be a wonderful year."

21

When we had left school in mid-December, the weather was crisp, and the mood was relaxed. We returned to a town blanketed in snow and a dormitory blanketed in panic. Final exams were just ten days away, and these were the tests that would count for at least half the overall grade in every class. Except for my four-day trip to see Beth, I had spent most of my Christmas vacation studying and writing my history paper.

I thought I had a chance to do well, but I knew I couldn't afford to do anything except work for the next two weeks. Beth's exams were scheduled similarly, so when we said goodbye in Scranton, we knew we wouldn't be seeing each other until late January.

I returned to a crisis. My roommate came back with the news that his parents were divorcing. "I didn't know anything about it," Danny said in an anguished voice.

I looked up from my biology textbook for what seemed like the tenth time. Danny was trying to study, but it was obvious he couldn't concentrate. I knew if this happened too many more times, I'd have to go over to the library to get anything done. "How could you not know?

Weren't they having problems before you left?"

He shrugged. "They've always fought on and off. That's just the way they are, but this time I got home for Christmas and found out my dad had moved into an apartment."

"But you call home at least once a week, don't you?" He nodded. "And they never said anything?"

Danny looked at me glumly. "My mother said they knew I was having a hard time and they didn't want to worry me."

It sounded awful, and I was sympathetic. At least I thought I was. I couldn't deal with it, though. It wasn't my problem and I had to study. "Uh, Danny, I've got to get this reading done."

"Oh, sure. Sorry I bothered you, Rob." He went back to his own reading, but five minutes later I heard a loud sigh. I braced myself for another interruption, but he just got up and left. I found myself hoping he would stay away until I had made it through my biology.

For the next week, I studied harder than I ever had in my life. Our biology study group got together three or four times, and I spent hours drilling French vocabulary and grammar with Andy Lynch.

Each morning I dragged myself out of bed at 6 o'clock. The heat in the dormitory was still turned down at that hour and I shivered my way down the hall to the bathroom for a hot shower. After I dressed, I dragged myself over to the cafeteria for breakfast; my nose buried in a book the whole time. Once I looked up and realized that almost everyone else who had gotten up to eat breakfast was doing the same thing. I didn't think I had ever heard the cafeteria so quiet.

I got into the habit of doing all my studying in the library, and I was generally there from the time I got out of classes in early afternoon until they locked it up at midnight. Then I would trudge through the snow to my room, pull off my clothes and fall into bed. Just about the only exceptions to my schedule were the brief visits I made to the fraternity house to let them know I hadn't died, dropped out or quit.

Every time I stopped by, I was amazed to see some of my pledge brothers just hanging out. I figured these guys must be a lot smarter than I was. I had studied my ass off just to get B's on midterms, and all I was hoping to do was maintain those grades.

Everyone talks about how tough the first year of law school is, and mine was a bear, but it wasn't half as tough as my first year of college. That was the year I had to make all my adjustments, the year I had to grow up in more ways than one. I guess you could say that was the year I stopped being a kid.

I didn't see much of my roommate. That was the way I wanted it. Every time I found myself wondering how he was doing—which wasn't often—I pushed him out of my mind by telling myself his problems weren't my responsibility. I knew if I didn't do well on my exams, I would have enough problems of my own.

When I slept, no more than five or six hours a night, I slept like the dead. I didn't know what he was or wasn't doing, which suited me fine. I had been thinking about forfeiting my room deposit and moving into the SPO house. It seemed like a good idea, but a hundred dollars was a lot of money, and the thought of just throwing it away didn't thrill me. Besides, I had promised my mom I would stay in the dorms for the whole year. I decided to put up with my roommate for another four months.

Exams were scheduled over a ten-day period, and mine were well spaced. I had my American History final on Monday the 18th, the first day of the exam period, French on the 21st and calculus on the 22nd. After a weekend break, I had English composition—which would be an in-class essay—on the 25th and biology on the 27th. I knew that once I had calculus out of the way, I could basically devote most of five days to studying for that last final.

Beth's exams started a little later and ended on Friday the 29th. We had decided to get together that Saturday for a post-exam blowout. By then it would have been nearly four weeks since Scranton, so we were both looking forward to it. We talked on the phone a few times, and she sent me a couple of nice letters. Still, our relationship was mostly on hold in January 1968.

The Friday before exams started, I found out that I had gotten an A-minus on my history paper, so I was right on the borderline between an A and a B there. I knew I had a solid B in composition, so there were two classes in which I was in really good shape. It would be the other three—calculus, French and biology—that would determine whether I held my 3.0 average from midterms.

Danny disappeared the weekend before finals. He hadn't told

me he was going anywhere, but he left on Thursday afternoon and didn't sleep in his bed for the next three nights. I was glad to have the room to myself. It saved me from battling through the snow and trying to find a place to study in the library. Alderman was packed every day.

The dorm was mostly quiet, but the tension was almost palpable. All the bills for months of carousing were coming due, and a lot of guys were beginning to realize they didn't have enough in their study accounts to cover the checks they had to write.

Danny came back at around 10 o'clock Sunday night. I didn't ask him where he had been, and he didn't volunteer anything. I learned later that he had gone home to spend time with his dad. He didn't look happy, but I couldn't remember the last time my roommate had looked happy. Maybe October. Maybe when he had the hometown girl down for Homecomings.

My first final went smoothly. After the midterm, I felt as if I knew what my history professor wanted to see in the way of answers. I did my best to give it to him and I felt pretty good when I came out of the classroom.

The second and third ones didn't go badly, either. The hours I had spent drilling French vocabulary with Andy had helped, and I felt certain I had maintained my B. As for calculus, I was daring to dream that maybe I had gotten an A. I felt like I understood everything on the final, but I knew that didn't mean I had gotten everything right. Regardless, my B was safe, and I felt satisfied I had survived the first week of exams in good shape.

There was nothing I needed to study for composition, so all that left was biology, five days in the future. I decided I could afford to take a night off from studying, and I went over to the fraternity house after dinner. "Hey, Rob," Lonnie Edwards greeted me. "We were beginning to wonder if you were still alive."

I laughed. "Well, you know how it is during finals."

Lonnie nodded. "Got a stick of gum for me?"

I reached into my pocket and pulled out a pack of Wrigley's Spearmint. Lonnie frowned a little. "Gee, Rob. I was really hoping for Juicy Fruit."

"Yeah," one of the other brothers said as he walked by. "That's because you are a juicy fruit, Edwards."

I knew better than to laugh. The other brother said he would take the gum, and he pulled a stick out of the full pack. Then he said he had better take the other four sticks in case he wanted more later. I handed over the entire pack and he walked off.

"So, Rob," Lonnie said, grinning. "Have you got a stick of gum for me?"

"He just took it all."

"Who's he?" I couldn't remember. "All right, get your notebook out and write this down. Greg Garber. Third year. Business major. Hometown is Columbia, South Carolina. Girlfriend's name is Andrea Donaldson at Longwood."

I scribbled as quickly as I could. "What about his birthday?"

Lonnie looked at me sternly. "I can't give you everything. Now about that gum..."

"I don't have any."

He shook his head. "Why don't you get down and give me twenty pushups then." It wasn't a question. I took off my jacket and fell to the floor. I did ten quickly and then he stopped me. "You're not counting them out loud."

"How would you like me to do that, Brother Edwards?"

I was catching on. "Good question," he said, grinning. "It never hurts to ask. I would like to hear the number of each pushup, and I want to know that you're doing them for me. Start at the beginning, please."

"One, Brother Edwards. Two, Brother Edwards. Three, Brother Edwards..."

I was glad I had practiced while I was home for Christmas. By the time I finished counting my twentieth pushup, I had actually done thirty. "Good job, Rob," he said.

With the obligatory hazing out of the way, we sat down and talked for a while. Lonnie was fourth year and heading into his final semester of college, so exams weren't quite as ominous for him. "Most of my work is research papers now."

I dreamed of being that far along, and I hoped I would be able to relax. I was enjoying being at the house, but there was still a part of me that thought I should be studying. "How's that girlfriend of yours?" he asked me.

"Beth? Oh, she's fine. We're getting together again next weekend."

"You bringing her down for Midwinters?"

The next big weekend. The third weekend of February. Midwinters fell after two weeks of the second semester, and it was supposed to break up the boredom of winter. "We haven't talked about it yet. I think we've both been assuming it."

"She seems really special. Don't screw it up. Girls like her are tough to find."

I stayed at the house until about midnight, although I did make a quick trip to the Corner after my conversation with Lonnie. It was only a block away, and I knew if I was going to be around the brothers, I'd better have some gum. I bought six packs and hid them in various pockets. I was going to make sure I didn't get caught short again.

Saturday was spent in the library, although I did go to the Virginian with Bruce Saturday night. We drank a couple of beers and swapped stories about pledging. He told me Dave was one of the strictest taskmasters toward the Kappa Sigma Kappa pledge class. "He's always asking us for gum or making sure we've got our notebooks."

I wasn't surprised that a lot of the same rituals were used at different houses. I also had heard that the second-year brothers were usually the toughest on the pledges. That made sense. They were the ones who had gone through it the year before, so it was probably a matter of getting a little revenge for their own suffering.

We talked some about our vacation and we talked a little about girls. He said he had stopped seeing Nancy, the girl he brought down for both party weekends in the fall. "I guess I'll make a road trip and try to meet someone else. Ed told me he could get me a date if I wanted to go down to Lynchburg the next time he goes home to see his girl."

"Hey. Let me know if you want to go along to Madison the next time I go."

Bruce shook his head. "That's not a good idea. You'll be with

Dave. If I'm along, too, he'll have me giving him gum and doing push-ups all evening."

I laughed. "You're right. Madison is out until you've finished pledging."

We ordered more beer. I was starting to feel very relaxed, and after I finished the fourth beer, I did something I would later wish I hadn't done. I had wanted to talk to someone about this for a long time, so I asked Bruce what he would do if he knew his roommate was masturbating in bed at night.

"Is this hypothetical or do you know something about the Colonel that I don't?"

I should have stopped there, but I forged ahead. "No, it's not Dick. It's Danny. At least three times and probably more. Those are only the ones I know about." He had a shocked look on his face and all of a sudden, I started to feel bad about it, as if I had somehow betrayed a confidence. "Hey, Bruce. Never mind. It's not that big a deal."

He shook his head. "That kid is really fucked up."

"Please don't tell anybody I told you."

He nodded absent-mindedly. "Sure. Don't worry about it. It's no big deal."

Sunday it was back to the grind, and I knew I wouldn't relax again until noon on Wednesday. I'd study biology for three solid days, breaking only for meals, sleep, and my composition final Monday. None of the grades from the first week had been posted yet. I had been told to expect them starting early in the second week of exams, so I made plans to start going past the history, math and foreign language departments.

By Tuesday night, I felt as though I couldn't possibly cram any more science into my head, but I felt pretty good about hanging onto the B-minus I'd eked out on the midterm. My lab grades were a solid B, but they were only going to be ten percent of the final grade. I knew I needed at least an 80 on the final to be sure.

Two of my grades were posted Tuesday morning, and they lifted my spirits tremendously. I had gotten a 94 on the history final, and that was enough to give me an A-minus for the semester. It was my first college A—the only one I would earn my first year—and it made me feel terrific. Then I went by to see my French grade, and I saw that I had made an 87 on that final and a B-plus in the class. Biology was the last hurdle.

Danny mostly kept to himself. I did notice he spent a lot of time on the phone, but he didn't volunteer any information and I was far too engrossed in trying to remember thousands of obscure scientific terms. The biology midterm had been an hour long, with fifty questions. The final lasted three hours and had three times as many questions. It would take a score of 135 out of 150 for a 90 percent and an A, and I didn't think I was in the running for that. I had high hopes that I had made the necessary 80 percent for a B.

One day remained in the exam period, so there wasn't much noise in the dorms Wednesday. Most of us were finished, though, and about six of us went drinking that night. We closed two bars and wound up over at the Virginian at 3 o'clock in the morning. "God, am I glad that's over," Ed Randolph said.

"Amen, brother," chorused five other first-year men who were battling various degrees of intoxication.

After that we all staggered back across the grounds to our dorm and collapsed into our beds. I slept until noon, the latest I'd been in bed since coming to Charlottesville. I battled a hangover for about an hour, finally showering, shaving and dressing. I wanted to do was check to see if my grades were posted. Even though we'd taken our biology final just the day before, it had been a multiple-choice test that would be graded by a computer.

The calculus and English grades were both up. I got B's on both finals and as my final grade in both courses, and one day later I learned I had improved my midterm B-minus in biology to a solid B by getting a B-plus on the final. I had earned a 3.19 GPA for my first semester of college. I was more than a little stunned and extremely happy. Any doubts I'd had about being able to compete were gone. I had been within one A of making the Dean's List the first time out.

22

Because our Christmas break had been long, we only had one week off between semesters that year. Students were expected to make their living arrangements, get their meal plans set and register for their spring classes. I knew I would be staying in the dorms and eating my meals at the fraternity house, so all I really had to do was register. I had taken the first half of two-semester courses in English composition, French and biology, and I still had to complete all three to fulfill the prerequisites in those areas.

American History was a full-year course, but I didn't have to take the second half. My math course had been calculus the first semester, and it would be statistics the second. I decided I would try to sign up for government instead of history, making it just a matter of trying to get favorable sections in the classes. My fraternity brothers steered me away from one section of government and told me I ought to sign up for another one. When I sat down and worked things out, I realized I'd have three of the five professors I'd had for first-semester classes if things went as I planned in registration. Of course, they rarely do. I had been fortunate in one respect during the first semester. Except for my biology lab, all my classes had been finished by noon. I wasn't as lucky this time. I wound up with a French class that met at 2 o'clock four days a week.

All my others were the same, giving me English at 8 a.m., three days a week. Mondays, Wednesdays and Fridays were going to be weird. I'd have English at 8, biology at 11 and French at 2. I had my new government class at 9 and statistics at 10 the other three days, and my biology lab was at 2 o'clock on Thursday.

It was irritating. It meant I would be in class until at least 3 o'clock in the afternoon every day of the week from Monday through Friday. I was going to have to get into the habit of using the time between classes to study, something I hadn't done a whole lot of during the first semester. Most days after my last class, I had to go to the SPO house to work for a few hours as part of pledging. If I didn't study between classes, it would be evening before I could hit the books.

Dave and I drove up to Madison for a double date right after exams ended, and I borrowed his car and went alone the next Saturday night. On the second weekend, Beth and I spent a very interesting hour parked in a secluded spot behind the gymnasium.

Except for those two trips, I was busy in Charlottesville. The brothers had assigned the pledge class a total housecleaning, and all twenty-one of us worked at least part of every day getting things squared away for second semester. Four beds were open on the third floor of the house because of winter graduation, and they were offered to the pledges based on grade point average. My average, rounded to a 3.2, was the second highest in the pledge class, so I had the chance to move in if I wanted.

I thought about it again. I wanted to live in the house, but I decided to wait until my second year. Nine guys were interested, so the beds didn't go begging.

Most of the guys who weren't pledging went home between semesters. The only others who didn't were the ones who lived too far away. Bruce and Dick both had gone back to Austin for Christmas, so they weren't going again less than a month later. Bruce wound up staying in town for pledge duties over at KSK, and Dick went to visit his uncle in South Carolina. That left the dorm almost deserted.

The kitchen was staying open at the house, so I ate most of my meals there. Occasionally I would go down to the Corner with Dave or Bruce for a sandwich at the Virginian. We would play soul music on the jukebox and drink beer while we talked about the upcoming semester and all the things we wanted to do. It was probably the most idyllic week of the year. No schedules. No classes. Nothing to worry about except pledge duties. It didn't last long.

The new semester was due to start the first Monday in February, and the dorm filled up fast the night before. Danny returned in late afternoon. This time he came on the bus and caught a cab over from the terminal. "How's it going, Danny?" I asked him, more out of politeness than anything else. He shook his head. "My dad filed for divorce. Since he was the one who moved out, I thought he might change his mind and come home. I talked to him a lot, but it turned out my mom doesn't want him to come home. I think they're through. I feel like shit."

I didn't know what to say, so I made sympathetic noises and buried my head in a magazine.

Things stayed about the same in the three weeks leading up to Midwinters Weekend. Classes started, and most of us got into our routines easily. A lot of guys who hadn't started studying till too late in the fall had paid for it. More than half the guys on our hall wound up with less than a 2.0 average. That wasn't all that much of an aberration for first semester. It was a tough adjustment from high school to college, especially at Virginia, which combined tough academics and a killer social life.

Most of the guys seemed to have figured out what they had done wrong. The hall was a lot quieter in February than it had been in September as a lot of guys tried to hit the ground running the second time around the track.

Not Danny. I didn't know if it was stubbornness or the depression he was feeling over his parents' problems, but Danny wasn't working any harder. His grades hadn't been good, with one exception. Danny Jacobs had been one of only three guys in our 200-person class to get an A in biology. That was impressive, but one C, two D's and an F in his other four classes left him with a 1.7 average.

He was starting to keep more and more to himself. The only guy on the hall he was hanging out with was Leo Mitchell. The Germ was a scuzzy guy, and there were rumors he had been fooling around with marijuana. I didn't warn Danny off, though. It was none of my affair, and I was just glad he was bothering someone other than me.

Leo's roommate was Billy Ray Stokes, an Old South type from Mississippi who absolutely hated the longhaired New Yorker. Billy Ray was from a wealthy old family, and he had one of the best wardrobes of anyone in the dorm. It infuriated him that Leo wore the same clothes day after day, and his dirty underwear and socks always found their way into a growing pile at the foot of the bed.

"I just want to take that stuff outside and burn it," he said in his deep southern drawl. "It stinks. I talk to him about it, but he ignores me."

I sympathized. As big a pain as my own roommate could be, I knew it would be a lot worse if the Germ were sharing my room. Billy Ray was trying to figure out a way he could get out. He had pledged Kappa Alpha, but his grade point average hadn't been high enough to get him a room in the house. "Rooter?"

God, I hated that nickname. I knew it was only a matter of time before someone said it around Beth. I wasn't going to let on, though. I always had known that the best way to get a group of guys fired up about teasing you was to let them know it bothered you. "Yeah, Billy Ray?"

"What would you say about trading roommates?"

"Trade Danny for Germ?"

He shook his head. "I said that wrong. What I meant was what if we could get Danny and Germ to room together and I moved in here with you?"

I wasn't quite sure what to say. I wasn't that fond of Billy Ray, although he'd be a lot more agreeable as a roommate than Danny. After my conversation with Dave, though, I knew it would be very difficult to switch roommates in the middle of the year. Besides, I really didn't know if I wanted to add to Danny's problems by letting him think I wanted him out of the room. "I don't know, Billy Ray."

"Why not? I know you don't like your roommate."

I shook my head. "Danny's having a rough time with his folks splitting up, and I don't want to make it any worse for him."

Billy Ray shrugged. "Maybe I can find somebody. Maybe if I offer some money."

He was right about one thing, even if I hadn't wanted to admit it. I didn't like Danny. It was a pain in the ass to have a roommate who was an outcast, but I just figured it was my cross to bear. I wasn't spending that much time in the room anyway. Between classes and pledge duties, and the fact that several hours a night of my studying was in an enforced study hall at the SPO house, I wasn't seeing nearly as much of my roommate as I had during the first semester.

I went up to visit Beth the weekend before Midwinters. Dave went along to see Marianne. He was bringing her down for the weekend, and we got everything set. It was much colder in Harrisonburg than in Charlottesville, so we didn't go far off campus. We went to dinner and then took our dates to a mixer-type dance they were having in the gym.

By now I thought Beth was terrific. We had been dating for nearly three months, and I thought she felt the same way about me. We were still going slowly in some ways, although our physical relationship had reached the point that was euphemistically known as "heavy petting" by late January. I didn't want to put any pressure on her to take it further than that, at least not yet. I was at least a little crazy with wanting to make love to her, but at that point I was willing to wait as long as it took. I knew it was a big step for both of us, and I cared enough about her not to want to rush her into anything.

"I wish we could see each other more often," she said.

"I know. Two or three times a month really isn't enough."

This was becoming a familiar refrain for us, one of our favorite topics of conversation. If we had been in high school and lived in the same town, we would be seeing each other every day. Neither of us had said anything about love yet. I guess we were both afraid. I had rehearsed it in my mind a couple of times, standing in front of the mirror in my room when I was alone and saying, "I love you, Beth."

I spent a lot of time wondering how I would have the nerve to say it when I finally felt ready. Wondering if I would ever be ready. Wondering if this really was love, and if it wasn't, what was? I was thinking about it so much it was making my head spin. We had gotten to the point where we said we really liked each other. I even told her once that I was crazy about her. Both of us knew what was happening and we were both scared to death. "Have you ever been in love?" she asked me.

I shook my head. "I never really dated anybody that seriously in high school. I suppose I had a crush or two, but I never told anyone I loved her. How about you? With all those boys chasing you all the time back home, did you ever fall in love?"

"No. It never felt right. This might sound silly, but I always wanted to hear bells ringing. I always wanted to see fireworks the first time I was in love with a boy."

"Shoot," I said. "Just my luck it's four months till the Fourth of July."

She smiled and put her head on my shoulder. "You know what I mean, Rob."

I almost said it then. I almost told her I was starting to fall in love with her. It felt like she was ready to hear those words, but I just couldn't get them out yet. I didn't know if it was because I was afraid that I was judging the mood wrong, or if I wasn't sure I loved Beth Erickson yet. Apparently, I still had a few things to figure out. I was spending a lot of time thinking about her these days, and it was taking me longer to do the same amount of studying I had done first semester because my concentration level seemed worse.

The Wednesday night before Midwinters brought a shock. I returned from study hall at the SPO house to find my roommate sprawled out on his bed looking drunk. Upon closer examination, he looked different. He had a big goofy grin on his face, and he seemed out of it, but I couldn't smell the ever-familiar scent of alcohol, and in addition, I knew Danny didn't drink. "Rob," he slurred. "The old Roo-teroni. Rootie Kazootie. My good and faithful Indian companion. What the fuck are you doing here?"

"Are you drunk, Danny?"

"Drunk? Me? No way. I've had something wonderful. Something much, much, much better than demon alcohol. I'm talking about grass. Pot. Weed. Mar-i-ju-ana."

"You smoked pot?" I asked him, shocked. "You can go to jail for that."

"Ease off, old Root. There's nothing wrong with grass. It just makes you feel wonderful."

"Where did you get it?"

He shook his head in an exaggerated fashion. "It's a secret."

I was getting furious. "You didn't smoke that shit in here, did you? In our room?"

He shook his head again. "No way."

"Thank you for that," I said disgustedly. "Why did you want to smoke pot anyway?"

Danny couldn't seem to get his mind focused. He blinked once or twice. "I just wanted to feel good, Rob. Everything's been so fucked up lately, I just thought it would be fun to get stoned and forget about it all."

"Are you all right?" Even as I asked him, I found myself feeling like a hypocrite, wondering if I really cared.

"I'm fine, but I'm really hungry. I think I'll get some change and go down to the vending machines." Danny somehow got himself up off his bed and staggered over to his desk. He found his change and promptly knocked it all over the floor. "Shit."

I couldn't help it. I laughed. "What's so fucking funny?" he asked me drunkenly.

"You are," I said, not unkindly. "You're acting like your hands don't work right."

I helped him pick his change up off the floor and pointed him in the direction of the stairs. I didn't go with him, but I listened for loud noises to see if he had fallen down the steps. When he didn't, I decided to take a shower and get ready for bed.

The next morning, Danny seemed almost embarrassed. "Rob, I'm sorry if I was a pain last night. It's just that ... well, I just felt like I needed to do something to take my mind off what's been happening at home and all that stuff."

I nodded. "Sure, Danny. Just try and remember you can get

kicked out of school."

"It's not an Honor Code violation, is it?" He seemed worried.

I shook my head. "Those aren't the only rules. It's against the law, Danny. Doesn't that bother you at all?"

"It's a stupid law. Marijuana doesn't hurt anybody. It's a lot better than alcohol."

"Oh?" I asked sarcastically. "Is that so? You don't drink. Then you smoke pot once and suddenly, you're an expert? Look, I'm not trying to run your life. I don't give a rat's ass what you do, but I don't want any pot in our room. I don't want anybody thinking I'm mixed up with that stuff." He nodded. "Where did you get it anyway? From that fucking Germ across the hall?"

"Don't call him that. He hates that name. His name is Leo."

"I know what his name is, but I'll bet he was the one who gave you that stuff, wasn't he?" Danny shrugged. "Just keep that shit out of our room."

I went over to the library to study. Some of the guys in the dorm were planning the standard pre-big weekend Thursday night bash, but that was already starting to wear a little thin for me. After eating dinner at the house, I went back to the library and studied until they kicked us out at midnight. Danny wasn't in the room when I got back, and I didn't care at all. I changed for bed and went right to sleep. When my alarm went off at 6 o'clock, I noticed he hadn't slept in his bed. That aroused a little interest, but not much. I had my own life to lead, and I was tired of worrying about Danny.

23

My black mood started lifting a bit when I got out of French class Friday afternoon. Beth was due to arrive in a couple of hours and I was eager to forget about everything except having a good time. Danny still hadn't put in an appearance. He hadn't said anything about having a date, so I found myself hoping he had gone home. I took a short nap and awakened in plenty of time to take a shower. I was shaved, dressed and headed down the street to the Downtowner with plenty of time to spare.

Beth and Marianne arrived on time, and Dave showed up a few minutes later to get his date and take her over to her motel. That left Beth and me alone. Bruce's date wasn't scheduled to arrive until after dinner. "Let's go upstairs," she said. "I'll put my stuff away and then we can go have a drink."

"I can wait for you here." I laughed. "An All-American boy's got to protect his virtue."

I picked up her suitcase and carried it to her room on the third floor. As soon as we were inside the room, she was in my arms. "I've missed you so much, baby."

"Me too," I said, kissing her hungrily. "I wish we could see each other more often."

We knew we would have some time alone, but both of us figured if we started getting too intimate it would be just our luck to be interrupted. We stayed dressed, even though both of us were getting to the point where we were curious about what it would be like to be together without clothes in the way. Beth knew I wanted to make love to her, and she felt the same way. "I want to too," she said after our kisses had been particularly hot for a while. "I want to be with you so badly. I'm just so scared I can hardly believe it."

"I know, sweetheart," I said, stroking her face. "I don't want to do anything to make you frightened or uncomfortable. You know how much I care about you. I'm not going to make love to you until I know it's what you want. Until we know it's right for both of us."

"You're so good to me, Rob. I feel so safe with you."

After that we just held each other for a while and talked about things that had been happening. I told her about my run-in with my roommate. "Have I ever met him?"

I shook my head. "We didn't run into him back at Homecomings, and Danny wasn't around for Openings. He didn't have a date, so he went home for the weekend."

"You don't like him much, do you?"

I shook my head. "It's hard to explain sometime. I'm not even sure I understand it myself. I don't dislike Danny. I don't really have anything against him. He's a bright kid, and there's nothing wrong with him. He's just way too desperate. He's afraid to relax and be himself. Does that make any sense or am I sounding stupid?"

Beth shook her head. "We've got girls like that. They try to fit in, but somehow, they always seem to do something wrong. They only make it worse for themselves."

After that we didn't talk about anything serious for the rest of the evening. We went from the room to dinner to the dance in the gym. I always enjoyed dancing with Beth. She was so uninhibited when she got out on a dance floor. I asked her once why that was, why she was able to relax so easily. She shrugged, a little embarrassed at the compliment. "I don't know. Must have been those seven years of ballet lessons."

It was a terrific weekend. Beth and I had been dating for nearly four months, and if I had had a fraternity pin I would have offered it to her. I had come to see I really was falling in love, and now it was only a question of getting up my courage enough to say the words.

Three little words, but let me tell you, there aren't three tougher words to say to someone for the first time. Except maybe for doctors telling people they have cancer. I kept hoping for the right moment, for a perfect situation when my three words would flow naturally and sound right. By Saturday evening, though, I knew that perfect moment wasn't going to come. I would have to go out on a limb and jump off.

We sat through a terrific concert. It wasn't the usual concert fare for a big weekend, but Simon and Garfunkel put on a great show and Beth and I both were big fans. When we came out of the concert at a little after 10 o'clock Saturday evening and headed for the fraternity house, Beth snuggled against me and put her arm around my waist.

"Isn't this a wonderful weekend, Rob?" She was radiant with pleasure.

"It's almost perfect."

"Uh huh," she said, kissing me on the cheek and snuggling a little closer. "I know what you want to do to me to make it completely perfect."

"Beth!" I tried to sound shocked. "That isn't what I meant at all."

She giggled. "Relax, Rob. Isn't a girl allowed to tease her boy-friend?"

I pulled her to me tightly. "Beth, these last four months have been so wonderful."

"I know. I don't think I've ever been happier than I am when I'm with you."

There was a pregnant pause, as if each of us was waiting for the other to say something more. Just about the time it started getting un-comfortable, I said something. "You're so wonderful, Beth. I hope you and I are together for a long time." I looked and saw tears in her eyes. "Is something wrong, angel?"

She shook her head. "I'm just a sentimental dope. I can't help crying."

I wanted to kiss her tears away. We were standing on a street in Charlottesville, snow on the ground and frost in the air, but all of a sudden, the moment seemed as right as it was ever going to get. I took a deep breath and blurted out the three words I had wanted to say for so long. "I love you, Beth."

The mixture of shock and ecstasy I saw in her expression made me feel terrific. The tears started flowing more freely as she threw her arms around my neck and hugged me tightly. "Oh, Rob. I love you, too. I love you so much."

Suddenly, life was perfect. All my problems had vanished, and I was the happiest guy on earth. Beth Erickson loved me. I held her close and kissed her. "I meant what I said before, angel. I hope we're together a long, long time."

"So do I, sweetheart," she whispered. "So do I."

It was obvious to everyone that weekend that we had passed a big hurdle. We were constantly hugging and touching each other, and there wasn't a single slow dance that didn't end with us in each other's arms, kissing as if the world was ending. We didn't get much of a chance to be alone Saturday night, so we weren't faced with the next hurdle. We didn't talk about sex, but I was pretty sure both of us were thinking about it.

I wanted her so badly I thought I was going to burst. I was sure she felt the same way. We had agreed that nothing would happen until we both felt it was right, and I thought that moment was going to come very soon. We stayed up all night Saturday. It was as though we knew it had been such a special day that we wanted to keep it from ending. The fraternity party broke up a little after 3 o'clock, and we walked to the Virginian and sat and talked for another hour before they closed for the night.

Even though it couldn't have been more than 20 degrees outside, we walked for a little while after that. We talked of everything and nothing, and we hugged a lot. Between the two of us, we must have said, "I love you" fifty times.

A little before five, we walked back to the fraternity house. Things were dead there, so we sat in the living room and talked some more. Both of us were so wired, sleep was out of the question. About half an hour before sunup, we went down to the Corner and ate breakfast at a hole-in-the-wall called The White Spot. After we ate, fatigue started setting in. I looked at the clock and saw that it was 7:30. "We stayed up all night."

Beth smiled a tired smile. "I didn't want to sleep unless it was in your arms."

I groaned. "That would have been so wonderful."

We both knew that staying up all night basically made this the end of the weekend. Her ride was leaving at 4 o'clock, and both of us were running on fumes. I tried to think of a way we could sleep—really sleep—together. I knew I couldn't take her back to the dormitory, and the only other option was the room she was sharing with Bruce's date.

Beth smiled at me. "Darlene said she had to leave early. I think she was planning to leave at 10 o'clock."

That was still more than two hours away. Checkout time at the Downtowner was noon, but I figured it would be worth paying the $18 for another night if it meant I could be alone in the room with Beth from 10 until four. I certainly didn't expect anything more to happen. Both of us were exhausted, and it certainly wasn't the way I was envisioning our first time. I just thought it would be wonderful to sleep with Beth in my arms.

We managed to stay awake for another two hours, and we showed up at the room just as Bruce was helping Darlene get ready to leave. "Where have you two been?" he asked me incredulously. "You look like you haven't slept at all."

I shrugged. "I'll get some sleep later."

"Well, Darlene's ride is here. Can you check out?"

"Sure," I said. Bruce didn't need to know that I already had stopped by the front desk and paid for an extra night for Beth.

As soon as they left, Beth yawned. "Excuse me. I didn't mean to do that."

"No problem. When was the last time you stayed up all night?"

"Prom night. That was the only time. How about you?"

I shook my head. "My prom date was lousy. This is the first time

I ever stayed out all night with anybody."

We thought for a minute about the logistics. We hadn't reached a point in our relationship where we were ready to undress in front of each other, and I didn't expect us to end up naked. Beth reached into her suitcase and pulled out a T-shirt. "I don't think I really want to change into my nightgown. If it's all right with you, I'll just wear this and panties to bed."

I nodded. "I'll just take off my shirt and tie and keep my slacks on."

Beth giggled. "They'll get all wrinkled. What's the matter, Rob? Don't you have clean underwear?" I must have blushed because she laughed. "Don't worry, honey. I'm not going to attack you."

"All right. I'll take my pants off, as long as you promise to keep your hands to yourself."

"I'll be right back," she whispered as she went into the bathroom to change. I put the "Do Not Disturb" sign on the door, quickly shucked everything except my shorts and got under the covers. I hadn't realized how exhausted I was. I dozed off almost as soon as my head hit the pillow and I almost didn't notice when Beth lifted the sheet and crawled under the covers with me.

"Rob?" she whispered. "Are you asleep?"

I shook my head and cleared the cobwebs. I felt like an idiot. "No, I was just thinking with my eyes closed."

She laughed and kissed my chest softly. "Liar. The first time you get me in bed with you and you fall asleep. I'm never going to let you live this one down."

Her kisses were helping me awaken quickly. "I'm awake now."

"Yes, you certainly are," she said, smiling as we kissed. "Maybe a little too awake."

The idea had been to get some sleep, but we knew it wasn't going to happen right away. Beth started to set her travel alarm for 3:30, so that once we did fall asleep, she wouldn't oversleep and miss her ride. Then I had a brilliant idea. "Beth? What time is your first class on Monday?"

She thought for a minute. She was tired, too. "Nine o'clock."

"Give me a second here while I figure this out." I thought it over, and it seemed like a good idea. "What if I drove you back to Harrisonburg first thing in the morning? I could borrow Dave's car, and we could leave really early. Say about 6 o'clock. That way you'd be back in time to change and still make it to class."

I could tell she liked the idea. "What about your classes?"

"I'd only have to miss one. I've got an 8 o'clock, but then my others are at 11 and 2. I'd be back in time for both. You don't have any studying you have to do tonight?"

Beth looked at me as if I was from another planet. "Rob, I don't think I've done any studying Sunday nights after any of our dates. I end up thinking about you. It always takes me till Monday to get my mind back on school."

I phoned over to the KSK house and I was lucky. Dave hadn't left to go see Marianne yet. I explained my plan, and he agreed with one slight modification. He wanted to ask his date if she wanted to stay. If she did, I would drive both girls up to Madison. "Fair enough, but no matter what happens, I can use your car tomorrow morning?"

"Sure. Come by and get it and have fun tonight." I could swear I heard a leer.

Once Beth had called to tell her ride to leave without her, she settled into my arms. "I guess I can turn the alarm off," she said. "There's no reason to wake up at 3:30."

I nodded. "Why don't you set it a couple hours later? That way we can get up and go somewhere for dinner."

"We could just order room service if you want," she said as she changed the setting on her clock. "That way we wouldn't have to put our clothes back on." I feigned shock, but she just smiled and snuggled into my arms. "We don't have to decide now. We can make up our minds later."

I had thought we would go right to sleep, but of course that didn't happen. We were so stimulated by the fact that we were finally alone together that we got one last rush of adrenaline. We spent nearly an hour kissing and touching each other, and the T-shirt she had worn to bed wound up crumpled on the floor. It was incredibly exciting to be in bed with Beth and for both of us to be so nearly naked. Her bare breasts were pressing against my chest, and I knew I would never again in my life be as excited as I was right then.

Somehow, we kept our underwear on; although our heavy petting progressed another step as Beth reached inside my shorts and touched me for the first time. She slipped her tongue into my mouth as she stroked me. "Oh, Rob. You feel so good."

I was touching her too, and she was so wet and hot inside. She wasn't the first girl I ever touched there, and she wasn't the first ever to touch me. It was the first time I really thought something more might come of it, though, and I wasn't sure how I felt about that. For one thing, I hadn't expected us to wind up in bed together.

I had carried a rubber in my wallet for two years in high school. I hadn't discarded it until there was a little circle embedded in the leather, but I had stopped carrying one when I arrived at college. It seemed like one of those childish high school tricks I wanted to forget. I didn't want to carry a rubber because if I whipped one out at the right moment, Beth might think I'd been expecting this. "Beth? You'd better stop, angel."

"Why? Don't you enjoy what I'm doing?"

"That's the problem. I'm enjoying it too much. It's making me want to..."

She nodded. "I know. It's making me want to, too."

"Yeah, but I don't have anything with me. I didn't expect this to happen."

She giggled. "Neither did I, but isn't it wonderful?"

"God, yes," I moaned. "But..."

"I know," she said, kissing me softly as she took her hand away. "We really ought to wait. It wouldn't be safe."

"Maybe we should just sleep for a while."

"Uh huh," she said, snuggling her head against the crook of my neck. "And baby? Maybe we should go out to dinner tonight." She giggled as she moved up to whisper in my ear. "Because that way, after we're done, we can go by the drugstore, and you can get what you for-got to bring with you."

I was pleasantly shocked. "Are you sure you're ready?"

"Yes," she said solemnly. "I am ready for you to be my very first lover."

We slept until the alarm awakened us at 5:30. Actually, she slept until the alarm went off. I slept until she awakened me with some very interesting kisses. I was disoriented at first, but it didn't take me long to realize I had slept nearly naked with Beth Erickson for the last six hours.

We fumbled around for a minute or two and then I said I thought I might like to take a shower. "It's going to be tough enough putting those same clothes back on. Maybe sometime this evening I could go by my room and get some clothes."

We looked at each other for an embarrassing moment. Both of us wanted the same thing, but neither of us wanted to be the one to suggest it. Finally, she laughed. "We've got three choices here," she said with mock gravity. "You first, me first or both of us together."

After almost four months, Beth and I finally were going to see each other completely naked. It was a little nerve-wracking. I knew I was in pretty good shape. I hadn't been getting as much physical exercise as I had at home, but I had done a decent job of staying in shape and keeping my weight under control. Still, it was scary. Neither one of us seemed to want to be the first to get out from under the covers. "Rob? We're not going to be able to get all nice and clean unless we get out of bed first."

"You first." She moaned. "See. You're nervous, too."

"All of a sudden I feel fat."

"Beth, you don't have an ounce of fat anywhere on you. You're gorgeous, and I've been dying to see you naked ever since I met you."

"All right," she said dubiously. "We'll both get out of bed and take off our underwear at the same time." We did exactly that, and we managed to fight through our embarrassment long enough to go into the bathroom and get under the shower. It was the first time either of us had ever showered with anyone else, and it was a lot of fun. We spent about half the time kissing and caressing each other and the other half soaping each other clean. As a result, we probably spent twice as much time in the shower as necessary. She washed my hair, which turned out to be an incredibly sensual feeling. Then I washed hers and she enjoyed it just as much.

After we got out of the tub, I asked her if I could borrow some toothpaste. She laughed as she watched me brush my teeth with my finger, but using her toothbrush seemed too much and I wasn't about to inflict my breath upon her any longer. I towel-dried my short hair and watched as she used her blow drier to get her long blonde hair dry. It was an extremely intimate experience to be together like this and I told her so.

She nodded. "I know. It almost feels like we're an old married couple."

Once we were dressed, we walked across the street and had dinner. We held hands through most of the meal, and we were constantly gazing into each other's eyes. Maybe it was because we knew we already had taken a big step and were about to take another one. Maybe it was just because we were happy. I wasn't about to question it.

After dinner we walked down to the Corner, which was the only place in town I'd be able to buy contraceptives on a Sunday evening. We went into Mincer's, and she pretended to be looking at magazines while I walked up to the counter to order prophylactics.

"Get more than one," she whispered to me, giggling.

I turned beet red.

After I made my purchase, I decided I ought to call Dave. He wasn't in, but he had left me a message. Marianne hadn't been able to stay, so I could come by the house and get the car anytime. I thought it probably would be smarter to get it right away than to interrupt the evening later, and Beth agreed. We walked over to the Kappa Sigma Kappa house, and I got the keys from one of his brothers. Then we drove by the dorms so that I could get a change of clothes and my toothbrush and razor.

"All set, baby," I said, sliding into the driver's seat. "Onward to destiny."

When we got back to the motel, I realized I was beginning to feel nervous. I knew it was because I was worried about taking such a big step so soon. I was afraid it would change things. I was frightened that once Beth and I made love, the fragile chemistry we were building between us would somehow be shattered. I told myself that was silly, that this was the logical next step in our relationship. I told myself how much I wanted this, and how good it would feel not to be a virgin anymore.

I couldn't get rid of the nervousness, though, and when I took Beth in my arms and kissed her, I could tell she was nervous too. "Are you all right?"

She nodded weakly. "I'm fine." She paused. "Well, maybe I'm a little scared."

I kissed her again and stroked her cheek gently. "That's natural. Hey, I'm scared too."

"Are you? I thought only girls got scared about this."

"Who told you that? I'll bet guys get every bit as frightened. At least this guy does."

"You're so sweet, Rob. And I love you so much. But I'm terrified."

We sat on the edge of the bed, holding hands and looking into each other's eyes. I kissed her, but it was a non-sexual kiss. "Beth, honey. This doesn't have to happen tonight. We've got lots of time. We've got all the time in the world to get to know each other. You're going to be part of my life for a very long time if I have anything to say about it." She started crying. "What's wrong?"

"Nothing's wrong," she said, swatting angrily at her tears. "You make me so happy. You're so understanding." She hugged me tightly. "Let's just hold each other for a while and see what happens."

We got out of our clothes and got under the covers. I put the rubbers on the floor on my side of the bed, just in case we found ourselves swept away with the passions of the moment.

We didn't make love that night. We snuggled for an hour or so, kissing and caressing each other, and then we watched television. We didn't get dressed. We were really enjoying being naked together, and it was nice not to feel the pressure of our first time. Of course, it was only pressure deferred. We knew we would face the same fears the next time we decided to do this, but I thought the fact we hadn't jumped right into it might make things a little easier.

Beth started nodding off during "Mission: Impossible," and she fell asleep quickly. I wanted to hold out until I saw how the IMF team resolved its weekly adventure, but I was asleep long before the show ended.

It was the second time—that afternoon had been the first—that I had slept in the same bed with a woman, and I had thought it might be difficult. It wasn't. I was so exhausted from everything that had happened over the weekend that I slept as soundly as usual.

24

Beth must have awakened during the night, because when the alarm went off at 6 o'clock, the television had been turned off and she was wearing her nightgown. "I got cold," she whispered to me when I asked her where that had come from.

I jumped out of bed, trying to get my blood circulating as fast as possible. It was cold, and I found myself wishing I had thought to bring pajamas. We showered together and dressed quickly. There wasn't as much time for the playfulness of the previous day, but we did share a few exciting kisses in the shower. Somehow, we made it out into the frigid morning by 6:30, and Dave's car started without any problems. We made a quick stop at a convenience store for coffee and donuts and then left for the two-hour trip to Harrisonburg.

Both of us were quiet on the way up. A lot had happened, and now it was starting to sink in. I didn't think either of us was sorry about anything; we were just tired and that made us quiet. When we did talk, most of our conversation was about our friends and our classes, and about how we were going to miss each other until we saw each other again.

"Next year I'll have my own car, Beth. I've got to finish the year with a 3.0 average, but if I do, I'll get to buy a car this summer and bring it down to school in the fall. Once I don't have to borrow someone else's car, we can get together a lot more often."

She snuggled against me and I put my arm around her. "That sounds wonderful," she said. "I miss you so much when we're not together. I wish we went to the same school. It's so silly that Virginia's not coeducational."

We talked about the possibility of getting together in two weeks. There was something going on up at Madison, and she wanted me to come up. I told her I would be there, one way or the other. I looked at my watch and saw that it was a little past eight. We were still about fifteen miles from Harrisonburg, and I knew Beth wasn't going to have much time to change before her first class. "I'm sorry you're going to be late."

"I won't be late. All I've got to do is pick up my books."

"You mean you go to class dressed like that?"

"And what's wrong with the way I'm dressed?" She was wearing a nice blouse and a pair of jeans. "This is fine for classes at most schools."

I had to laugh. She was right. Only at Virginia did we wear our Sunday best to class every day. Ah, tradition. I dropped her off at her dormitory at 8:30. She kissed me hard before getting out of the car. "Call me soon," she said.

"You know it." I watched as she hurried across the parking lot to her dorm and then turned the car around for the return trip to school.

25

Euphoria got me through the next week. The knowledge that, for the first time in my life, I was in love helped me deal with the depths of winter. It was still more than a month to midterms, so there wasn't a lot of immediate motivation. I was keeping up, but I didn't feel quite the same urgency I had in the fall.

I told myself I knew how to manage my time better, and I knew more of what my professors expected of me. That was certainly true. It was also true that having access to older guys who had taken the same classes before helped. In between pledge duties I was able to ask the brothers a lot of questions. Sometimes I got answers that helped, but I sure spent a lot of money on gum. I did a lot of pushups, too, but in the process, I got to know more and more about the house I had chosen to join. I didn't like all the brothers—I hadn't expected to—but nothing happened that winter to make me regret the decision I had made to follow my grandfather and my father into Sigma Phi Omicron.

Classes weren't going badly for me, but things were getting worse for Danny. Part of that was my fault, the aftermath of letting slip the fact that Danny was masturbating in his bed at night. I had regretted it almost as soon as the words were out of my mouth, and I had hoped Bruce somehow would forget it. I knew he didn't have anything against Danny, so I didn't think he would tell anyone. Unfortunately, he passed the information along to the very worst possible person—his roommate. I came home from class one afternoon to find the door to my room locked and Dick Simpson outside it taunting Danny.

"You're whacking it in there, aren't you, Jacobs?" Dick said gleefully. "Beat your meat! Beat your meat! Beat your meat!" He stopped for a moment when he saw me walking up, key in hand. "Hey, Rooter. I think your roommate's playing with himself."

I frowned. "What makes you think that, Dick?"

"Why else would he have the door locked? He's got to be jerking off."

"You must not be very busy if all you've got to do is spy on my roommate."

Dick shook his head. "Fuck that," he said angrily. "I told you guys I was going to get him back for that time he jumped me. He's not going to be able to show his face around this dorm after today."

"Jeez, Dick. He lives here. Where's he supposed to go?"

"I don't give a shit where that fucking Hebe goes."

Dick wasn't about to quit, and he started chanting even louder than before. I realized there was no possible way to go into my room without totally humiliating my roommate, so I turned around and walked out of the dorm and over to the SPO house. The only book I had with me was my French text, but I figured I could study vocabulary for a couple of hours before dinner. I would go back to the room sometime in the evening, and that might give Danny a chance to save face.

When I finally returned a little after 8 o'clock, Danny wasn't there. I wondered briefly what had happened after I had left, but I knew sooner or later, someone would tell me more than I wanted to know.

I studied in the room all evening. For the first time that I could remember, no one came in looking for conversation. The dorm seemed more subdued than usual, and I wondered if that was because of what had happened earlier. I made it through all my work by midnight and I got ready for bed. Danny still hadn't returned, and I went to sleep easily. When my alarm went off at 6 a.m., I noticed that Danny had come in sometime during the night. He was sleeping soundly, and I didn't have any desire to awaken him.

Bruce came up to me just before biology to apologize for what had happened. "It just slipped out, Rob. We had had a couple of beers, and I wasn't being careful. If I'd been thinking, I never would have told Dick. I know how much he hates Danny."

I shrugged. "I can't blame you for it. If I hadn't told you, there's no way that Dick could have found out. What finally happened yesterday afternoon after I left?" He shook his head. "You mean it got worse?"

Bruce nodded. "Dick just wasn't going to let up. He kept banging and banging on the door, and by the time he stopped, half the guys on the hall were outside the door. I can just imagine what must have been going through Danny's mind. I guess everybody knows about it now."

"Did Danny ever come out?"

Bruce shook his head. "Not until after Dick finally got tired of it and went to dinner. I heard the door open, and I heard him run down the hall and out of the building."

"How's he going to face anybody after that?"

"I don't know. I sure don't think I'd be able to show my face."

Danny did show his face, but it wasn't easy. He got through the worst of it by keeping his mouth shut and completely ignoring people. He took a lot of crap, but he didn't react to any of it. I don't think he said a word to anyone—including me—for the rest of the week, and despite Dick's efforts to keep it alive, the incident blew over.

Nobody in the dorm liked Danny much, but Dick wasn't the most popular guy himself, and Danny had become something of an underdog. I was surprised one evening to hear Joe Del Rio tell Dick to leave Danny alone.

My roommate was spending as little time as possible in the room, and there were nights he didn't return home until after I went to bed. I didn't know what to say and I didn't want to make it worse. Eventually, he started talking again. We never broached the subject of his embarrassment, and it was obvious things were strained. He had to know that I was the only one who could have revealed his activities. I felt bad about that.

I realized later that things were really piling up on him. His parents' divorce, his own bad grades, his problems in the dorm. If he had a close friend, he might have been able to talk about it. He didn't even seem to be hanging out with Leo Mitchell anymore, so he had no one at all. He had gone home a few times to see Natalie, the girl he'd brought down to school in October, but by early February he had stopped seeing her. He told me her parents hadn't wanted her getting serious with a college guy.

I offered once to have Beth get him a date up at Madison, but he turned me down. I guess by then he didn't like me very much either. I never confronted him. Of course, I never helped him, either.

As Danny's life was falling apart, my own seemed to be getting better and better. My classes were going well. I was making friends in the fraternity. And of course, there was Beth. We were writing to each other three or four times a week and talking on the phone almost as often. It was the first time either of us had been in love, and we were enjoying it tremendously.

I went up to Madison the second weekend in March, and we spent the better part of forty-eight hours together. I took her to a dance, and we were on the dance floor together for hours. We went parking in Dave's car, and we worked each other up to a fever pitch. I didn't want our first time to be in a car, though. I wanted it to be special for her, something she would remember happily. That meant the car was out and so was the cheap motel I stayed in. She couldn't stay out all night, either. She would have had to sign out for the weekend to go out of town, and I didn't want her to lie to be with me. I slept alone.

Easters Weekend, the last big weekend of the year, was a month away, and we figured that would be when we'd finally find the time and the opportunity. I told her I would work something out with Bruce so that she could have the room at the Downtowner to herself. If that didn't work, I would pay the half I owed and find her a room at another motel. I wanted us to be alone together, whatever it took.

"That's what I want too," she said. "I'm still a little nervous about it, but I really want you to make love to me. I think about it all the time and it's driving me crazy."

One of the nicest things about our relationship was that we had become close enough to talk about almost anything. I had never had a girl for a friend, and even though Beth and I were more than friends, we were friends too. I even talked with her about Danny. I didn't want to become too involved in his problems, but I asked her if she knew anything I could do to make things easier for him.

She didn't have any bright ideas. She knew I felt guilty for letting my knowledge of his masturbation slip out. "It's not your fault, Rob."

"No?" I said bitterly. "There's no way Dick would have found out if I hadn't told Bruce."

"You don't know that. Somebody might have walked in on him when you weren't even there."

"I wish I had moved into the house at midyear."

Beth nodded. "It would have made it a lot easier, I'm sure. But you told me you promised your mom you'd stay in the dorms, didn't you?" I nodded. "I'll bet your grades are going to be better than they'd have been if you moved into the house."

She had a point. I knew the pledges that had moved into the house were having trouble studying. They were constantly getting drawn into poker games or marathon television-watching sessions. I was getting a lot more work done in the dorms. "Besides," she said. "The year will be over in less than three months."

26

It wasn't as if we were in the home stretch. Midterms hadn't even arrived, but the school year was almost two-thirds complete. I had been a college student for more than six months. It felt like much longer.

Some of the guys who weren't planning to live in fraternity houses their second year already were apartment hunting for the fall semester. Dave had told me he was tired of living at KSK and might move off campus. He wondered if I might want to share an apartment. It sounded like a terrific idea, but I wanted to live in the fraternity house at least one year. I told him I would think about it.

The weather turned warm by mid-March and a major case of spring fever hit the first-year class. Cuts were up and study time was down, even though midterms were approaching. I made my classes, but I remember spending as much time looking out the window as I did concentrating on the lectures.

Even Danny seemed to perk up some. Dick had pledged a fraternity during winter rush, so he wasn't around the dorms as much anymore. With his chief tormentor absent most of the time, my roommate seemed a little happier.

I wasn't around much to see him. Between classes, studying and my pledge duties, I didn't have much free time. When I did, usually on weekends, I went to Harrisonburg.

Madison's spring break fell the week before ours that year. Beth's parents were expecting her to come home, and I was planning to go to Florida with Dave and two of his fraternity brothers the following week. That meant we wouldn't see each other for most of March. She had midterms one week and spring break the next and my schedule was running one week behind hers. We kept writing and trading phone calls, but it wasn't the same. Both of us were looking forward to Easters Weekend as the high point of the year.

Midterms went surprisingly well. I breezed through my exams with two A-minuses and three B's, topping my first semester performance. I knew if I could hold my grades, I had a chance to make the Dean's List. That was beyond the wildest dreams I had for my first year. It didn't happen, but it was the only time in four years of college I finished a semester unhappy with my grades..

Florida wasn't much fun as I had expected. We had a nine-day break, and we drove for a day and a half to get to Fort Lauderdale. I had never been that far south, and it was wild to leave the near-freezing temperatures of early spring and suddenly be on the beach in 90-degree weather. We laid out a lot and we drank a lot of beer. Dave and his brothers spent the week chasing women and I didn't see much point to it.

Sure, I was still a virgin. And yes, there were a lot of women available. I knew I wanted my first time to be with Beth, though, and I knew it would happen. She was back at school by then, and I called her three or four times.

"You're crazy, Rob," she said. "You're down there in Florida, with all those half-naked girls in bikinis, and you're wasting your time calling me."

"You want me to chase women? Is that it? You want me to get some experience so I'll be a better lover for you?" I asked, teasing her a little.

"No way. If you get to be my first, I want to be your first, too."

So I concentrated on getting a tan and thinking about my roommate as little as possible. Danny had gone to Bermuda with his mother and sisters, and I hoped he would come back tanned, relaxed and ready somehow to make it through the last two months. When Dave and I got back to Charlottesville, I realized I hadn't done any studying for nine days. I hadn't even taken any books to Florida. It was my longest real vacation since the beginning of the school year.

We returned to a city in full bloom. The dogwoods were flowering, and the grounds looked incredibly beautiful, even prettier than the first time I had seen them in September. It was only two weeks till Easters, but I made plans to borrow Dave's car and go up to Madison the next weekend anyway. I hadn't seen my lovely girlfriend for three weeks, and the thought of waiting two more was almost unbearable.

Things seemed to have loosened up a great deal. All that remained of the school year for me was a research paper in government and final exams. The paper was due May 1, and exams would start on the 15th of the month and run for the next twelve days. The end was in sight. The week before Easters was Hell Week in the various fraternities, and we would be initiated as full brothers the Thursday before the final party weekend.

Hell Week isn't as bad now as it was then, and we were assured it was nothing compared to the way it had been in the good old days. A friend of mine joined the Marine Corps out of high school, and he told me all the older marines ever talked about was the "old Corps" and how things were so much tougher. I guess it was a variation on the old theme. Millions of fathers around the world told their children of the old days, when they walked five miles in the snow to get to school. It seems that each generation gets softer than the one that went before, at least if you can believe those old stories.

But if there's one thing I've learned in 56 years, it's that people don't change much from generation to generation. Only the music does.

Hell Week was fun. We spent a lot of time cleaning the house, and I lost count after I had done three hundred pushups the first three days. Finally, on the last night of Hell Week, we got some of what we were dreading. We assembled down in the basement to find a huge block of ice and a jar of olives. The rest, as they say, was history.

The humiliation was all in good fun, all in the interest of bringing us together as brothers. We all heard stories about what was going
on at some of the other houses, and it was obvious that Sigma Zoo had
taken the lead in teasing its initiates. The members of their pledge class
were told to strip and to stick their sexual organs through a hole in a
sheet that blocked off a corner of the basement. On the other side of
the sheet, a prostitute had been hired to perform fellatio on the pledges.

As the story went, all of them enjoyed it tremendously. When
they were finished, the hooker sneaked out through a back door and
a guy who had been sitting there watching came out from behind
the sheet. One big football player fainted from embarrassment at the
thought that he had enjoyed oral sex with another man. We didn't have
to undergo anything that humiliating. A little frostbite of the buttocks
never killed anyone. Believe me, I know.

It all ended on Thursday night, when we were initiated as life-
time brothers in Sigma Phi Omicron and were given the pins we had
ordered weeks before.

I wouldn't have my pin long. I had bought a small box and some
gift-wrap, and I planned to give it to Beth when she came down for
Easters. I left the house at midnight and walked back to the dorm, excited about the upcoming weekend. I loved Beth so much, and we had
been dating for five months. It didn't fulfill the one-year rule from back
home, but both of us were ready for what would happen sometime in
the next three days.

Bruce and I had worked things out as far as the room. He had
been able to find someone in his fraternity who needed someone to
share the cost of a motel room, so Beth and I would have the room at
the Downtowner all to ourselves for Easters Weekend.

When I look back on it, I laugh at my lack of spontaneity. I was
trying to work out every detail, every possible contingency, to make
sure I lost my virginity.

Of course, there's no possible way to plan for everything. Beth
arrived at 6 o'clock Friday afternoon, and we went to dinner and the
dance at the gym before moving on to the fraternity party. By about 1
a.m., we were ready to leave the party and go back to our room to be
alone together. When we started walking, I realized I had forgotten to
bring my toothbrush and shaving kit. Since it wasn't that much out of

the way, we decided to walk past the dorm so I could get what I needed.

Women weren't allowed upstairs, so Beth waited in the main doorway while I bounded up the stairs two at a time. A few more strides got me down the hall to my room, and I opened the door and walked into the middle of a crisis. Danny was curled up on his bed, sobbing and moaning and pulling at his hair. My first reaction was to back out the door, close it quickly and walk away. I could always buy another toothbrush, and the last thing I needed with Beth waiting downstairs was to get caught up in some sort of psychodrama. I couldn't, though. I felt awful about all he had been through because of my mistake, and this looked serious. "Danny, are you all right?" No response. "Danny?"

Still no response. He seemed to be lost in his own little universe. I walked across the room so that I could see his face better. "Danny?" I asked, looking into his eyes. "What the hell is going on?"

Not only was there no response, there wasn't even any look of recognition in his wide, staring eyes. I didn't think Danny even knew I was there. Now I was starting to get scared. "Danny?"

My face was only a few inches away from his. I was shouting, but there wasn't anyone else around to hear me. The third floor was all but deserted. I had no idea what was happening. Then Danny moaned. It was a scary, blood-curdling sound. "Danny?" I was starting to sound like a broken record, and I was getting really tired of the sound of my own voice. "Talk to me, Danny."

Finally, he said something. "My fingers are melting," he whispered. "It's so hot in here that my fingers are melting."

It wasn't hot. It hadn't been hot since the end of the previous summer, and I had no idea what he meant. I reached out to feel his forehead to see if he had a fever, and he didn't even respond to being touched. His forehead felt cold and clammy. I jerked my hand back and repeated my most common line. "Danny?"

"It's too hot," he moaned. "I've got to cool down." He started tearing at his shirt. He ripped the buttons and pulled it open. He didn't seem to know what he was doing, because he succeeded only in getting it twisted up around his shoulders.

I thought about Beth waiting downstairs for me. I knew I

couldn't leave Danny, even for a minute, and I hoped she would eventually come upstairs to see what was keeping me.

In retrospect, it was amazing it took me as long as it did to realize what had happened. I kept thinking Danny somehow had snapped, that the pressures had driven him over the edge. I didn't know how to deal with it. Of course, that wasn't what it was. I kept trying to get Danny to talk, and he kept moaning about how hot it was in the room. I helped him out of his shirt, and he immediately started clawing at his pants. Once he was down to his underwear he started shivering. "I'm cold. So cold."

At least that seemed rational. Our dorm was always cold. I helped him wrap his blanket around himself, and he curled into a fetal position and started whimpering. Most of his words weren't even coherent, so I wasn't any closer than before to understanding what was happening.

It was Beth who finally figured it out. She had been taking a psychology course and had heard a lecture about psychedelic drugs. After I had been upstairs for nearly twenty minutes, she walked up the steps and knocked on my door. "Come in," I shouted.

She pushed the door open and started kiddingly to ask me what was keeping me. She didn't get more than two or three words of it out before she saw Danny curled up in his blanket. He didn't even realize someone else had come into the room. I wasn't sure he even knew I was there. "Rob, what on earth ..."

"I don't know, Beth. I've been trying to ask him what's wrong, but he doesn't say anything. You'd better close the door. It's against the rules for you to be up here."

Beth nodded and stepped into the room. I motioned to her to sit down on my bed, and she did. "He hasn't said anything?"

I shook my head. "Not much. He said something about it being so hot that his fingers were melting, and then he started tearing off his clothes. I don't know what the hell that means."

She apparently did. "It sounds like he's tripping. Could he possibly have taken some drug?"

"I don't know. He smoked marijuana a couple of months ago and got silly. That wasn't anything like this, though."

Beth shook her head. "It wouldn't be pot. This has got to be something stronger."

Danny interrupted us at that point, moaning out something that was mostly gibberish. I did make out the word "lizards," and I knew there weren't any lizards anywhere on the grounds except maybe the biology labs.

"It sounds like he took LSD," Beth said. "He looks like he's freaking out."

I didn't know anything about LSD. Later I learned about some of its properties in classes, and I was frightened enough by what I heard that I never felt any compulsion to try it. Even if I had, what I saw that night would have scared me straight for life. "What does that mean?" I asked her.

"I don't know much. They told us that a trip could last as long as eight hours. Do you have any idea when he took it?"

"Beth, honey. I've been with you for the last eight hours. How could I know?"

She shrugged. "Sorry, I forgot. Anyway, if he took it recently, he could be like this all night. Somebody's got to stay with him. If he hallucinates badly enough, he could try to jump out a window. My psychology teacher told us a story about a girl who took LSD and thought she could fly. She jumped off the roof of a building."

I groaned. "All night?"

"Somebody has to stay with him till it wears off. Is there anyone we could call? Could we get the paramedics here? Maybe they could take him to the hospital."

I shook my head. "I can't do that. If he's caught like this, high on some drug, he could get kicked out of school. I'll have to stay with him."

Beth was disappointed, but she took it well. "Well," she said, smiling sadly. "I guess there's always tomorrow night."

I felt like an idiot. I had forgotten what I'd be doing if I weren't trying to help my roommate. "Do you know anything I can do to help him?"

"Not much," she said, shaking her head. "We really didn't

get into it that much. The lecture we had was mostly about how we shouldn't get mixed up with drugs like LSD. I think it might help him to get some fluids into him."

"Like what? Water?"

She nodded. "And maybe fruit juice. I think Vitamin C is supposed to help. Is there anywhere around here you can get orange juice?"

I looked at my clock radio and saw that it was nearly 2 a.m. "The grill should be open for another few minutes. They sell orange juice." She looked at me quizzically. "It's down at the north end of the complex. In the basement of Latimer House." I reached for my wallet and pulled out a five. "Get as much as you can."

"I'll be right back."

Beth returned ten minutes later carrying four Dixie cups full of orange juice. "Don't give him any of this now. We should wait until he starts acting thirsty."

I hadn't been doing much more than trying to make my roommate comfortable. He had quieted down some, and he seemed a lot closer to catatonic than he had been when I came into the room. "He's not responding at all."

Beth nodded. "It's one of the stages. I think."

"Danny?" I asked him softly. There was no response.

"Relax, Rob. Just sit and wait. We'll know if he needs anything." She started looking around my room. "God, these rooms are ugly. Those walls look like..."

"I know. They look like they were painted by our old friend Rick Arbogast."

It wasn't a very funny joke, but we were in desperate need of comic relief, and she giggled. "And those posters. I can't believe you've got that same stupid Raquel Welch poster that every horny college freshman boy in America has."

"Hey, it could be worse. A couple of the guys on the hall have Playboy centerfolds on their walls."

"That's really disgusting," she said, but I noticed she couldn't hide a smile.

Danny was quiet for the next half-hour or so, and we didn't say much of anything either. With nothing happening, Beth was starting to get tired, and she put her head on my pillow. "I'm sorry, sweetheart. I'm starting to conk out."

"That's all right, but we've got a problem. You can't sleep here. We're not allowed to have girls in the dorms, and I could get kicked out of school for having you up here."

That brought her awake with a start. "Oh, God. You're right. What should we do?"

"Let me see if Bruce is back yet. Keep an eye on Danny for a minute." I went next door and knocked on Bruce's door, but there was no answer. In fact, I still didn't hear anyone stirring anywhere else on the hall. "There's nobody around."

"Should I leave?"

I thought about it for a minute. The motel was only two blocks away, but I hated to have her walking alone in the middle of the night. "Stay a while. Maybe Bruce will come back and he can walk you down there."

Three o'clock passed and then 3:30. I heard one or two guys come in from their dates, but they weren't guys I would trust with the fact that Beth was in my room and Danny was freaked out on drugs. I had been in the room for two hours, and the four Dixie cups full of orange juice still were sitting on my desk. Condensation was dripping down the outside of the cups and Beth had dozed off on my bed. Danny hadn't done anything.

I thought maybe he had fallen asleep. His eyes were wide-open, though. It gave me the creeps. By now I was totally angry. If I'd had a rope or a pair of handcuffs, I'd have bound him to his bed and walked Beth down to the motel myself. I knew I couldn't leave him, though, and a little past four, I finally heard noise in the room next door. I said a quick prayer that it was Bruce and not Dick. I knew I'd never be able to trust the Colonel with this, and I was pretty sure Beth would remember Dick enough not to want him walking her to her motel room.

Fortunately, it was Bruce. "What's up?" he asked. "I thought you'd be at the motel."

"Yeah, well..." I shrugged. "I need a big favor. Something's wrong with Danny," I said, not mentioning the fact that it was drugs. "I can't leave him right now, and Beth is asleep on my bed." He raised an eyebrow but didn't say anything. "I've got to get her out of here before I get caught with her in my room. Would you walk her down to the motel?"

He nodded. "Sure."

"Bruce? Thanks for not asking me what's going on."

He shrugged. "I know you'd tell me if you could."

I awakened Beth and told her Bruce was here. Then I kissed her. She threw her arms around my neck. "Call me when you can."

After she left, things got boring. Five o'clock passed and then six. By then I was having trouble staying awake, and I used one of the cups of orange juice to swallow a couple of No-Doz. I knew they would make me sick to my stomach, but at that point there was no other way to stay awake.

The sun had risen, and I was feeling totally miserable when Danny stirred. I could tell the effects of the drug were starting to wear off. It was 7:15. He didn't seem to know where he was at first, but he realized I was looking at him. "Rob?"

"Yeah, Danny. It's me. Do you want some orange juice?"

He nodded gratefully and I handed him one of the three remaining cups. He drank it down quickly. "God, I'm thirsty." I handed him another cup and he drank about half of it.

"Are you all right?"

Danny thought about that one for a moment. "I don't know. I don't remember much. What are you doing here? Aren't you supposed to be with your girlfriend?"

"Yeah, I was. I stopped by here last night to get something I'd forgotten, and I walked in on you. You were moaning something about your fingers melting." He looked embarrassed. "Danny, you were freaking out! You were acting nuts. What the hell did you do last night?"

He shook his head quickly. "I don't remember."

"The fuck you don't! You took some drug, didn't you? You took LSD."

Danny wouldn't meet my eyes. "I'm not saying."

I figured that was a good sign. At least he remembered that if he went to the trouble of lying about it, he would be out because of the Honor System. "Where did you get it?"

"I can't tell you that either."

"I'm so tired of you, Danny. You've been nothing but trouble all year. Then last night my weekend gets fucked up because I had to keep you from jumping out the window. Well, forget it. Fuck you and the horse you rode in on. I wish I didn't ever have to look at you again. I wish we'd never met."

He looked stricken, but I wasn't giving an inch. I was completely exhausted, but it would be another hour or two before the No-Doz would wear off enough for me to get any sleep. It was already morning, and I didn't see much hope of getting more than a couple of hours unless I wanted to write off the whole day. I thought I might as well take a shower. I grabbed my towel and some soap and stomped out of the room. The No-Doz was starting to make me nauseous. I thought I might have to throw up, and a minute or two later I found myself hunched over the toilet with the dry heaves. It was a perfectly awful ending to a horrible night.

I stayed in the shower a long time, letting the hot water cascade over my body. Danny was gone by the time I got back.

27

The alarm brought me out of a deep sleep at 11:30, and as soon as I was conscious, I realized I had a pounding headache. I blamed Danny. He still wasn't around, which suited me fine. I would have wanted to deck him. Another shower made me feel better, and I took two aspirin in hopes that they might solve the rest of the problem. I phoned down to the Downtowner a little after noon. The operator put me through to Beth's room.

"Hello?" She sounded as though she hadn't slept too well.

"Hi. It's me. A little worse for the wear, but I'll live. I think. I got about three hours sleep. I finally made it to bed about 8:30."

"Oh, God. That sounds awful. Is Danny all right?"

"I suppose so. He seems like he's back to normal. He's not talking about it at all. I yelled at him for being evasive and when I got back from taking a shower he was gone. I don't know where he is. I might have been too rough on him."

"Don't blame yourself," she said softly.

"Don't worry. I don't. I was mad at him for screwing up our big night."

She giggled and suddenly, I felt a little better. "So was I. I felt so lonely. I really wanted you with me last night." I groaned. "Poor baby. Well, there's always tonight."

We decided to get together for lunch and then see what transpired. Our only real plans were the Beach Boys concert and the party that night, so the afternoon was open. We went across the street from the motel and had lunch. I still couldn't get rid of my headache, and it was obvious to Beth that I was feeling miserable. "Poor Rob. Maybe you should get some more sleep."

I didn't want to waste the time we had together, but I knew she was right. Three hours hadn't been enough. We decided to go back to her room. She looked through the paper and found an old movie on television. Right about the time Bacall was asking Bogey if he knew how to whistle, I fell asleep fully dressed on the double bed.

I slept all afternoon. I didn't even notice when Beth helped me out of my shirt so that it wouldn't wrinkle. I just slept. She awakened me at about six. We had two hours before the concert was supposed to start, and my beautiful girlfriend was famished. I shook my head to help some of the cobwebs break loose. "Did the nap help?" she asked me solicitously. "Are you feeling better?"

I thought about it for a minute and realized my headache was gone. I smiled for what seemed like the first time all day. "Uh huh. I'm still groggy, but I feel pretty good."

"That's good, because I'm ready to have some fun. Dinner, the concert, the party and..." She paused meaningfully.

I put Danny and his problems completely out of my mind and started thinking about the night ahead. If this really was going to be the night Beth and I were going to lose our virginity together, I wanted to make certain I remembered everything.

She was already dressed and ready to leave for dinner, and I took a quick shower and shaved before putting on the shirt she had hung over a chair. "Are my pants all right? Did they get wrinkled too badly? I could go back by the dorm and change."

Beth looked at me strangely and I realized what I had said. We both started laughing. "I guess going by the dorm wouldn't be such a great idea."

"You've got that right. If I have anything to say about it, you're not going back there until I leave to go back to school." She flew into my arms and I kissed her as we snuggled for a minute or two. "Oh, Rob. I've been looking forward to this night for so long."

"Me too. I hope you're not disappointed."

"You either. What if I'm not any good for you?"

I kissed her again. "I don't think there's much chance of that. You're so sexy," I said, leering at her in my best Groucho impression. "You've got a body that was made for love."

Beth looked at me skeptically. "Which one of the Marx brothers was that supposed to be? Karl?" I affected a hurt look. "That's the worst Groucho I've ever seen."

We kissed again, and for a minute it looked as though we might forget about dinner. Just when it started getting interesting, though, Beth pulled away. "I'm hungry, Miller. Feed me. If you expect me to make it through this wild night, I need food. Sustenance. Fuel. Otherwise, I might fall asleep before you get a chance to..."

"Let's eat."

At that point, the evening started gathering momentum. We had dinner and then walked to University Hall for the concert. It was funny. The Beach Boys had lost a lot of favor in the last year or so, and their music seemed curiously dated. Within the last month alone, Lyndon Johnson had said he wouldn't run for re-election as our president and Martin Luther King had been assassinated in Memphis.

The world was changing so rapidly. I had seen a good example of that just the night before. A year ago, I had never even heard of LSD and now I had helped someone through a bad trip. It seemed strange to be sitting there listening to "Surfin' USA" and "I Get Around," songs I grew up with on the radio back home. It seemed almost as if the last year hadn't happened, as if I was back home in Johnstown cruising with my buddies.

It probably would have been more fitting if we had been listening to Jefferson Airplane or the Doors. That's the music I remember when I think of the spring of 1968. That and "A Whiter Shade of Pale." The plaintive lyrics of Procol Harum's hit record from the fall before were still in my memory.

"...we skipped the light fandango, turned cartwheels cross the floor. I was feelin' kind of seasick..."

For a moment I almost felt seasick myself. So much had happened that I felt like I was losing my moorings. One thing hadn't changed, though. There was still Beth, sitting next to me and clinging to my arm. I knew I never wanted to go back, even if it meant being able to forget everything I had seen. She made it all worth it. The Beach Boys swung into "California Girls," and the crowd was on its feet, clapping and singing along.

"Well, East Coast girls are hip; I really dig the styles they wear ..."

I was starting to feel better. No matter what happened in the outside world, and no matter how badly my roommate was screwing up his life, I knew I didn't have any complaints. My life was terrific. I started singing along with everyone else in the crowd.

"... I wish they all could be California girls..."

It was a terrific evening; one I've never forgotten. We went from the concert directly over to the fraternity house, and it was there I took the little gift-wrapped box from my jacket pocket and handed it to Beth. "Is this what I think it is?" she asked me, smiling.

I smiled back. "How would I know what you're thinking? Open the box and find out."

She tore the wrapping off the box and opened it. Inside was the fraternity pin I'd been given only two days previously. "Oh, Rob. It's beautiful, but didn't you just get this?"

I nodded. "I haven't even worn it. I wanted you to be the first one to wear it."

She kissed me passionately. "Put it on for me, will you?" I unfastened the clasp in the back and pinned it to her sweater just over her left breast. She looked down at it. "I wish there was a mirror around so I could see it."

"There's a big mirror over the bar," I said, taking her by the arm and leading her across the room. It was dark in the party room, not the best place to see something as small as a fraternity pin on a sweater. I could see it, though, and it looked perfect.

"This is a pretty big step, isn't it? Isn't being pinned sort of like..."

"I think they call it being engaged to be engaged. Just tell me if you don't want it. I can always go into the kitchen and find a knife so I can cut my throat."

Beth kissed me. "Sometimes you're so strange, Rob. Of course, I want to wear your pin. I was afraid you wouldn't want to give it to me."

I shook my head. "I can't imagine not giving it to you. I can't imagine not having you in my life right now. Beth, I'm crazy about you."

She kissed me again. "I love you too, but I don't have anything to give you."

I leered at her. "You certainly do."

Beth blushed deeply as I put my arms around her and held her close. The dance band was starting a slow song, and I was ready to dance with the woman I loved. "You know something?" I whispered in her ear. "It looks like it's turning out to be a pretty good weekend after all."

We stayed at the party until a little after two. Most of my brothers had noticed that Beth was wearing my pin, and we fielded quite a few congratulations. I found myself thinking how terrific it was to be part of a group of great guys like this, and how wonderful it was to have a girlfriend like Beth. The thought of how I spent the previous night crossed my mind, but I was far too happy to dwell on Danny. If he wasn't smart enough to stay away from LSD after what had happened, it certainly wasn't my problem.

After we left the party, we walked arm in arm to our motel room. I already had arranged with Dave to use his car early Monday morning, so our weekend wasn't going to end until then.

Beth and I had been planning to spend both Saturday and Sunday night together. We knew we were about to take a major step. Just the fact that we both had reached 19 as virgins showed that it meant something. We were both excited, nervous, and yes, scared now that the time finally had arrived. We arrived at the room, opened the door, and walked inside. As soon as the door was closed, I took Beth in my arms and kissed her. She was shaking. I wasn't sure if it was with passion or fright.

"Rob? I'm so afraid I won't be good for you. I want it to be special for you and I'm afraid I won't know what to do."

I kissed her softly. "Don't worry, angel. Let's just try to do what comes naturally. Just relax and enjoy yourself. So what if it's awkward at first? We'll both learn together."

It was awkward. Neither one of us knew what we were doing. I had asked Dave a few questions, and I figured Beth probably had discussed the subject with her more experienced girlfriends.

We were babies when it came to lovemaking, but we were so much in love with each other and that made a big difference. We made it through the embarrassing moments with a minimum of distress. I had a tough time getting the condom on, and the first time was pretty painful for her.

A few years later, I remember hearing someone on a talk show saying the only good thing about the first time was getting it out of the way. I had to agree. I was glad my first time was with Beth, though. I loved her a lot and having my first time be with her meant so much more to me than if it had come in the back seat of a car with the town punchboard.

It lasted only a couple of minutes. When it was over, I held her and kissed her as we talked about it. It had been good enough for both of us that we felt a sense of relief. I must have told her I loved her a dozen times. I knew she wanted to hear it and I was ready to say it as often as she wanted. She fell asleep in my arms a little before 5 a.m.

We showered together in the morning and went right back to bed. The second time was a lot better than the first, and the third and fourth times were approaching fantastic. "God, I can't get enough of you," she whispered as she snuggled against me.

"Sweetheart, you can call me Rob."

She chortled. "You really think you're something, don't you?" I nodded. "You give a guy your virginity and all of a sudden he thinks he's the Supreme Being."

We stayed in bed most of the day. We ordered lunch from room service and sent out for pizza in the evening. We watched some television and talked some. Mostly, though, we made love.

It's funny. Once you're past forty, you're amazed at the sexual vitality of your youth. I'm lucky now if I can manage it twice in an evening and remembering that first marathon makes me wonder if I inhabited a different body in my late teens.

"You know, I think we're getting the hang of this," I said after what must have been our sixth or seventh time. "What do you think?" Beth didn't say anything. She was having a hard time getting her heartbeat under two hundred beats a minute. "I guess you liked it."

She laughed. "If I'd known you were going to turn out to be such a stud, we'd have started doing this a lot sooner."

We set the alarm for Monday morning and woke up for one last encounter before I had to drive her back to school. Beth snuggled against me for the entire two hours. We had reached the point where we could read each other's moods, and the closer we got to Harrisonburg, the more obvious it was that I was getting upset. Once I dropped her off, I had to turn around and drive back to school. I had to deal with my roommate again, and I was so tired of Danny.

"Are you all right, sweetheart?" Her voice was full of the sleep she hadn't had.

"I'm still irritated about what happened Friday night."

Beth nodded. "It's not your problem. One more month and you won't be his roommate anymore."

"I feel like I'm getting dragged into things I don't want any part of."

"You're not." She stroked my cheek. "You're just worrying too much about things you shouldn't be worrying about."

I wasn't that easily placated. "You told me some of the stuff you knew about LSD. Well, what if I'd gotten there a little later. What if I walked in and he'd been clawing his eyes out ... or demolishing the room ... or jumping out the window thinking he could fly?"

"He wasn't. You got there and everything was all right."

"No thanks to me. I didn't have any idea what was going on. If you hadn't come up, I wouldn't have known what to do at all."

"Sweetheart, stop worrying. And anyway, I hope that won't be your most lasting memory of Easters. I hope you'll find something ...

some better memory ... that you can keep."

"Well," I drawled. "Maybe I can think of something else."

She played with the pin that was attached to her sweater. "I know I will."

"And what would that be?" I asked her teasingly.

"Well, for one thing, it's not every weekend a girl gets to see the Beach Boys." I must have looked crestfallen. "Rob, sweetheart. It serves you right for asking."

28

On the way back to Charlottesville, I started thinking about Danny again. I knew he had been lucky, and I wondered what in the hell had made him take LSD. Beth had told me enough about the destructive capabilities of the drug that I doubted I would ever have any interest in trying it. She said most of the early testing had been under carefully supervised laboratory conditions, and people always were watched through each step of their trips.

I was beginning to think Danny was a real idiot. He might be a bright kid, but if street smarts or common sense could be measured like earthquakes, I knew he would barely register on the Richter scale.

I made it back to school in plenty of time to change and go to biology. There was a folded note on my desk, and I figured it was from my roommate. I stuffed it into my pocket without reading it, planning to look at it when I was waiting for the biology lecture to start.

It slipped my mind. I didn't get to it until lunch, when I reached into my pocket for some gum and came out with the note. When I opened it and looked at it, I got a nasty surprise. It was from Jack Mathews, our resident advisor, and it was short and to the point.

"Rob. There has been an accusation made. I need to see you ASAP. Jack."

As best as I could figure, there was only one possible thing it could be. Someone must have told him Beth had been in my room on Friday night. I wondered how much else he knew. I also wondered who had told him. Bruce had promised me he wouldn't say anything. As far as I knew, Danny was the only other person who had seen her. I hadn't even realized he knew she was there. The odds were it was one of those two, although I knew someone else could have seen her or heard us talking as they walked by the room.

I caught up with Jack in the early evening and it was exactly what I had thought. "Rob, I have to ask you one question." He looked at me solemnly. "Did you have a girl in your room at any time on Easters Weekend?"

He didn't have to remind me that a lie would bring far worse punishment than anything he could do to me if I admitted my guilt. I knew I wasn't going to lie about it, anyway. "Yes, I did. Friday night, from about 1:30 to ... oh, I think it was a little after four. I'm sorry, but I can't tell you why."

He looked at me quizzically. "Rob, this is serious. You can be kicked out of the dorms for this."

I was relieved he hadn't said I could be kicked out of school. "I understand, Jack. I will tell you that I wasn't doing anything illicit."

"You didn't bring her up here for sex?" I shook my head. "Then why?"

I shook my head again. "I can't tell you."

"But you're not denying the accusation?"

"No, I'm not. I'm guilty, but would you tell me who made the accusation?"

"The accuser requested that he be allowed to remain anonymous. He can do that under certain circumstances. If it was something for which we could kick you out of school, you would have the right to face your accuser."

"That's nice," I said dryly. "But I can be kicked out of the dorms strictly on the basis of an anonymous accusation?"

"Relax, Rob. I'm not going to kick you out. I do have to punish you, though."

"All right." I wanted to hear what it would cost me.

"I'm putting you on dormitory probation for the remainder of the semester. Any repeat of this, or any other violation, and I will kick you out of the dorms." Jack looked at me thoughtfully. "There's something about this that doesn't figure. I'm getting the feeling there's more to this than I've been told, either by you or by ... your accuser."

I thought he had been about to say the name but had caught himself in time. "Why would you think that?"

"You didn't sleep in your room Saturday night or Sunday night, did you?" I shrugged. "When I asked one of the guys where you were, he said he thought you were staying with your girlfriend at a motel."

"Is that against the rules, too?"

Jack smiled. "Cool it, Rob. The case is settled. I'm just trying to understand what happened. Did you stay in a motel room with your girlfriend?"

I hated it when people asked questions so directly. The Honor System was so binding, even when it came to trying to protect Beth's reputation. "I can't deny that," I said, trying to avoid confirming it as well.

Jack smiled again. "That's a good answer, Rob. I like that. But if you had a room, then why in the world would you bring her to the dorm?" I didn't say anything. "Are you protecting someone? Is there something going on that I don't know about?"

This time I grinned. "Which question do you want me to answer, Jack?"

"Hell, Rob. I didn't like bringing you in here like this. You've been a model citizen all year as far as I'm concerned. Good grades, good behavior, a good fraternity ... you've been less trouble than anybody else on the hall. Just do me one favor. If you are protecting someone for whatever reason, and if it gets to be too much for you to handle, come to me. Maybe I can give you some help ... off the record."

He extended his hand to me, and I shook it. "Thanks, Jack."

I had gotten off easy and I knew it. I supposed I had earned the right to screw up once, but I wasn't happy to have been called on the carpet. I still wondered who had turned me in. I didn't think it was Bruce. I trusted him as much as anyone I knew except for Dave, and I had known Dave for almost thirteen years.

I could see Bruce turning me in for an honor violation, even if I didn't know if I could do the same thing. We'd had several discussions throughout the year—after girls and fraternities, the Honor System was the chief topic in first-year bull sessions. I knew Bruce believed in the system with all his heart and was completely intolerant of anyone who would violate it. I hadn't done that, though. The rule I had broken had nothing to do with the Honor System.

I thought about asking him, but I decided I didn't want to know. It had to be either him or Danny, and I preferred to think that my roommate had been so angry at my outburst that he had struck back in the only way he could. The idea that Danny had been the one to turn me in didn't bother me. As far as I was concerned, I didn't care what he did anymore.

I never asked either of them, but I did mention what had happened the next time I went to Madison to see Beth. I told her I was pretty sure Danny had turned me in. She shook her head. "I'm not so sure, Rob. I was there. I saw what he was like. I don't think Danny had any idea I was in the room. I'm not even sure he knew you were there. I think his conscious mind was way off somewhere."

"But if it wasn't him..."

"... then it had to be Bruce. Why do you have trouble believing that he could do something like that?"

"I don't know. I guess because I thought he was my friend."

Beth put her hand on my arm. She measured her words carefully. "Did you ever consider the possibility that maybe he was a little jealous?"

"Jealous? Of me?" I laughed. "Why would Bruce be jealous of me?"

"Rob, sometimes you're so naive." She kissed me, as if to remove the sting of what she had said. "Think about this. You've got a girlfriend and he doesn't. Right?" I nodded. "And how did his first-semester grades turn out?" I shook my head. "And you did well." I nodded.

"Didn't you help him get into his fraternity through your friend Dave?" I nodded again. "Maybe he resents that a little. Maybe he wishes he had done it on his own."

"But he did. I just introduced him to Dave. I didn't do anything else to help him."

"He might not see it that way. Now can you see why he might be jealous?"

That was the end of that conversation. It was months before I found out who turned me in, and by then it didn't matter.

By late April, the days were flipping by almost as quickly as those old movies where you see the pages of the calendar flying away like autumn leaves on a tree. I wrote a government paper that wasn't as good as I could have done and settled for a B. I was getting to the point where B's were disappointing grades.

The only thing I remember about early May was going to Beth's spring formal dance. She wore a pale green dress she had bought for the occasion, and I was certain my girlfriend was the most beautiful woman in the world. We sneaked off after the dance and made love in Dave's car. The one thing we learned was that both of us preferred making love in a bed.

We had started talking about our plans for summer. Beth was thinking of staying in Harrisonburg and going to summer school. She was doing well—her grade point average was higher than mine was— and her faculty advisor had told her that she could finish her under-graduate degree in three years if she went every summer.

I told her I was going home and planned to work construction again that summer. "I've got to make a lot of money to pay for this wild social life."

I was planning to buy a car as soon as I got home, and I figured I could drive from Johnstown to Harrisonburg every couple of week-ends. Summer school would be finished by early August, and Beth would have nearly a month at home with her family. "You'll come see me again, won't you?"

"Sure, but this time I might have to sneak into your room."

She kissed me. "We'll see," she said skeptically. "I still think my dad would kill you."

Back at school, everyone was making their living arrangements. Dave had found a terrific apartment three blocks from Fraternity Row, and he pitched the idea to me again. "Think about it, Bobby," he said as we toured the two-bedroom apartment. "Close enough to be at the house whenever you want, but all the privacy you'll never have if you live in the SPO house."

I shrugged. "It sounds good."

"You're not even thinking about the best part. No more motel rooms for you and Beth. Whenever she comes down, the two of you can just stay in your room. The landlord said he'd put double beds in the bedrooms for $20 extra a month." It certainly sounded interesting. I asked Dave if I could think about it. "Yeah, for three days. That's how long the guy said he'd hold the apartment. If you say no, I've got to find a roommate quickly."

I was beginning to think I might say yes. I'd have to talk it over with my mother, because it would cost me considerably more to live off-campus than in the house. I'd also have to check with my fraternity brothers. I knew a certain number of people were required to live in the house. I told Dave I'd let him know.

With ten days left before exams, it was time to start studying harder. I'd kept up well, even if I hadn't been studying as much since midterms. Now I had to buckle down. Most of my studying was with my pledge brothers, although I still felt I had an obligation to the other three members of my biology study group in the dorm. We got together two or three times during the next week. Bruce was spending most of his time at KSK, but Ed Randolph and Joe Del Rio hadn't pledged anywhere. They were still in the dorms and needed us to study with them.

I talked to Beth twice to get her opinion about the apartment. It didn't surprise me a bit that she liked the idea. She told me she thought I'd have an easier time studying if I was living off-campus and I had to agree. After finding out from my brothers that I didn't have to live in the house, I decided I could always move back my third year if I felt I was missing the pleasures of fraternity living. I told Dave I'd be glad to share a place with him and we signed a twelve-month lease that would start in September.

I hardly saw Danny at all anymore. We hadn't had a conversation since I'd told him off on the Saturday of Easters, and that suited me fine. Our room was empty most of the time. I studied at the library, and he was nowhere to be found either.

29

Three days before the start of exams, Danny broke the silence. "Can we talk? I want to see if we can straighten things out between us."

I put my French book down and turned toward him. "All right, Danny. I'm listening."

I didn't think it would take long. I didn't think we had that much to say, but we wound up talking for hours. Danny started by apologizing for what had happened in April, and he assured me that was his one and only experience with hallucinogens. It was obvious that it had been a rough year for him, from his problems during rush to his parents' divorce, from his poor grades to his problems with Dick. "I always used to be able to ignore guys like that. I don't know why I couldn't this time."

"I think Dick is pretty tough to ignore when he doesn't want to be ignored."

Danny told me he had talked with his parents. They weren't getting back together, but they had assured him he would be able to spend as much time with either of them as he wanted. "I know I'm lucky still to have both of my parents alive."

I nodded. I still missed my dad as much as ever, even though it had been more than two years since his death.

"I even think I'm starting to get my grades straightened out. I ought to wind up with about a 2.5 this semester. I don't know if I'll ever have much of a social life here. It's pretty obvious that I don't fit in all that well with most of these guys."

"Not everybody at this school is alike. Just because you didn't get along with the guys in your dorm this year doesn't mean you won't make friends next year."

Danny shrugged. "I think I'll probably get an apartment. I've been checking the bulletin boards to see if there's anyone looking for roommates for next year."

I nodded. "There are plenty. Just make sure you find someone you'll get along with."

"Yeah, and if I have an apartment, I'll have my own bedroom. I suppose a lot of the problems I had this year wouldn't have happened if I had my own room." It was the closest either one of us ever came to talking about the fact I'd heard him masturbating in bed. I didn't say anything.

Danny even said there was a chance he might be able to get into a fraternity. He had met a guy in his biology lab section who was having trouble. Danny had started tutoring the guy, and they had become friends. "He's in a fraternity. Delta Lambda Chi."

DLC had a terrible reputation. The house itself was run down, and the fraternity always seemed to be battling social probation. It was one of a handful of houses that hadn't filled its pledge quota, but that didn't seem to bother Danny. "Don't worry, Rob. I'm not fooling myself. I know it's not a good house."

"You'd rather go there than a good Jewish house like Phi Ep?"

He nodded. "It's hard to explain."

I wanted to ask him about the night Beth had been in our room, and if he had been the one to turn me in to Jack Mathews. I didn't, though. I didn't want to spoil the mood. It didn't really matter all that much anymore, either.

"Rob, how come you didn't turn me in when you found me tripping?"

"I didn't want to see you get kicked out just because you made a mistake."

"Thanks. One thing I've seen is that they're not too tolerant around here."

I was glad we had talked things out. I figured one of the worst things about my first year, the single thing I felt guiltiest about, had been straightened out. When I called Beth the next day, I told her how glad I was we had talked.

"Did he tell you if he was the one who turned you in?"

"No, and I didn't ask."

"Rob, you're so silly. I'd be going nuts if something like that happened and I didn't know who was responsible."

"I know who was responsible. I was. I broke a rule by having you in my room and I deserved to be punished for it."

She didn't see it that way, but I had enough Catholic guilt drummed into me from an early age to believe that I had to do penance for every sin. I hadn't been going to confession as much lately, though. Part of it had to do with Beth. I knew that according to the Church, it was a sin for me to be making love with Beth. It didn't feel like a sin, though. It felt wonderful, and in more than a physical sense. I loved Beth and I didn't want to be told I was committing a sin. I knew I would do my best to avoid Father Cepicki that summer at home.

One thing I was learning in college was that not everything was black and white. There were so many shades of gray, and even though I was at a school that saw honor in strict black and white terms, I knew there was more to it. I was soon to learn how much more. It's a lesson I've never forgotten.

My exam schedule was like first semester in that my tests were spread out well and the toughest one—biology—would be the last one. It was scheduled for May 26, 1968. That's a day I remember as well as my wedding day or the days my children were born.

30

My first three exams went smoothly, if not quite as well as I would have liked. I had A's in government and statistics after midterms, but my B's on those two finals pulled my grade in both courses down to B-pluses for the semester. I had another B in English, and French turned out to be a B as well. Unless I screwed up the biology final badly, I'd have a B in that course, too. Two B-pluses and three B's weren't what I'd wanted, but I figured with all else that had happened since the beginning of February, making it out of my first year with a 3.1 average was perfectly acceptable.

Things weren't going as well for some of the other guys. Most of them had struggled in the fall and more than a few needed good performances on their finals to stay off academic probation. Statistics showed in those days that only about three percent of the students who ever landed on academic probation wound up completing their degrees, so these guys were in big trouble.

Danny apparently wasn't one of them. He had told me he thought his spring grades would be considerably better, and I didn't think he'd lie about it. He was studying hard for his biology final, tutoring three guys from the DLC house. I knew two of them from my lab section. They were athletes and neither one of them seemed to know much about biology. They had squeaked through the first semester with D's and needed to do better this time.

It was obvious that my roommate saw this as his entry into the DLC pledge class. He was giving it everything he had, but when I walked into a study session they were holding in our room, it seemed more like an animal trainer trying to teach gorillas something that was beyond their capability to learn.

The biology final was scheduled for a Wednesday, with grades to be posted by Friday. Dave and I were planning to leave for home that afternoon. We would stop by Harrisonburg to see Beth and Marianne and would go on to Pennsylvania on Saturday. I had come up with an interesting idea. Beth was going to ride with us to Johnstown. She would spend a couple of days with us and get to know my mother. Then I could drive her home to Scranton, where she would have a week or so before coming back down to summer school.

Both of us were excited about it, even though we knew we probably wouldn't have much opportunity to get physical with each other. She joked about sneaking into my room and laughed when I reacted with shock. We hadn't seen much of each other the last few weeks, and neither of us was all that excited about spending the summer two hundred miles apart. I figured to be putting a lot of miles on the car I'd be buying.

By Tuesday night at midnight, I felt as ready for the exam as I ever would. I had studied, restudied, and crammed everything from two semesters of elementary biology into my brain and I thought I could retain enough of it not to embarrass myself. I slept the sleep of the just and awakened quickly when my alarm went off at 7 o'clock. I didn't realize I was about to begin the longest day of my life.

Bruce got up at about the same time, so we went to the cafeteria for breakfast together and got in a little last-minute reviewing. He needed a C to assure himself a 2.0 for his first year, while I wanted at least a B to wrap up my 3.0 for the second straight semester. "Tell me, Root. How did you stay focused all year? I'm going to be grinding for two years to bring up my bad first-year grades."

I shrugged. "I had a good teacher. Dave hammered it into me

all summer that I had to start working right from the beginning, and I guess getting the message from somebody who went through the same thing the year before made a big difference."

We walked over to the lecture hall together and sat down in our seats with ten minutes to spare. There was no assigned seating, but most people seemed to gravitate toward the same seats they occupied all year. There were two hundred in our class, and the auditorium was big enough to hold twice that many. We had been instructed to leave empty seats on each side of us, so even the back rows were occupied. I looked around for familiar faces, and I saw a couple of my pledge brothers.

I also saw Danny sitting about three rows in front of me and off to the left. He was surrounded by the guys he had been tutoring. I thought that was a little odd, but quickly dismissed the thought. I didn't want anything distracting me.

The professor walked into the hall at exactly 9 o'clock and the class fell silent. Three graduate assistants came in with the exam booklets and began handing them out. We all had the computer answer sheets we had purchased at the bookstore, and everyone had two or three well-sharpened No. 2 pencils.

"Gentlemen, this is your final examination. There are a total of 150 questions, and all are multiple choice. You will have exactly three hours to complete those questions. I will be calling time at approximately..." He looked at his watch. "... ten minutes past noon. I hope many of you do better than you did on the first-semester final. I'm never eager to see repeat faces. Thank you for your cooperation throughout the academic year, and good luck on your exam." Two hundred heads bent over two hundred booklets. "You may open your booklets now and ... begin."

I looked at the first question and realized I knew the answer. I checked the five choices given, found the appropriate one and blacked in the letter "C" on the first line. After about half an hour, I was already nearly a third of the way through the final. I was stunned to realize that I was breezing, and that I hadn't come across one question that had stumped me. I lifted my head from the exam booklet for a moment, figuring I would catch my breath and slow down. I didn't want to go too fast. I could make mistakes that way, too.

Just before I was about to read the next question, I noticed something odd. Danny had his hand on top of his head. He wasn't scratching or anything. He just had his hand resting there. Without even looking in that direction, I saw out of the corner of my eye that one of the DLC brothers was glancing over at him. I wasn't sure what to think, but I kept watching for a little while. Danny tugged at his left ear once and stroked his chin twice. The guys he had tutored were watching him intently.

Suddenly, I felt a sick feeling in my stomach. I thought I was going to throw up, so I turned my paper over and stood up to leave the room. Because of the Honor System, there weren't any proctors. The professor trusted us not to look up answers if we left the examination room for a drink of water or a trip to the bathroom. I walked out of the room quickly and found a water fountain. I had a drink and then splashed some water on my face. It helped. The sick feeling lessened, but I knew if I went back to my seat, I'd have to look at Danny again. If I saw what I was afraid I had seen, I didn't know what I would do.

Could it be possible that my roommate was helping the guys he had tutored cheat on the biology final? The thought of it stunned me. It was incredibly stupid if it was true. What could Danny possibly gain by putting himself at such a risk? Was it worth getting kicked out of school for good to get into a sleazy fraternity like DLC? I didn't think so, but I didn't have the same desperate need for acceptance as my roommate. I told myself I would ignore it, that it was none of my business. We weren't being graded on a curve, so even if this far-fetched thing really was happening, it couldn't possibly hurt my grade.

I took a deep breath and gathered my thoughts. I had been out of the room for five minutes, and I didn't want to waste any more time. As soon as I opened the door, though, I knew I would have to see if I was right.

After watching Danny for about five more minutes, I knew I was right. He touched the top of his head twice more, and he gave four other distinct hand signals that would cover every one of the five multiple choice possibilities. The three sleazoids he had been tutoring all kept glancing at him, and every glance they took was accompanied by a mark on their answer sheets.

I was stunned. My roommate was violating the Honor System.

There was nothing I could do to stop him, no action I could take to save him from his stupidity. It seemed so obvious to me, and I couldn't believe it wasn't obvious to everyone in the room. As best as I could tell, no one else was watching. No one else seemed to have figured out what was happening, that amid two hundred of us, there were four students cheating.

I felt heartsick. I wished there were some way I could forget what I had seen. If I was the only one who had figured out what was happening, I was going to have to accuse Danny and his three friends of an honor violation. Everything Dave and I had talked about last September, everything that had come up in countless dormitory and fraternity bull sessions, was coming to pass. I had made it through the school year without lying, cheating or stealing. That never had been an issue for me. What had bothered me all along about the system was my role as an enforcer. I didn't want the responsibility of essentially being the one to kick someone else out of school, but my worst nightmare in the world had come to pass.

Somehow I forced myself to return to my own exam paper. I wouldn't be doing anyone any good if I spent so much time watching to catch the four cheaters that I left myself no time to take my own exam. I looked at the 61st question and saw that I had finally come across one I didn't know.

I had to work hard to make myself concentrate for the two hours remaining in the exam period. Somehow I managed to answer every question, although I never regained the feeling I had before I looked up and saw Danny that first time. From time to time, I glanced down at him again. He was still giving hand signals and the three other guys were still taking their cues from him.

When the professor called time, I turned my paper in and quickly left the lecture hall without saying a word. Bruce and I had planned to meet for lunch to talk about how we thought we had done, but I hurried off before he came out. I had to be alone. I couldn't face him suspecting what I did about Danny. I hurried back to my room at a half-run, dropped off my books and left the dorm. I walked down the street, searching for a place I could sit and think without being bothered. I decided to go into the stacks at the library. It was the most private place I could think of, and no one would be looking for me there now that my exams were finished for the year. I found a deserted spot and sat down at a desk in a secluded corner, where I sat quietly for about ten minutes before I realized I was crying. Pulling a grubby handkerchief out of my hip pocket, I dried my eyes.

The last time I could remember feeling this bad was the day my dad died. He had had a heart attack, and it had come as a complete surprise to everyone. I was a junior at Johnstown High and was in the middle of gym class when they called my name over the public address system and asked me to report to the main office immediately. I hadn't even changed into my street clothes. I trotted down the hall in my T-shirt and shorts, and when I walked into the outer office, I noticed that my mother was standing there.

I couldn't remember ever seeing her at school in the middle of the day before. I knew something must be wrong, but I didn't have any idea what. "Mom?" She smiled sadly at me. "What are you doing here?"

My mother reached out and gently put her hand on my arm. Her expression was noncommittal, with none of the overwhelming grief I knew later she must have been feeling. "Bobby, I'm not going to beat around the bush. Your dad is dead."

At first it didn't register, but after a second or two I felt as if a mountain had fallen on me. "What?"

"Your father had a heart attack this morning in court. There wasn't anything they could do for him. They tell me it was over very quickly, and he didn't suffer."

"No. There must be some mistake. Dad…"

The principal was standing there, too. I didn't know why I hadn't noticed him before. "Robert, your mother has asked us to excuse you for the rest of the day. You can leave any time."

I just nodded. I couldn't think of anything to say that would be appropriate. Then I remembered I was wearing my gym clothes. "I better go get dressed."

I ran down the hall with tears streaming down my face. By the time I got back to the locker room, the period was almost over, and my classmates were getting ready to take their showers. "Is everything all right, Bobby?" the gym teacher asked me. Ken Curran was the varsity football coach, and I had known him since my freshman year.

I shook my head. "No, Coach Curran. It's not all right. My dad is dead." I couldn't think of anything else to say.

The coach didn't know what to say, either. "I'm sorry," he said in a low voice.

The three days that followed had passed in a blur. There was a wake, a memorial service and burial in the family plot. I felt like I remembered all of it and I didn't remember any of it. If that sounds strange to you, I'm not sure anyone who hasn't lost a parent unexpectedly could understand.

I hadn't cried much as a kid. I never did get into a lot of fights, and most of the ones I couldn't avoid I had managed to win. Our family hadn't been big on displaying emotion anyway. I cried some on each of those next three days, though. I felt as if I'd lost my best friend in the world. My dad and I always had been exceptionally close, even though I don't think I realized just how close until I had to live without him.

We had talked about every subject imaginable, from the history of the law to Santa Claus to the Pittsburgh Steelers. He always treated me as if I were an intelligent person. He never talked down to me and he never lied. I can't think of a question I asked that he didn't give me a straight answer. I missed him so much. Hell, he's been dead nearly forty years and I still miss him. I've never met anyone like him, before or since.

A lot of kids idolize their dads when they're little. Most of them outgrow it. I never did. I'm nearly sixty now, and my father still is my hero. My biggest regret is that he died too soon to meet his grandchildren, and that my kids never got the chance to learn from him all those things he taught me.

I felt so desolate when he died, and as I sat in the stacks in Alderman Library on that late May afternoon in 1968 wondering what to do about Danny Jacobs, I felt every bit as empty. A part of me wanted to stay there forever, to remain deep in the stacks until the situation somehow resolved itself in some other way. I knew I couldn't do that, though. I knew I had to face Danny, man to man, and confront him with what I had seen.

I hoped beyond hoping that there was some logical explanation, that Danny would laugh and tell me I was wrong. At that point I would have given anything if I could just go back and take the exam again. Given a second chance, I knew I'd never lift my head from my own paper.

It was nearly 4 o'clock before I convinced myself I couldn't wait any longer. I had to get back to the dorms and talk to Danny before he left. If I had to deal with him long distance, it would be far too complicated.

With exams all but finished, there were several impromptu celebrations taking place on our hall. I quickly moved past the parties and headed through the open door into my own room. Danny was on his bed, reading a magazine. He looked up when I walked in and greeted me with a smile. "Rob, hi. Where have you been? Bruce Benson was looking for you. He said you were supposed to meet him for lunch."

I took a deep breath and closed the door to the room. Danny looked at me quizzically as I locked the door and slowly walked over to my bed. "Is something wrong?"

I nodded and sat down. "I've got to talk to you about the biology exam, Danny."

For an instant I thought I could see fear in his eyes, but he covered it quickly. "Sure, Rob. How do you think you did?"

I shook my head. "That's not what I need to ask you about."

This time I was sure I saw a furtive look. He covered again, though. "Oh?" he asked with what seemed like forced calm.

"Danny," I said slowly. "You were behaving strangely during the exam."

He seemed to force himself to respond with an equal slowness. "I don't know what you mean."

"All right, then. Explain this." I showed him each of the five different hand signals I'd seen him making again and again during the exam.

Danny looked stricken and his response was a whisper. "You saw that?"

"Uh huh. Can you tell me what it means? I'd like to know. I hope to God you can give me some explanation for it." Danny just sat there. "Well? I'm waiting."

"I don't know what to say."

"Were you cheating on the exam?"

He tried to cover. He really tried. "Rob, why on earth would I cheat on the exam? You know I got an A last semester and I'm going to get an A again. Why would I cheat?"

I shook my head angrily. "You know what I mean, Danny. You were helping those sleazoids from DLC pass the exam, weren't you?"

Danny took a different tack. "Were you the only one who saw this?"

"What difference does that make?" I asked in an exasperated tone. "And anyway, how would I know if anyone else saw you?"

"I don't know." I could almost see his mind working. He thought for a few seconds and then he broached the subject. "What are you going to do about what you think you saw?"

"Danny, I know what I saw. I saw you helping your buddies cheat."

"You don't have any proof of that."

"No, I don't have any proof, but I imagine if the subject comes up, there might have been other people in the room who would remember they saw something strange."

He knew I was right. There might have been any number of people who had noticed something but had been too concerned with their own exam papers to spend much time thinking about it. He didn't say anything. He just sat there looking at me, and finally I broke the silence. "Why, Danny?"

He shook his head. "You wouldn't understand. How could you possibly understand? You've been Joe College ever since you got here. Good grades, good fraternity, everybody's buddy and a beautiful girlfriend."

"I've been lucky."

"That's not it at all. I don't think luck has anything to do with it. You just seem to know the right way to do things. I don't. I'm a total fuckup."

I sighed. "You try too hard. People don't like that."

He nodded. "I know that, and I try to make myself relax. It doesn't work. I wanted everybody to like me when I came down here, but I don't fit in at all. Not even a little bit."

"Maybe you should have gone to Michigan State. Things probably are different there. This is such a party school, and it's so southern. There are probably more..."

"... Jews up there?" he completed my sentence bitterly, although a little different from what I was saying. "Like I said, you wouldn't understand."

The two of us sat there for a minute. This time it was Danny who broke the silence. "I wanted to get into a fraternity so bad. And those guys liked me. I know they did."

"I don't know if they liked you or not, but they sure did use you, didn't they?" He gave me a quizzical look. "Danny, I would be really surprised if all this was your idea. I doubt you went to these guys and offered to help them cheat on the exam. Did you?"

He shook his head. "No," he said in a small voice. "I really don't remember which one of them suggested it, but it definitely wasn't my idea. It was something the three of them worked up between themselves. Does that make any difference?"

"Not really. All four of you are guilty of cheating."

"Yeah." Danny had admitted it. It didn't make me feel any better. "Now what?"

"You know the system as well as I do. You can admit what you did and withdraw, or you can deny it and go through a trial."

"I lose either way. Even if I withdraw, it goes on my record that I committed an honor violation and I can never come back to school here."

I nodded. "Yeah, that's the way it works."

"There is one other option."

I didn't know what he meant. "No, unless there's something I haven't thought of, those are the only two."

"No, Rob. There's one other option. You can forget what you saw and not turn me in. You know it'll ruin my life, and you don't want to do that. I've heard you talk about the Honor System enough that

I know you don't like the part about turning other people in." I just sat there, feeling totally humiliated that he would ask me this. I didn't know what to say. "Rob, I'll do anything. I'll give you anything you want ... money, whatever."

I shook my head angrily. "Is that it, Danny? You want to buy me off?"

He knew immediately that he had said the wrong thing. "No, that's not it at all. I was stupid to say that, but I'm desperate. I've heard you say you think the system is too harsh, that kicking somebody out for good the first time they make a mistake is ridiculous. Well, this is my first mistake, and you can give me a second chance by letting it slide."

"Danny..."

"If you can't do that, then how about this one? There is a fourth option. The semester is over now. I'm all finished with my exams. I'll go home and I won't come back. I'll withdraw from school and transfer somewhere else. Just don't make me do it with an honor violation on my record. Can you at least cut me that much slack?"

I thought for a moment. "I don't know. What's to stop you from coming back?"

"I'll give you my word."

"Even if you do, I've got to go to school here for three more years. I've got to live under the Honor System all that time, and I'd know I violated it by not turning you in for cheating. And even if you left, those other three guys would still be here."

"Please, Rob." He was almost crying now. "For the love of God, don't do this."

"How would you explain it to your parents if you just didn't come back?"

"I'd tell them I hated it here and decided to transfer."

"But you don't hate it here."

He shook his head. "No, I don't. I don't know why I don't after everything went so badly this year, but I love it here." I nodded slowly without saying anything. "But I know I can't stay. There's no way of that now." He paused. "Is there?"

I didn't say anything. I just sat there and looked at him. He looked so totally pathetic, and at that moment I hated Danny Jacobs for dragging me into this. I hated myself for looking up and I hated the university for having such a rigid, unbending system. I wished I could find a way in my mind to justify letting Danny off the hook.

"Rob? You've got my whole life in your hands right now." I really needed to hear that at this moment. "Don't ruin my life. Let me just drop out of school quietly."

"What about the other three guys?"

"What if I could talk to them? I could tell them that somebody caught us without telling them who it was, and I could tell them they'd have to drop out, too."

"I doubt if they'd go along with that."

"They might. I'll talk to them. I'll try. The system gives you twenty-four hours to report an honor violation, doesn't it?" I nodded. "Then give me till tomorrow morning. Let me talk to them and see what they say."

It was certainly within my power to do that much without compromising myself. I didn't think much of his chances of getting the three sleazoids to go along with him, and I didn't know if I could let them withdraw even if they did. I didn't know what to think. I felt horrible about the prospect of having to be judge, jury and executioner for this misfit kid I had been rooming with since September. Danny had been right about one thing. I hated the part of the system that required students to police themselves. It was too much pressure to put on 18-year-old kids to ask them to leave home with a mature, fully developed sense of honor. And it was far too harsh to make permanent expulsion the single sanction for all offenses. When Dave had told me the story of the kid who had been expelled for lying about his age to buy a beer, I had been horrified. I didn't know if I would violate the system myself to let Danny escape punishment, but I didn't know that I wouldn't, either. "All right, Danny. You talk to them and get back to me. I won't do anything until tomorrow morning."

Danny smiled for what seemed like the first time in hours. "Thanks, Rob."

31

Danny headed for the phones to call the DLC house, and I left for a walk. I didn't want to talk to anyone else, and I didn't want to be faced with Danny until I had more of an idea of what I was going to do. It was dinnertime, but I wasn't hungry. I hadn't eaten since breakfast, but even the thought of food was making me nauseous. I decided I'd see how far I could walk.

I walked across the grounds to the Corner and kept heading east. I walked past Sears, past the liquor store and on past the Trailways station. By then I had covered almost two miles, but I wasn't ready to stop walking. I headed east, on into the old downtown section. The sun would be setting soon, and the lights were coming on. I passed the old movie theatres where several guys in the dorm had come for occasional matinees, and it surprised me to realize I had been in Charlottesville nearly nine months and had never been inside these theatres.

I walked past the downtown area and into a residential section. I went on past the houses until I realized I was nearing the outskirts of town, with gas stations and cheap motels the main sights along the highway. It was getting dark by then, and for the first time I started feeling pangs of hunger. I saw a little diner up the road and stopped there for something to eat. The clock behind the counter said it was about 8:15. I had been walking for the better part of two hours.

I looked at the menu and ordered a hamburger and some fries. As I waited for my order to come, I stared out the window at the trucks driving past on State Route 250. At the other end of town, the west end, 250 headed toward Staunton. It was the first leg of the trip to Harrisonburg, and I had made it countless times since September. I hadn't seen this end of town before, though. Here the big trucks were heading east toward Richmond and Interstate 95. From there they could go all the way north into New England. The interstate wasn't completed all the way to the south in those days, but I remembered the leg of it Dave and I had traveled to Fort Lauderdale for spring break and I found myself wishing I could have just stayed on the beach in Florida and never come back.

I finished eating and decided I had better start walking back to school. As it was, it would be nearly 11 o'clock when I got back. I had been tossing and turning mentally ever since I left the dorm, trying to figure out what I would do in all possible contingencies. If all four agreed to withdraw. If they didn't. If Danny changed his tune and started denying it. I knew at the beginning, at least, it was my word against his. I knew he wouldn't do that, though. He and I were members of the two most guilt-ridden ethnic groups in the world—Irish Catholics and Jews. Once he had admitted to me what had happened, there was no way he would deny it later.

I thought about turning him in and what it would mean. I thought about him leaving school forever with that irreversible blot on his transcript.

The true believers in the system often talked of how the university helped students get into other schools after expulsion, but I had asked a dean about that once and he had told me that was strictly fantasy. Once a student was separated from the university community, the school had no further interest in that student. Danny would be on his own.

I wished my dad were alive so I could call him. I somehow knew he would have been able to put it all into perspective for me, and I wasn't certain he would have taken the hard line, either. He had always been merciful as a judge in situations where mercy was appropriate. When I had read Shakespeare's "Merchant of Venice" my freshman year in high school, my dad and I had a long discussion about Portia's famous "quality of mercy is not strained" speech. I remembered some of what my dad had said. He told me honor had to be an absolute thing, but forgiveness was important as well. You can expect people to behave honorably, but sometimes you must be prepared to forgive them when they don't.

I thought of another story I had read, Poe's eerie "Cask of Amontillado," about a man who was trapped behind a wall that grew slowly, brick by brick. At that moment I felt as if I were the man behind the wall, and each step I took was another brick. Each minute closer to the grounds closed off another option and brought me closer to the time the last brick was in place and I would have to make my decision. Of course, I wasn't the one who was trapped, but at that moment I didn't see it that way.

It was a little before ten when I got back to the downtown area. One of the theatres was disgorging its crowd from the early show, and I stood and watched for a minute or two as the townspeople of Charlottesville came out discussing the film. The downtown theatres were frequented more by townies than students, and as I watched I realized how little contact I had had with anyone outside the university community.

A couple of giggling high school girls walked past, and one of them smiled at me flirtatiously. I must not have smiled back, because she turned and walked away quickly.

I thought about Beth and how much I wished I could discuss this with her. I knew she still had one more exam, though, and I didn't want to disrupt her studying. I knew I was on my own, anyway. I knew I was the only one who could decide what to do.

My feet were starting to hurt as I neared the grounds. I wasn't one bit closer to understanding what I would do. Would I turn Danny in? Would I let him withdraw quietly, or would I back down and let it slide? I had told him I would let him know in the morning, but I wasn't sure I would have any better handle on my feelings in twelve hours.

I couldn't talk to any of my friends. Dave wouldn't be any help at all, because if he didn't tell me to turn Danny in, he'd be part of an honor violation as well. The same went for Bruce or for any of my pledge brothers. I suppose I could have made the question hypothetical, but a hypothetical question wouldn't have been nearly as difficult for anyone to answer. If someone had given me the situation in that form, I'd have said to turn the guy in. A hypothetical question wasn't real. You couldn't feel Danny's pain and you couldn't realize just how serious the consequences were.

As I approached the dorms after nearly five hours of walking, I looked up at the third floor of Kent House and counted down to the window of the room I shared with Danny. The light was off. I figured he wasn't there, but I opened the door to find that he was in his bed. I decided he must have been emotionally exhausted, and I wondered if he had talked to those three guys yet. I tiptoed across the room and turned on my desk lamp.

There was an envelope sitting against the lamp, the same place Danny had put my mail all year on the days he'd been the first one to check our mailbox. This one didn't have a stamp on it, so I figured it was from him. I sat down and opened the envelope.

Rob—I talked to the guys earlier in the evening and they told me there was no way you could prove anything. I argued with them and told them we had to leave school, but they told me to get fucked. I'm sorry, Rob. I'm so sorry. Danny

He had risked everything to help these guys he thought were his friends, and when things had gotten tough, they had cut him loose without a second thought. The fact was, they were probably right. I probably couldn't prove anything. Danny had known that too, but he had enough of a sense of honor to admit what he had done. The three DLC brothers lacked even that.

I looked across the room in the dim light and suddenly something seemed strange. All year long, Danny had snored softly when he slept. It hadn't bothered me. I was such a sound sleeper he could have talked in his sleep and it wouldn't have fazed me. In fact, the only times I ever noticed had been the times he had gone to bed before me. But this time he wasn't snoring. This time I couldn't even see his chest rising and falling as he breathed. Danny was a restless sleeper, but now I couldn't remember him moving at all since I came into the room.

I felt like an idiot. I thought I was being melodramatic, and that if I went over and shook Danny awake, he would ask me what the hell I was doing. I looked at him for another minute or so, though, and he still didn't move. I felt a chill in the room, even though it was almost summer, and I got up and turned on the overhead light. Danny didn't stir.

I went over to his bed and looked down at him. He was flat on his back, and he looked really pale. For a moment I thought of the song from the previous fall. As I stared at Danny, I thought his face was a whiter shade of pale. Almost without thinking, I reached down to touch him. As soon as I felt the coolness of his skin, I knew my roommate had made his decision to answer to a higher justice than the university's honor system.

I stood there for what seemed like an eternity but must have been only a few seconds. Catholic to the core, I crossed myself and said a Hail Mary. I didn't know what to do. I grabbed the note off my desk and jammed it into my pocket. I didn't know then why I was doing it, but I figured it out later. Then I ran down the hall and started pounding on the resident advisor's door. It was nearly midnight, but Jack Mathews was still up studying. I heard him push his chair back and walk across the room to open the door.

He looked at me strangely. "Rob? Is something wrong?"

"Come quickly. It's Danny."

I knew in my heart Danny was dead, but I couldn't bring myself to say it. Jack followed me down the hall quickly. "What is it?" he asked as we approached the room.

I just shook my head and gestured toward the doorway. He walked in first and looked at Danny's body. "Is he...?"

I nodded. "I think so. His skin felt cooler than it should."

He reached down and touched Danny's face lightly. He jerked his hand back and moaned. "Oh, God! I'd better call someone. Stay here with him."

Jack took off down the hall to his room, where he had a private phone line. I stood there looking at Danny. I hadn't realized that we had caused something of a commotion, and I was surprised to see two or three guys standing in the open doorway looking in at Danny. "What's wrong with Jacobs?" Joe Del Rio asked.

Ed Randolph looked as if he knew. "Is he ...?"

Bruce Benson was the one who noticed I seemed to be slipping into a state of shock. He came up to me and touched my arm. "Are you all right, Rob?"

I shook my head sadly. "He's dead, Bruce. Danny's dead."

Bruce led me over to my chair and sat me down. He motioned for the others to leave us, and they vacated the doorway. I wasn't thinking too clearly, but I somehow knew it would take only a few minutes before everyone in the dorm knew Danny Jacobs was dead in his bed. "What happened?" Bruce asked me softly.

"I don't know. I came back a few minutes ago and I thought he was asleep. He wasn't snoring, though. The little bastard always snores and that's how I knew something was wrong."

My voice was creeping up toward hysteria and Bruce calmed me down. At that moment, Jack Mathews came back. "I called security. They're getting an ambulance."

"Why?" I asked.

"Maybe there's some way. Maybe he hasn't been dead that long."

"You felt his skin, Jack. Do you think they're going to be able to bring him back?"

I must have sounded bitter. "I don't know, Rob. I was just following the procedures they tell us to follow. I've never seen anything like this before."

Bruce put his arm around my shoulders. "Do you want me to call Dave? I know he was over at the KSK house when I left there a few minutes ago."

I nodded. "Yeah, call him. Please."

"Use the phone in my room," Jack said as Bruce took off down the hall. He came over and sat down on my bed. "Rob, I need to ask you something before security gets here. Do you think there's any chance that this was a suicide?"

I sighed. I knew the note I'd jammed into my pocket was a pretty good indication Danny had killed himself, but I wasn't sure. I wasn't going to slander my dead roommate at this late date, so I told the first lie I could remember. "I don't know, Jack," I said in a voice little more than a whisper. "I don't know why Danny would want to kill himself."

I knew I would have to destroy the note and that it was almost certain the three guys who had brought this on Danny would walk away completely free from cheating on the biology final. I realized then that honor isn't always measured in easy ways.

Somehow, I got through the next few hours. Dave got there shortly after the ambulance arrived. We watched with morbid fascination as the paramedics futilely tried to revive Danny. "Any idea what killed him?" Jack asked them.

One paramedic shook his head. "There's no way of telling until they do an autopsy, but my guess is that it was a drug overdose. Was there a suicide note?"

Everyone looked at me as the one who had discovered the body. I just shook my head sadly and told another lie. "I didn't see one."

"Has anyone called the parents yet?"

Jack shook his head. "God, it's late," he said, looking at his watch. "I hate to call anybody with news like this in the middle of the night, but I'd better go and do it."

As he left the room, a uniformed university policeman knocked on the door and poked his head through the doorway. The paramedic motioned for him to come into the room, and the cop looked around and saw me. "You the one who found him?"

I nodded. "I'm Rob Miller. He was my roommate. He was awake when I left here a little before six, and I was gone until about eleven."

"Where were you?"

"I went for a walk."

The cop gave me an incredulous look. "For five hours?"

I realized how stupid it sounded, but I nodded. "I walked out to the east end of town. I ate dinner out there around eight or 8:30 and then I walked back."

"Mind if I ask why you went for this little ... hike of yours?"

I wasn't thinking too clearly, but Dave jumped in. "Does that matter, officer? It's obvious the kid wasn't murdered, so why does it matter what Rob was doing?"

"Who are you, son?"

"David Lyons. I'm Rob's friend from back home in Pennsylvania. I'm second year, and I came over from my fraternity house when one of my brothers called and told me what happened. I thought my friend could use some emotional support."

"Uh huh. And what was your relationship to the dead boy, Mr. Lyons?"

"I didn't even know him. Rob is my friend from back home."

The cop seemed caught up in his routine and appeared unable to vary it at all. I tried as best I could to tune him out and found my mind wandering. I wondered what had happened. It was obvious Danny had felt crushed, but had he been so certain I would turn him in that he saw suicide as his only honorable way out?

Jack had returned, and the cop asked him if anyone had looked through Danny's things. He had the resident advisor open some drawers and search them. I figured they were looking for pills or other drugs. They didn't find anything, so they went to search the trashcans in the bathroom. A few minutes later, the cop came back with an empty pill bottle he was carrying on the end of a pencil. "You ever see this before?"

I shook my head. "No, but how do you know it was his? It doesn't have a label."

"We don't, but we'll dust it for prints and see if the lab in Richmond can pick up any trace evidence. It's all we've got to go on until we get the autopsy back."

I wasn't going to say anything. I hoped somehow the autopsy would be inconclusive and Danny's parents could be spared the knowledge that their son had killed himself.

The cop handed me his business card. "We're through here, son, but if you think of anything at all that might help us figure out what happened..."

I promised I'd call. Another lie. No matter what happened, I knew at that point I would never reveal what I knew about Danny and the circumstances of his death. He left and Jack Mathews followed him out. The paramedics had taken Danny's body away a few minutes earlier, so Dave and I were left alone in the room.

"Are you all right?"

I shrugged. "I don't know," I said dully. "I was sitting there at my desk, and I didn't even know he was dead. Maybe if I'd checked sooner..."

"God. It must have been terrible. If it was suicide, it's the first one they've had in the dorms in three years." He paused. "Do you think it was?"

"I don't know, Dave." My voice was completely flat and totally without emotion. "I forgot to ask him."

32

It's funny. I remember so much about the day Danny died, from feelings and conversations all the way down to what I ate at the diner on the east end of town. That day is forever emblazoned on my mind, but I remember very little about the next two.

I slept in a spare bed in Dave's room at KSK. He called my mother Thursday morning to tell her what had happened, and to let her know we might be delayed. I didn't talk to her. I was still sleeping. He called Beth, too. She was shocked and offered to come down, but Dave told her to stay in Harrisonburg and finish her exams. He said we would pick her up as soon as we could get away.

By the time I awakened around noon, Jack Mathews had called to let us know that Danny's parents had arrived a few minutes earlier. He said he would tell them what he knew, and he promised to direct them to the officer who was investigating the case. Yvette Jacobs had asked if they could talk to me. Jack said she suspected suicide and wanted to ask me if I knew of anything that had been bothering Danny.

That was the third of the three messages Dave gave me when I dragged myself out of bed and into the shower. He said he had told Jack we would be at Kent House at 1:30 to meet with Mr. and Mrs. Jacobs.

I didn't have any of my clothes with me, so Dave loaned me some of his. We went to lunch at the Corner. I didn't have any appetite at all, but Dave made me eat a hamburger. We didn't talk much. He told me about the calls he had made, and he said he had told my mother and Beth that I would call them that evening. I just nodded. "Are you all right, Bobby? Do you have any idea what you're going to tell Danny's folks?"

I shook my head and told another lie. I was surprised at how easy it was getting, but by then I had decided to do whatever it took to keep the truth from coming out about Danny. "I don't know what I could tell them."

I already had torn the note into little pieces and thrown it away. If I had anything to say about it, no one was going to know that Danny had violated the Honor System. What was the use of persecuting a dead kid? By any possible standard, honor had gotten its pound of flesh from Danny Jacobs.

When we got to the dorm, and I saw Irv and Yvette for the first time since September, it was easy to see that both had been crying. Neither of them looked as though it was something they did a lot, either. "Oh, Rob," Danny's mother said after I greeted her. "He liked you so much. He talked about you all the time when he was home."

I hadn't thought anything would surprise me, but that did. "I liked him, too," I said, stretching the truth a little. "Danny was a good kid."

"They're saying he might have killed himself. They say they found something that shows it might have been drugs. Was Danny taking drugs?"

I didn't have to lie, at least technically. "No. I never saw Danny take drugs."

She started crying again, and her husband put his arm around her. I wondered if they still were getting a divorce. "Was he unhappy, Rob?" Irv asked.

I nodded. "I think so, sir. Danny had a pretty rough time of it this year."

"I know. He told me he was having some trouble, and it was obvious from his first-semester grades that something was wrong. Danny never got grades like that before."

"Did a lot of the guys have trouble with their grades this year?" Yvette asked.

"Sure. It's a tough adjustment, going from high school to college. I think half the guys on our hall were below a 2.0 first semester."

"If you don't mind us asking, how did you do?"

"I did pretty well. I had a 3.2 average, but my best friend was a year ahead of me and he gave me a lot of good advice."

Dave hadn't said a word up to that point, but he chimed in. "Yeah, Mrs. Jacobs. Bobby learned from my mistakes. I had a rough first semester, and I didn't want him to have the same problems."

Irv smiled a sad smile. "It sounds as if you two are really good friends. I wish Danny could have had a friend like you to show him the ropes. My son was so sheltered."

They said they were staying in town for a couple of days to await the results of the autopsy. Under Jewish ritual, they would have buried Danny as soon as possible, but the state laws regarding deaths under suspicious circumstances would force them to wait. The police had promised to release the body to them by Monday, and they were hoping to have the funeral in Annandale on Tuesday.

"Do you think you could make it to the funeral, Rob?" his mother asked. "We would really like it if you could be there. He thought so highly of you."

I had hoped to be back in Johnstown with Beth by Saturday night. I didn't know how I could possibly juggle everything and make it all work, but I felt I owed it to Danny to come to his funeral if that was what his parents wanted. I told them I would be going home to Pennsylvania, but that I would be honored to make the trip down for the funeral on Tuesday. They thanked me and started to leave. "Mr. and Mrs. Jacobs?"

"Yes, Rob?"

"I don't know what the autopsy is going to show. But if it should turn out it was a drug overdose that killed Danny, that doesn't automatically mean it was suicide. Lots of kids try things and don't know how they will affect them. Danny might have been depressed and tried a drug just hoping it would make him feel better. And if he took too much, he probably never knew it."

"That's possible," Irv said thoughtfully.

Those were the last words we ever exchanged, except when they greeted me cordially at their son's funeral Tuesday. Of course, the autopsy showed that Daniel Aaron Jacobs had died of a drug overdose. He apparently had taken too many Seconals. It was a peaceful way to die. Danny went to sleep and never woke up. At first the coroner wanted to rule it suicide, but someone talked him out of it. The death certificate finally said Danny Jacobs had died of an accidental overdose. I spent a lot of time hoping that made his parents feel a little better.

Dave and I left for home Friday, right after I checked my biology grade. I had gotten a solid B. I knew I should be proud, but nothing was further from my mind. We picked up Beth and she rode with us to Johnstown. She spent the weekend with us. I felt guilty because I loved her and there was so much I didn't know if I could ever tell her.

I drove her to Scranton on Monday and left from there for Washington, D.C., and Danny's funeral. The services were set for 11 a.m. on Tuesday. They had a closed casket. I was relieved. I already had seen Danny dead and had been dreading the thought of having to look at him again. The ritual was unfamiliar, and I sat there with half my mind on what the rabbi was saying and the other half on what I remembered about him.

Danny had been miscast from the start as a college freshman at a southern party school. He should have gone somewhere up north where there were lots of other kids like him. He should never have been thrown in with guys who were more concerned with how they dressed or which fraternity they were pledging than they were with their grades. It was culture shock of the worst kind and Danny never got over it.

He wasn't a bad kid. His biggest fault was that he wanted so badly for people to like him, and the harder he tried to make that happen, the worse things got. So much had happened. His disastrous experience with fraternity rush ... his clash with Dick Simpson ... his poor first-semester grades ... his parents' divorce. All of it had resulted in more pressure than he could handle. And when I had caught him helping his new friends cheat on the biology final, for Danny it had been the last brick in the wall. I had been wrong. I wasn't the one trapped at all. Danny had been trapped somewhere he couldn't escape, like the guy in that story.

And even though I had never heard the words from Poe's famous story, they echoed in my mind.

"For the love of God, Montresor!"

Maybe if I had let him off the hook right away, if I had allowed him to leave school without being accused of cheating ... maybe then Danny still would be alive. I didn't know, and as I sat there listening to the rabbi perform his funeral service, I still didn't know what I would have done. I remember hoping I would be able to figure it out someday.

EPILOGUE

Of course, all that happened a long, long time ago.

Within days of Danny's funeral, Bobby Kennedy was assassinated in Los Angeles. And by the time I returned to Charlottesville in September after the most agonizing summer of my life, Nixon and Agnew were running for office by verbally bashing college kids. Turbulent times were upon us.

I could count the times I slept well that summer on one hand, and when I did sleep, as often as not I found myself in nightmares standing over Danny Jacobs, dead in his bed. More than once that summer, I wished it had been me who had died. Maybe if I had been a person who obsessed over things, I would have had an easier time dealing with it, but that just wasn't me. I thought things through or discussed them with people I loved and then let them go.

Not this time. I was devastated by the role I believed I had played in Danny's death. What made it worse was that technically, I had committed an honor violation by not accusing the three guys Danny had been talked into helping.

Worst of all? I had no one to discuss it with. I couldn't tell Dave. He was governed by the same rules I was, and while I didn't really believe he would turn me in, I would be sticking him with a similar level of guilt on that score. I couldn't tell my mother, although I don't think she would have been upset I didn't turn anyone in. She might have been bothered by the fact that I let it go so far that Danny could see no way forward. I knew she would forgive me, though, but that didn't mean I could forgive myself.

That was why I couldn't tell Beth either. For some reason, I remembered the old Groucho Marx line about not wanting to belong to a club that would have someone like him as a member. How could I love or respect someone who would let me off the hook on this?

I broke up with Beth in late August while I was visiting her family at the Jersey Shore. Several things went wrong, but the one insurmountable problem was that I was tired of measuring my words and I couldn't stand having such a dark, nasty secret between us. I felt like every time I saw her and didn't tell her, it was as if I was cheating on her. Two days into our week at the shore, she blew up at me.

"Rob, you have got to tell me what's wrong. This doesn't make any sense at all. Have I done something to offend you?"

"No," I said glumly.

"You're damn right I haven't. I have been a perfect girlfriend."

In spite of myself, I laughed and smiled at her. She smiled back hopefully, but the moment didn't last. My smile disappeared and hers faded.

"Rob, I love you. Please tell me what's wrong."

I let out a long breath. I thought for a moment and then I shook my head. "I can't."

She sighed. Her look changed from quizzical to annoyed. "Can't? Or won't?"

"Does it matter?" I asked her.

She shook her head. Then she turned quickly and ran back down the beach toward her parents' house. I could tell she was crying. I left that night, five days earlier than scheduled, and I felt as though I had aged five years in the twelve months since I had left for college the first time.

I had thought long and hard about not returning to Virginia at all, but I knew there was at least one insurmountable problem with changing colleges at such a late date. I had made a phone call to see if it was possible, only to learn it was too late to get into Penn State for the fall semester. They said they would be happy to accept me as a midyear transfer, but I knew if I was at home in the fall, I would be hearing from the draft board that I had lost my 2-S student deferment and would be classified 1-A and on my way to Saigon by Christmas.

And while that might be the perfect way to do penance for Danny, how could I explain that to my mother?

I drove back to Charlottesville for my second year, and the toughest moment was when Dave learned I had broken up with Beth.

"Are you crazy?" he asked me. "She is the greatest girl you ever met, except for maybe your mom."

I shrugged. "Yeah, she is definitely special."

"Then why would you break up with her?"

Another shrug. "It's too soon for me to feel happy after what happened with Danny."

Dave sighed. "You didn't kill him." He paused. "Or did you?"

He knew I hadn't, so he passed it off as just what he called my journey to the kingdom of weirdness.

Bruce Benson and I finally made it down to Hollins for a mixer in September. On the drive down, he told me he owed me an apology and that he had been the one to turn me in for having Beth in my room on the Friday night of Easters Weekend. He said he was glad I hadn't gotten into any real trouble. I told him it was no big deal, but of course Beth had been right when she said he must have been the one to report me.

I met an interesting girl at the mixer, and we dated through the fall. I brought her up for Homecomings and Openings and she was the second girl I had sex with. It bothers me that I can't even remember her name. Hayley something or other is the best I can do. It wasn't her fault. She was certainly nice enough, but she wasn't Beth Erickson. She wasn't the first woman I ever loved, the woman I still loved.

By March of 1969, I couldn't stand it any longer. I phoned Beth one Friday and asked if I could come up and talk with her. I told her there were things she didn't know and that I hadn't been completely honest with her. She said she didn't think there was any point to it at such a late date. She was dating a Kappa Sigma from Washington and Lee, and she thought that rehashing problems with last year's love affair—no matter how special it had seemed at the time—would be pointless. I said I wouldn't take no for an answer, and I would be there at noon the next day.

She was even lovelier than I remembered. I knew I was viewing her through the eyes of love, but I also knew this woman well enough to know she really was beautiful in more ways than just physical.

She told me her boyfriend was arriving at 5 o'clock, and that I would have to be gone by then. I said all I wanted to do was tell her the truth and leave. I didn't leave anything out. I told her I had caught Danny cheating on the exam, that I had confronted him and had given him the evening to decide what he would do. I explained that I had gone for a walk and returned hours later to find him dead. I said I had destroyed the suicide note and had lied to protect his memory, and I told her about the guilt I felt every time I saw the DLC brothers who had escaped punishment.

I talked a lot, maybe more than I ever had at one time in my life. I told her I had been an idiot not to tell her all this the previous summer, that she had been the best thing that ever happened to me and that my life had been a mess since we broke up. I told her I loved her, and that I always would regret throwing away what we had.

Beth didn't say much, although there were a few times I saw tears in her eyes. She thanked me for being honest with her, and said she hoped finally talking about it would help me get over my feelings of guilt. She said she would always care about me and that she forgave me for hurting her. I knew a brush-off when I heard one, so I thanked her and left to go back to school.

My grades were pretty good my second year. I lifted my overall GPA to 3.3 and I made the Dean's List both semesters. My mom was proud, and I knew my dad would have been, too. I followed my dad and my grandfather into one other extracurricular activity, joining the Jefferson Literary and Debating Society. It had been around since 1825 and was the oldest student organization at the university, meeting every Friday evening to drink beer and argue the issues of the day. I caused a controversy when I delivered my probationary speech on why the single sanction of the Honor System was a bad thing.

I still dreamed about Danny, and every time I saw one of the three other guys who had been involved, I remember feeling that justice hadn't been served. Two of them flunked out that spring, and I heard through the grapevine they both wound up in the Army. With Vietnam at full blast in 1969, I thought maybe justice was finally having its say. The third guy eventually made it through school and graduated, but that didn't bother me as much as it would have earlier. I was starting to put the incident behind me.

I still missed Beth. I sent her a birthday card in September 1969 when she turned 21, and she sent me a nice note thanking me for remembering. Dave was still dating Marianne—they wound up getting married after college, although it didn't last—and when she told him the following spring that Beth was pinned to the guy from W&L, that was enough to spark an evening of heavy drinking on my part.

Of course, eventually things do work out the way they should if you stick with it. Sometimes they just take a lot more time than you wish they would. At the end of my third year, after two more semesters on the Dean's List and grades in honors territory, I was elected president of my fraternity. That didn't come as a great surprise. I had been a good friend to most of my brothers in the chapter, and I was willing to take on the work associated with the position. The best part of it for me was that I hadn't even pursued it. Several of my brothers had asked me to run.

Two greater surprises were still to come. My grades, my fraternity work and the Jefferson Society apparently meant enough that my application for a room on the Lawn was approved. My dad hadn't had a room on the Lawn, but my grandfather had occupied one 55 years earlier. I was given the same room. Family tradition.

But best of all, in December 1970, halfway through my final year of undergraduate studies, Beth wrote to me. It was only a birthday card with Snoopy on it, but I was 22 years old and had never stopped missing her. I drove up to Harrisonburg the next day and this time she did most of the talking. She told me her boyfriend had asked her to marry him, and that was when she realized she didn't love him. It had been nearly two and a half years since we had stopped seeing each other, but she admitted to me a lot of the same feelings were still there.

What I remember most about that moment was the incredible feeling of relief that overwhelmed me. Heck, I even cried a little. I said I knew there was a lot to live down, but that what I wanted more than anything else in the world was to start again and rebuild our relationship.

I said I thought I had matured enough from 19 to 22 to make a difference and I was right.

Except for one or two outliers, we got together every weekend of our final semester of college. Mostly I drove up to see her, but she came down to Charlottesville for Midwinters and Easters. I gave her my fraternity pin again in February and an engagement ring in April, three years to the day after I had given her my pin the first time. We were married in Scranton in August, the summer after both of us became college graduates, my degree cum laude and my lovely bride's magna cum laude. I certainly appreciated the irony of my Bachelor of Arts degree from Virginia being "with honor."

We got an apartment in State College, Pa., and Beth spent three years teaching third graders while I earned my law degree at Penn State. I made the Law Review and was ranked second in my class, and a few months after I passed the bar and got a great job as an associate with a big law firm in Philadelphia, we started a family.

Beth and I have been married for 35 years and are more in love than ever. Whenever I get together with other governors, I remind them that the Keystone State has the most beautiful First Lady, a true Mrs. America. Nobody dares disagree with me, even the Mississippi governor married to a former beauty queen. Beth and I have four wonderful kids, two girls and two boys. We'll be 60 in less than three years and we're ready to be grandparents. Our daughters are adults now and they are both gorgeous.

Angela and Alicia take after their mother, and I put in a lot of wasted effort trying to keep the suburban Lotharios in line when my girls were in high school. The boys didn't laugh at all when I told them how much I love my daughters and if anyone did anything to hurt them, I had no problem with going back to prison. Angela didn't see the humor in that, but it made Alicia laugh.

Angela earned an MBA from the Wharton School of Finance at Penn and is one of the young superstars of a major brokerage firm on Wall Street. She's already making more money than I ever will. Alicia is living with her sister and taking acting lessons, working toward a career on Broadway.

Our sons came along later, and both are maturing into fine young men. Bobby hasn't decided whether to become a lawyer, but he's only 20. Give him time. I suppose it's a little intimidating when your lawyer father is governor of Pennsylvania. Of course, his full name is Robert Alan Miller III. As I said all the way back at the beginning of this story, I have always been a believer in family tradition. He did break one tradition with my blessing. I was the last of my family to go to Virginia. Bobby is halfway through his undergraduate studies at Yale.

Our other son, the youngest of our four kids, is a dreamer. He's a lot like his honorary Uncle Dave, who happens also to be his godfather. He's 18 and his name is David Daniel Miller. You see, I still haven't forgotten Danny Jacobs.

It took me a long time, but I finally came to terms with what happened on May 26, 1968, on the third floor of Kent House. I finally realized that if I had been given the chance to decide, I would have let my unhappy roommate withdraw from school and leave without being stigmatized for life. It was a shame Danny hadn't waited to get my answer, but it really is exactly like my dad told me in high school and what Shakespeare wrote hundreds of years earlier. The quality of mercy is not strained, and a system that doesn't allow for mercy is devoid of real honor.

I never ragged Danny, and except for letting slip that one unfortunate bit of information, I didn't contribute to the tormenting some of the other guys were doing. I thought that was enough, but it wasn't. Sometimes you've got to stand beside the underdog and fight the bully. I may have learned that lesson too late to help Danny, but I learned it.

I never wanted the life-or-death decision I faced with Danny, and I'm uncomfortable knowing that in ten minutes or so, they're going to execute Tommy Wood in Waynesburg unless I pick up the phone and stop them.

I did learn one other thing in college. When I was in my last semester at Virginia, I needed an elective to fill out my schedule. I signed up for an English course with a man who was reputed to be one of the most interesting professors at the school. It turned out to be a course in Chaucer, and one of the books we analyzed was "The Canterbury Tales." I had never read the book, and I smiled when I saw the Miller's Tale. I read it and I read the one after it, with the story of a crooked miller.

I had never really thought all that much about the derivation of my last name. Back in the old days, when names came from occupations, men named Miller helped feed their communities by milling wheat into grain.

It was then, in 1971, that I learned what the real lyrics of "A Whiter Shade of Pale" were. The line I had always thought spoke of the mirror telling its tale was Chaucer. It was "when the miller told his tale." I felt a certain sense of irony that I had never realized that in 1967. There was a lot I didn't realize then.

A few years back, before I got into politics, I did some legal work for a non-profit group that works to feed hungry people in the Philadelphia area. There's no more honorable goal, and one of my top priorities as governor has been making sure that the hungry children of Pennsylvania are fed. In fact, with our children all but grown, Beth has taken a major role in helping me accomplish that.

That's my story. This Miller has told his tale, and if you're looking for conclusions. I'll give you one.

I need to pick up the special phone and call Waynesburg to stop the execution. Maybe Tommy Wood doesn't deserve our mercy, but if we execute him, it makes it that much easier to execute the next person and he might be more deserving. It comes down to standing up for life, and that's the kind of governor—the kind of man—that I want to be. If that keeps me from being president or even costs me a second term in Harrisburg, then so be it.

I have had an amazing life. A wonderful wife, great kids, and good friends. I'll never forget standing in the dim light of that dormitory, though. I'll never forget looking down and seeing Danny Jacobs laying there dead, looking paler than pale. I didn't kill him, but I might have saved him, and I didn't.

Some years ago, Beth asked me why I was so passionate in my work. I told her I fought for the underdog because I owed it to Danny.

Now I know better.

I owed it to myself.